COMING UP ROSES

WILDFLOWER RIDGE 2

ELLE ASHWELL

GlitterInk
PRESS

For the anxious mamas out there,
You got this x

AUTHOR NOTE

While this is a sweet, sexy love story, some subjects may be upsetting for some readers. These include: brief mentions of a car accident causing death of both the main character's parents (in the past) and horse riding accident causing child injury (also in the past).

Depictions of anxiety, panic attacks, farming practises, sexually explicit content and coarse language are also included. Please read with care and reach out if you require further information.

GLOSSARY

Wildflower Ridge is a New Zealand based sheep and beef farm and as such, this book uses New Zealand spelling and language. I've included some Kiwi-isms and farming terms in this glossary to help you out.

> *Bale feeder - a farming implement for distributing large round silage or hay bales*
>
> *Bench - a kitchen counter*
>
> *Bush - native forest*
>
> *Feeding out - the process of delivering stock feed to the paddocks*
>
> *Fetlocks - joints in a horse's legs, essentially their ankles*
>
> *Gumboots - wellington/rubber boots*
>
> *Hereford - a breed of beef cattle that is a reddish colour with white face and markings*
>
> *Manual car - a vehicle with stick shift transmission*
>
> *Paddock - a fenced off field to keep stock in*
>
> *Ranchslider - a sliding glass door*
>
> *Rippers and Power harrow - tractor-pulled farming implements for cultivating ground, ready for planting crops*
>
> *Sheep and Beef farm - a Kiwi farm that raises both sheep and cattle for beef*

Side-by-side - an all terrain farm vehicle
Silage - a grass-based feed for cattle
Toasted sandwich - like a grilled cheese
*Ute - a 'utility vehicle', commonly referred to as a
pick up truck in other parts of the world*

1

———

ABI

ANXIETY CLAWS AT MY THROAT, threatening chaos and tears and a really bad first day at my new job.

I take a deep breath, shove the panic down and follow Olivia Austin up the stairs.

"And this," Olivia, my new boss, says, "will be your office."

She pushes the timber door at the top of the stairs open. The office is a converted hayloft in a refurbished barn that's now a wedding and function venue. It has rustic timber floors and walls, with a window that looks out over the main reception room of the venue. Another window faces out at the end of the building with an incredible view of the wedding lawn, lake and the Wildflower Ridge farm sprawling out towards the horizon. It's a beautiful part of the country and I can see why my ex Dallas settled here, especially with the way the Austin family adopted him and our daughter Sadie like two of their own.

I shake thoughts of my ex out of my head and refocus on the room, taking yet another deep breath to steady my nerves.

A desk sits in the middle of the space, facing the door. A laptop and several files are lined up neatly across its surface, and the wall behind the desk has floor-to-ceiling shelves filled with books, bridal magazines, framed photographs, dried bouquets and aesthetic storage boxes with labels for ribbons, fairy lights, tealight candles and more. A couple of small couches sit in the corner, a coffee table between them. That must be where Olivia meets with potential clients.

Where *I'll* meet with potential clients, I suppose.

I trail my fingers along the edge of the desk. "It's gorgeous," I say. "The whole place is."

"Thanks," Olivia says, a blush hitting her cheeks. Her phone rings and she groans. "I need to get this," she says, glancing at the screen. "Can I leave you to review all that paperwork on the desk? Feel free to have a look around. I'll be back as soon as I can."

"Of course." I smile and I hope it looks genuine through all my nerves.

Olivia turns, her boots clunking on the stairs as she heads outside, leaving me standing in the middle of my new office, at my new job, in a new town.

I sink into the desk chair and rest my head in my hands, my elbows propped on the desk.

What have I got myself into?

This job is an incredible opportunity. It's an amazing role, managing the function centre. I'll get to help plan weddings and parties and be paid for it. Sure there's a lot of less exciting stuff like budgets and reports to Olivia, but she's giving me mostly free rein to run the place.

It was supposed to be her job, until her father passed away last summer and she was left with an entire sheep and beef farm to run. She told me she has a great team working the farm, but there still isn't enough of her to go around to run the farm and the venue. I can tell how disappointed she is that she doesn't get to be hands on running her dream, but I'm going to take care of it in the meantime. No matter what.

Part of it's for selfish reasons. I need to prove myself. Prove I'm reliable, responsible, fit to be a mother again. I'm done letting my daughter down.

I moved to Kauri Creek to be close to her, to try and reconnect. I didn't realise I'd end up with a job on the same property where Sadie lives with her dad, who manages the farming side of Olivia's operation.

When I found out Dallas and now five-year-old Sadie live here, I tried to walk away from the job, but Olivia wanted to interview me, regardless of my history of failing at the tasks most important in life.

When I sat down with Dallas to make a plan about reintroducing me to Sadie's life, he not only insisted I at least interview for the position, but then also encouraged me to take it.

He's the best person I've ever known, never once throwing my failures in my face, just wanting the best for me. And for Sadie, too.

I pull a file towards me and flick it open. Inside is a stack of new employee forms and documents, ranging from tax code declaration forms to a thick farm health and safety policy. Just some light reading then.

I settle into the chair and start working my way through the stack.

~

I DROP the page I've been trying to read for the last five minutes onto the desk and rub at my eyes.

"Words going blurry?" The voice startles me. I must have been really focussed on trying to read that document because I didn't hear anyone making their way up the stairs. My brain is already overflowing with new information.

"Yeah, too much reading," I say to Dallas, who's leaning in the doorway, his arms folded across his chest. God, he looks good. Sandy blond hair peeking out from under a faded cap, a blue shirt that matches his eyes and worn jeans stretching across his thighs. I shove the thoughts away. I can't think about Dallas like that. I don't even want to. He deserves everything. I'm not here to mess with his brand-new relationship. This place suits him though. He's happy here.

"From what I remember you could read a whole book in one sitting," Dallas says with a chuckle.

"I still can, but books have plots, and characters ... and kissing. This is just policy."

Dallas laughs. "That's true. How's it going?"

"This place is gorgeous," I say. "It's all a bit overwhelming but hopefully I'll figure it all out soon."

"You will," he says, absolute certainty in his tone. He opens his mouth to continue talking, but nothing comes out. He rubs his hand across the back of his neck. I wait. "Do you want to see Sadie this afternoon?"

I blink at him. My heart stutters and a hot flush races through my body. Anxiety. I haul in a deep breath, counting slowly as I release it.

Before I have a chance to reply, Dallas speaks again. "I know you've had a big day already, so I understand if you want to leave it for another time, but I don't want Sadie to feel like we're keeping you a secret over here."

"I thought you wanted to be certain I wasn't going to flake on you again."

He steps into the room and drops into a chair across the desk from me. "You've taken the job and Olivia mentioned you've rented a house in town."

I nod. It's an adorable little house and while I don't have a lot of stuff in it at the moment, I'm looking forward to furnishing it properly and hopefully, the second bedroom will become Sadie's when she stays with me. The thought makes my heart race again so I decide not to think about that just now.

"You're nervous, huh?" Dallas says, voice soft.

"Utterly terrified," I say.

A smile tugs at his lips at my brash confession. "You'll be fine. I've been bringing you up a little bit with her. She knows we've been in touch. I'll talk to her when she gets home from school and check she's in a good space to see you. If she isn't, don't take it personally. Some days when she gets home she can barely keep her eyes open."

"I don't want to cause her any stress," I say. "Any more stress, I mean." I lift my hand towards my mouth, the urge to bite my nails strong. But I catch sight of the shimmery gold polish on them and refrain. I paid for this manicure, I'm not ruining it on its second day.

"Abi," Dallas says and I drag my eyes back up to meet his. "I know this is easier said than done, but you've got to let the past go. It happened, none of it was your fault, and you're back now. That's what matters."

Heat prickles behind my eyes. Dallas has never held my failings against me, even when he should have, even when I abandoned him with a two-year-old. When I first realised he didn't hate me and wasn't going to keep Sadie away from me, I cried for an hour—full on, body wracking, eyes nearly falling out of my head, bawling.

"I'm trying," I whisper.

"I know. I need to keep moving, but I'll call you after Sadie gets home and let you know where things are at."

"Sounds good," I say, smiling through my nerves.

As Dallas descends the stairs, I pick up the document I've been trying to read. It's not any easier after taking a break, in fact, now that I'm thinking about possibly seeing Sadie this afternoon, it's a whole lot harder to concentrate.

2

FLYNN

I TURN off my motorbike and prop it on the stand, then swing my leg over and stare up at the sign hanging above the Wild-flower Ridge Function Centre door.

I'm here to introduce myself to the new manager, but I can't seem to make my feet move.

I might be nervous.

Scratch that, I'm super nervous.

I can't even understand why.

I've only seen Abigail once and all I can remember from that encounter is that she's gorgeous.

But surely that's not enough to make me *nervous*. I see good-looking women all the time. My two best friends are objectively hot women, and they don't make me nervous. The thought of being into either Olivia or Katie is ... well, *ew*.

It's not like I'm into Abigail either. She's so far out of my league *and* so completely off-limits it's laughable.

It's that realisation that finally gets my feet moving.

I kick my boots off at the door because there's still mud clinging to them from the farm and I know from experience Olivia will lose her shit if I track it through the building.

Abigail may not have my hide over it yet, but I don't want to get off on the wrong foot. Or speed up the process of her realising I'm an irresponsible pain-in-the-ass.

There's no sign of Abigail in the main room, so I head for the stairs at the back. My socks are quiet on the timber stairs and I knock on the open door as I reach the top, hoping I don't startle her.

She's facing away from me, both hands resting against the desk, her head lowered, like she's staring at something on the desktop.

She doesn't react to my knock. I wait for another moment. Maybe she's just focussed on something.

I try not to spend that entire moment staring at her ass, or her legs, or any other part of her. I force myself to look towards the window at the end of the room. In the distance I can just make out the Hereford cattle in their paddock.

A shuddering sound brings my focus back to Abigail. She stands up straight, waves her hands in front of her face and takes another gulping breath, except it doesn't sound like she pulled in much air.

Something isn't right here.

I knock again, louder this time, then stride right into the room.

"Abigail?"

She turns to face me and the full effect of the dress she's

wearing hits me. It's some kind of business-y style that's fitted to her body, ending just above her knees.

The expression on her face stops me from being completely distracted by the dress though.

Abigail tries to draw another breath, but it stutters and gets stuck in her throat. Panic flashes through her green eyes, staring up at me while filling with tears.

"Can you hear me?" I ask and she nods. "Okay, just listen to my voice." I hold out my hands, palms up. She hesitates, but places her shaking hands in mine. I lead her to the window. "You're going to be fine, okay? Everything will be all good."

I position Abigail in front of the window, then slip my hands free of her grasp. It's surprisingly hard to let go.

I step behind her, but she must think I'm moving away because her hand grips my wrist and she looks up at me with those pleading eyes.

"I'm right here," I say. "I'm not going anywhere." I place my hands on her shoulders, hoping I'm not crossing any lines. Her body is wound so tight she's almost quivering. I can feel every stilted breath. "What can you see?"

A shaky inhale. "Um ... grass."

I chuckle. "So much grass. I hope you like green."

Her hands land on top of mine and she grips tight. She makes a choked sound that I'm going to claim as a laugh.

"What else can you see?"

"Pond."

"We call it a lake for some reason, but you're right. It's a pond."

Another sound I'm taking as a laugh.

"There's some cows," she says, her voice shaky and breathy. "Way in the distance. They look red."

"They are red. They're Herefords. They're my favourite kind of cattle."

She twists her head around to look at me. "Favourite cattle?"

"Yes, favourite cattle. I'm a farmer, we all have our favourites. We also have favourite tractors. Don't judge."

"Do you like He-Heffalumps because you're a redhead?"

"Heffalumps?" I can't help myself and a cackle bursts out of me. "Herefords, I think you mean."

"Same difference," she says, her voice finally sounding more normal. Her grip softens on my hands.

"And no, they're not my favourite because I'm a redhead. They're big and chunky and hairy. They're cute."

"Cute? Nothing you just described is 'cute'."

"I'll take you to see the calves one day and change your mind. You know, Olivia's parents met and fell in love because of a Hereford bull."

"How did a bull play matchmaker?" she asks, leaning back into my hands. Her body is close enough to brush against mine and I'm going to have to end this contact before I really get myself in trouble.

"He was on the road when Violet came around the corner. She ended up in the fence, Henry came to her rescue. She never left."

"That's quite a story."

"Yep. They've always said they fell in love that day, right there in the middle of the road."

"If only it were that easy for the rest of us," she says.

She's been slowly relaxing as we've been talking, her body softening under my hands, her breathing returning to a normal rhythm. As she says those last words though, she stiffens again.

"Sorry," she says, stepping out from under my touch. I let her go and she takes several steps into the room—away from me—and smooths down her dress. Her mouth curves into a bright, and entirely fake, smile. "I'm Abigail." She holds out her hand.

I wrap my fingers around hers and let her shake my hand.

"Flynn," I say. "Farmhand, general dogsbody, here if you need help with anything."

"Oh, um, yes." Abigail rakes her fingers through her hair in an attempt to smooth the waves. "Olivia mentioned you. Nice to meet you."

"Are you okay?" I can't handle the false pleasantries. I just walked in on her having a panic attack and she's going to pretend like everything is fine.

"I'm fine," she says, giving me another fake smile.

"Do they happen often?"

She winces and looks away, the smile dropping from her full, red mouth.

I soften my voice. "I'm not asking to be an asshat. I'm asking so I can help you."

"I'm fine," she says, meeting my gaze again. There's determination blazing in her eyes. "I have to go. Did you need something?"

I shake my head. "No. I was just coming to introduce myself. Did Olivia give you my number?"

"Yeah, I think she gave me everyone's numbers. There's a massive list."

"She likes to cover her bases," I say with a smile. She returns it, but hers is tight. "I'll let you get back to it then. Just let me know if you need anything. Here to help. Best to call if there's a time crunch, though I'm not always in cell service. But I'll get here as soon as I can, so just let me know what you need." Wow, Flynn. Shut the hell up. "Right, okay. See ya."

I turn tail before she has the chance to reply. I don't need to see the look on her face as she dismisses me and my rambling.

I shove my feet back into my boots and swing my leg over my bike, stomping on the kickstart. I rev the engine and release the clutch, sending the bike shooting forward.

I need to not think about Abigail as an incredibly hot woman with an ass to dream about. I also need to not think about her having that panic attack, because it tugs at my heart in ways it definitely shouldn't. She also clearly wishes I wasn't there to witness it, so the sooner I can forget about it, the better.

I don't want to mess up our working relationship. I know why she's in town and I'll do everything in my power not to ruin that for her, or for one of my favourite people—her daughter.

3

—

ABI

DALLAS'S COTTAGE IS GORGEOUS. Situated across the paddock from the main Wildflower Ridge farmhouse, the cottage is surrounded by trees, mostly hiding it from view of the main driveway.

The house is small, smaller than the one I've rented in town, but it's well-maintained and charming. A couple of big wooden planters sit on the front porch and I wonder if Dallas has taken up gardening or if those are Katie's influence.

I haven't met Katie yet. I've seen her once in passing but she's kept herself scarce while I caught up with Dallas, and while I interviewed for the job. I'm not sure if it's because she doesn't want to meet me, or if she's simply giving me the space to settle in first. Either way I appreciate the chance to find my bearings without Dallas's new girlfriend watching my every move. Based on her relationship with him, and Olivia being her best friend, I'd say Katie's a lovely person, but her simply existing adds another layer of stress to this whole situation.

Because I abandoned Dallas and Sadie, and now he's found someone that can give them both the kind of love they deserve.

I'm under no illusions that I'm the best person for Sadie, but I'll try my damn hardest to repair what I broke.

I park beside Katie's car and Dallas appears around the side of the house. I take a few deep breaths and climb out of the car before another panic attack has a chance to take hold. I can't believe Flynn walked in on my one back at the office, and although his arrival had snapped me out of it, I still wish he hadn't seen it.

I wish no one had seen it.

Not worth stressing about it now. I'll save that anxiety spiral for tonight, when I'm alone in the dark.

"Hey. You ready for this?" Dallas asks as I approach him.

I want to say no. I want to disappear again. I knew seeing Sadie again would be hard. I didn't realise I'd want to throw up, run away, hide and cry, all at once.

I square my shoulders and stand tall. "Yep," I say. "How is she?"

"She's excited. She wants to show you the garden she's planting."

Oh. That's sweet. I don't know how to reply, so I keep my mouth shut as I follow Dallas around the house. There's a small lawn and an even tinier porch with a cozy looking outdoor chair taking up the majority of the space. At the end of the lawn are two raised garden beds and leaning over one, carefully inspecting the soil, is a little girl with two lopsided braids in her blonde hair.

She's wearing a flannel shirt with a tulle skirt and tiny pink gumboots. I love everything about her.

"Hey, Sadie girl. Someone's here to see you," Dallas says softly as we approach her.

My daughter spins around, her blue eyes—just like her dad's—widen as she takes me in.

"Hi, Sadie," I say, my voice coming out choked. "It's really nice to see you."

"Hi," she whispers, then chews on her bottom lip. Her gaze drops from me and focusses on the ground. She kicks a boot in the grass.

Silence extends between the three of us, the tension growing so taut it feels like the world could shatter with one wrong move.

Dallas gestures towards Sadie, encouraging me.

I take a wobbly step forward. These shoes are not designed for grass, or emotional meetings with your estranged five-year-old. I clear my throat. "What are you planting?" I ask, voice wobbling as much as my ankles.

"Vegetables," Sadie says. "Daddy says they're important." She pulls a face. "Do you like vegetables?"

"Some of them," I say, taking another step. "I like carrots, but I don't like cauliflower very much."

"Do you still have to eat it?"

"Sometimes."

She ponders that for a moment, then points to a couple of tiny seedlings. "Those two are cauliflower but I won't make you eat them. Dad can have them."

I smile. "Sounds like a good deal. What's your favourite vegetable?"

I can't believe I'm having a conversation about vegetables with my daughter.

I can't believe I'm having a conversation with her at all.

"I like carrots. They're Scout's favourite too."

"Scout must have good taste then."

Sadie nods. "Do you want to meet her?"

"Uh." I glance at Dallas, hoping he can read the confusion on my face. Who the heck is Scout and why would I want to meet her right now?

"Maybe you should tell Ab—uh, your m—. Maybe you should explain who Scout is."

He trips over what to call me and I realise it's one part of this we haven't discussed. What *is* Sadie going to call me?

"Oh," Sadie says. "Scout's my horse."

"*Your* horse?" Dallas questions.

Sadie pouts. "Okay she's Olivia's horse. But Katie rides her and she's teaching me to ride on her."

"I'd love to meet her," I say.

"I'll get a carrot for her," Sadie says, then races past us into the house, pausing just long enough to kick off her muddy boots at the back door.

"I guess we're meeting her right now?" I ask, turning to Dallas who's shaking his head with a fond smile on his lips.

"Looks that way." His gaze lands on my shoes. "Come on, I'm sure Katie left some shoes here you can wear. They'll be a little more suitable than those."

"Are you judging my shoes?"

"You know I'd never. If you want to walk down to the barn and meet a horse in them, be my guest."

"Katie's shoes would be great, thanks … if she won't mind."

"She won't mind, Abi. She's really happy you're here."

"She is?" I can't hide how unlikely I find this.

"Yeah. She wants what's best for Sadie."

"She knows what happened? What I did?"

"She knows," Dallas says. "Admittedly I didn't actually mean to tell her, but I was bleeding quite a lot, and in a fair amount of pain and then she made me get on the damn horse." He runs a finger down his forearm, where I've noticed a fresh scar runs up the inside. "She understands, Abi. Trust me."

We reach the house and he locates a pair of sneakers and socks. By the time I've pulled them on, Sadie is bouncing next to me, a carrot in her hand.

"Can we go now?" she asks the moment I stand upright again.

I glance down at my dress and sneakers combo. I look ridiculous. But I'm sure the horse won't care. "Yeah, sure."

Sadie skips along the driveway, leaving Dallas and I to walk side by side. By the time we pass by the main farmhouse, Sadie has settled into walking between us. She spends the time chattering about her riding lessons, Scout and another horse called Aurora.

We head down the hill to the barn, where two horses are grazing in the paddock off to the side.

"Oh, there's Flynn," Sadie says, waving enthusiastically even though he's not looking in our direction. He's doing something with a tractor. He might be … washing it? I've never considered washing tractors a thing, but I guess they need cleaning occasionally.

Sadie stops walking and I pause when I notice her presence missing beside me. I turn to find her staring up at me, confusion written in her expression.

"What's up, Sadie?" I ask, squatting down so I'm at her height.

"I don't know what to call you," she whispers, her eyes going a little glassy.

"Well, my name is Abigail, or Abi, and I am your mum. So you can call me any of those. Whichever one you prefer."

She mouths my name, then smiles and nods. "Okay." She grabs my hand and tugs me forward. "Flynn!"

He looks up from the tractor. "Sadie!" he calls back.

She releases my hand and races down the hill, straight into his arms. He scoops her up and spins her around, their laughter echoing.

By the time we approach, Flynn is listening raptly as Sadie tells him about her day at school. When she catches sight of us, she wriggles and Flynn sets her feet back on the ground. She takes his hand and drags him toward us.

"Come meet my mum," she says and my breath catches. They stop in front of us, Sadie clearly in charge of the introductions. "Flynn, this is my mum, Abigail." She grins up at me. "Flynn is one of my bestest friends."

He wraps a big hand around the end of one of her braids and gives it a gentle tug. "The feeling's mutual, sprout."

"I'm not a sprout," she grumbles.

"A sprout is just a little plant. And you're a little person. So sprout you are." He grins at her then meets my eyes. There's concern there. I don't want to see it. "Also, I met your mum a little earlier. Did you bring her to meet the horses?"

Sadie nods.

"I'll go grab Scout's lead," Dallas says, heading for the barn.

Flynn turns to me and watches me carefully for a moment. I shift uncertainly under his gaze. "You good?" he asks eventually, the concern in his eyes making my skin itch.

"I'm fine." I glance at Sadie, who's wandered towards the paddock, calling out to Scout. The horses are both slowly making their way across the paddock.

"Sure, okay. Let me know if you need anything." He smiles. "Catch you later, Sadie," he calls out and the grin he sends her way is a thousand times brighter than the one I got.

Whatever. I don't need some random farmhand in my business. I just need to focus on my job and on Sadie.

The panic attack makes sense. It's the first time I've seen Sadie in years. She doesn't remember me from before. Feeling anxiety over that makes sense.

What doesn't make sense is feeling jealous of my five-year-old because Flynn gave her a better smile than me.

4

———

FLYNN

"HOW'S IT GOING?"

"Shit!" I jerk in fright when I round the corner of the tractor and find Katie leaning up against the back wheel. The running hose in my hand jolts, and I somehow get soaked.

"Oops. Sorry," Katie says, only looking about five per cent apologetic. The rest of her looks highly amused. She's in jeans and work boots, a faded grey sweatshirt and the cap Dallas was wearing a few minutes ago when he walked down the driveway with Abigail and Sadie. Now I understand why he volunteered to get a lead rope they probably don't even need.

"I should get you," I grumble, shaking my now wet hair out of my eyes. "Why the hell are you hiding behind the tractor?"

"I'm not hiding exactly. More just, preferring not to be seen."

"Why? Dallas clearly knows you're here." I gesture toward her head, then glance back over my shoulder where I can just make out Dallas and Abigail standing at the fence, Sadie balanced on the railings between them. "Oh. You're spying."

"I am not. I'm making myself scarce." She sighs and slumps against the tractor. "I didn't realise they'd be coming down here. I wanted to give Abi a chance to hang out with Sadie without me around. Figured meeting the ex's new girlfriend on the same day as her daughter might be a little much."

"That's remarkably considerate of you," I say, then tauntingly flick the hose towards her, yanking it away just before the water hits Katie's boots.

"I'm a remarkably considerate person, thank you very much." She scowls at me, then redirects her attention. "So, how's it going?"

I glance back at the trio standing at the fence. Do I tell Katie about the panic attack Abigail had earlier? Is it even relevant? Maybe it's a one off and it was purely because she knew she was seeing Sadie for the first time in years.

I shrug. "Fine, I guess. Sadie seems excited. I hope Abigail doesn't let her down."

Damnit, that sounded more angsty than it was supposed to, I know it the moment Katie's attention, which has been mostly focussed across the yard, snaps to me.

"I know it's everyone's biggest concern. But Dallas is sure Abi's in it for the long haul."

"That's good," I say, finally returning my focus to washing down the tractor, trying to avoid the rest of this conversation.

"You all good, Flynny?" Katie's voice is soft, just like the hand that lands on my arm.

"Yep. Just tired. It's been a long day."

She purses her lips, but doesn't push. For that I'm grateful.

"Are you coming to Vi's for dinner tonight?"

I roll my eyes. "Katie Kat, when am I not at Violet's for dinner?"

She laughs. "This is true."

Violet is Olivia's mum and the owner of Wildflower Ridge. She's technically my boss, though Olivia is the one running the show around here, with her mum's full support. Violet has always had an open-door policy at the main house, for as long as I can remember.

My mum was her best friend, so I've always been around Wildflower Ridge. I learned to ride a motorbike on the driveway with my dad, Olivia, and her dad, Henry. I fell asleep on the worn couch in the living room more times than I could ever count. I met Katie on the front porch of the house, a boring old day that ended up changing my life in a way I didn't expect.

I worked at Wildflower Ridge after school, on weekends and every school holidays and went full-time straight out of high school. These days it's home too.

Violet's kitchen is always open, and she always cooks enough dinner to feed an army, so most of the time I eat there, rather than cooking for myself. Dallas, Sadie and Katie join us sometimes, though less often now they're their own little family.

Aside from my brother, who lives in a somewhat grimy flat above the mechanic's workshop he manages, all of my family is at Wildflower Ridge.

When my parents died, this is where we came, into the loving care of Violet and Henry, until legalities were sorted and

Hunter and I moved back to our home in town, my barely eighteen-year-old brother my legal guardian.

I hose down the tractor, using a soft brush to clean off any mud, while Katie stands and watches me. "You could help you know."

"Or I could watch you." She pokes out her tongue. "Oh, they're leaving. I can go feed the girls now."

Dallas, Abigail and Sadie are making their way back up the driveway. I guess they forgot I'm here, or just didn't bother to say goodbye. It's not like Sadie, but I guess she's got things on her mind right now.

As they disappear over the hill, Katie heads back to the barn and a moment later is out in the paddock, checking over the horses and giving them their dinner.

Once I'm finished with the tractor, I park it in the huge implements shed beside the barn.

It's really too early to finish work for the day. I have a list of things to do a mile long. But I wasn't lying to Katie when I said I was tired.

I can't stop thinking about Abigail and the way her green eyes looked up at me, pleading, while filled with tears. I don't know how I made it through that moment, I don't know how I managed to talk her through it and calm her down. I felt anything but calm, and now, I feel completely wrung out.

I need to get out of my head, and there's only ever two things that help me do that. One is sleep, but considering the time, if I sleep now, I'll never sleep tonight, and the second is a ride.

I should just go for a quick blast down the farm. I could

check the cattle while I'm out there. It would be a better use of my time.

But I need something more today.

I wheel my bike out of the shed, load it onto the back of my ute and strap it down. My riding gear is already in the backseat, so after sending a quick text to Violet to let her know I won't be there for dinner after all, I head out.

I roll my windows down and turn up the music as I pull out of the Wildflower Ridge gate. I love this time of year. It's coming into summer so the days are getting longer, the temperature's warmer and there's a bit more sun in my life. Though I'm grateful for the sun now, soon I'll be cursing it when it makes my freckles run rampant.

This is exactly what I needed. The wind on my face, a little bit of freedom. Not that Wildflower Ridge is stifling. Except when it is.

Sometimes the itch under my skin gets to be too much and I need to get away. Fortunately for me, the perfect spot for my escapes isn't too far from home.

It's a long stretch of beach that borders the neighbouring farm to Wildflower Ridge.

Constellation Station is another place I know like the back of my hand. The owners George and Clarissa Sheridan were also friends with my parents, and their twin sons are the same age as Olivia and me.

Max and Toby were my best friends through primary school. Toby died a few years ago, and Max had a personality transplant somewhere around the age of sixteen, so I have very little to do with him these days. I don't know what he'd say about me accessing the beach through his property, but I doubt he'd stop me. Being the orphan child of Trent and Isla Woods occasionally has perks, and people not wanting to say no to me is one of them.

I'm singing along to the music at the top of my lungs when I round a sweeping bend in the road. Pulled over on the narrow shoulder is a silver sedan, its hazard lights flashing.

I pull in behind the car and stride up to the driver's side window, knocking on the glass.

A muffled shriek comes from the person in the driver's seat, and a moment later the window rolls down.

Abigail stares up at me, her eyes wide and shocked. And teary. Really, really teary.

As I stand staring at her, a tear slips down her cheek.

"You gave me such a fright," she says, gasping down a breath.

I almost ask her if she's okay. I manage to stop myself before I let the words out. Of course she's not okay, you idiot. She's crying on the side of the road.

"What's wrong?" I manage to ask instead.

"Nothing."

"Let me guess, you're fine?" I arch an eyebrow at her.

"Yes."

"You're crying in your car."

She sniffles, then wipes at her face, smudging mascara along her cheek. "They're happy tears."

"Happy tears?"

"Yeah, you know when something's amazing and you can't help but cry?"

"Can't say I understand the feeling actually," I say, running a hand through my hair, before reaching it towards her. "You've got a little ..." I pause, my hand lingering in the air between us.

She doesn't move, doesn't tell me to stop, so I touch my fingers to her skin and swipe away the smudged makeup. She exhales at my touch and I feel her breath ghost over my skin.

I pull my hand back and she blinks a few times.

"You've never happy cried?"

"Nope. But I take it that means things went well with Sadie?"

Abigail nods, her dark hair spilling over her shoulders with the movement. Her smile dims though when she looks back at me. "Did you tell anyone about earlier?"

The panic attack. "No."

"Are you going to?" She bites down on her bottom lip. I try to focus on her eyes, not her mouth.

"Is Sadie at risk?"

"Never."

I let out a long exhale, thinking. "Then no. I won't tell anyone. Not unless I have to, for Sadie's sake."

"Thank you," she whispers. "I should go."

"Okay. I'll see you tomorrow."

Then she pulls back out onto the road and drives away, leaving me standing there with the biggest, stupidest, most embarrassing crush to ever exist.

5

—

ABI

COULD I time my breakdowns any worse?

First the panic attack that Flynn walked in on, then him finding me parked on the side of the road bawling my eyes out.

I wasn't lying to him though, they were happy tears. Okay, and maybe a few sad ones when I realised how much time I've missed.

How much I've missed of watching Sadie grow up. Yeah, she's only five and there's years left for me to learn everything about her and watch her grow from the precocious child she is now to an adult.

But I missed *three years*. Three years because I let anxiety rule my life.

The miracle of it all is neither Dallas nor Sadie seem to hold it against me. At all.

Sadie was a little shy to start with—who could blame her— but it didn't take long until she was chatting away, telling me all about school and the horses and how Katie is teaching her and Dallas to ride.

That little bit of information about Dallas surprised me. He knows how to ride. We've gone riding together in the past, but when Sadie dropped that comment and I met Dallas's eyes above her head, he just shook his head, dismissing my question. I'll get to that another time. I have all the time in the world to get to know them again. I'm looking forward to every moment.

I pull into the driveway of the little house I've rented.

It's an old-fashioned bungalow, but it's been kept in excellent repair and the interiors are in great condition considering it doesn't look like they've been updated for about fifteen years. There are three bedrooms, which seems like a lot for just me, but I hope Sadie will soon have a room here, and I can use the third room as an office.

Heading inside, I drop my keys onto the wide island bench and open the Ranchslider, stepping out onto the deck. I kick off the black patent heels I've been wearing all day and stretch my toes against the timber decking.

What sold me on the house, aside from the charm of the place as a whole—was the backyard, which has a gorgeous deck that catches so much sun and a large stretch of lawn with a few fruit trees dotted around the section.

It's the perfect family home and that's the reason I'm here. Family. It's time for me to stop letting down the people I care most about in this world.

I savour the late afternoon sun for a few more moments before heading inside and grabbing one of my pre-prepared meals for dinner. The relief at having thought ahead for this week is real, because I am exhausted.

I'm just pulling the heated food out of the microwave when my phone rings. My best friend's name appears on the screen and I swipe to answer the video call.

"Hey, Em," I say, grabbing a fork from the drawer and heading back to the deck to eat while we chat.

I met Emily in my antenatal parenting classes. We stayed in touch after the classes ended and our babies were born. We were the youngest in the class, me aged twenty-one, her twenty, and I think we bonded over being young mothers. Everyone else in the class was married, or settled in a long-term relationship and while Dallas and I had been together for a little while before Sadie came along, Emily's baby daddy wasn't a regular on the scene.

She's a great mum though, and now has a fiancé that loves Emily more than life itself, and treats her son, Cody, like he's her own.

"How's the wedding planner?" Emily asks through the phone. Her camera is shaking around all over the place and I give her a moment to situate herself. Her face steadies and as I take in her blonde hair piled on top of her head in the messiest messy bun and the freckles on her cheeks, I have a pang of homesickness so strong it brings tears to my eyes.

"I'm an events coordinator, thank you very much," I say. "I do more than just weddings."

"Oh, sorry, sorry. My apologies, madam events coordinator. But how was day one?"

"It was good. Exhausting, and I didn't even do anything."

"New jobs are always exhausting. Be prepared to be tired for at least the first month."

"Says the person who hasn't started a new job in years."

She grins. "What can I say? Trophy wife life suits me."

"Sure does," a voice echoes in the background. "Hi, Abi."

"Hi, Simone," I say, laughing as Emily preens under her affection.

I ignore the pang that shoots through my chest over the fact that I once had that. I once had the perfect partner and a delightful child. A family. And I let them both down and ruined *everything*. The only peace I get from the situation is that they're so incredibly happy here, and that they haven't completely written me off.

"Tell me about who you work with," Emily says, interrupting another thought spiral.

"Well, there's Olivia, who's my boss. The events part of the family business was supposed to be hers, but her dad died earlier this year and she's spending all her time dealing with farm stuff."

"Didn't you say Dallas was running the farm?"

"He's the manager yeah, but I guess there's still plenty for Olivia to be doing. Her mum, Violet, helps her a whole lot too."

"What're they like as people? Aside from badass business ladies?"

I laugh. My friend is right. Olivia and Violet are badass. And some of the loveliest people I've ever met.

"They're so nice," I say. "I don't think they have any nastiness in them. Olivia's so level-headed for her age especially considering what she's had land on her plate. I haven't spent much time with Violet yet. She keeps herself busy looking after everyone."

"How do you mean?"

"From what it sounds like, Violet is essentially everyone's mum. She's Olivia's actual mum and has kind of adopted Dallas and Katie and Flynn as her own. She spends a lot of time with Sadie."

"Speaking of Dallas and Sadie ..." Emily trails off.

"I saw her today," I whisper, my voice coming out thicker than I expected. Tears sit along my lashes. I've cried too much today already so I blink them back.

Emily's face goes soft. "How was it?"

"Perfect," I say, pushing the word through the block in my throat. "She's perfect, Em."

"Did you meet the new girlfriend?"

"Katie. No, not today. I think she made herself scarce on purpose."

"Scared of you?" Emily raises an eyebrow. I know she's standing up for me, but it's totally unnecessary.

"Em, you know it's not like that. I'm happy for Dallas. He's doing really well. I think she stayed away so she didn't over-whelm me."

Emily hums. "Maybe. I'm reserving judgement. Any cute guys? Aside from Dallas?"

I roll with the subject change. Emily's always flitted from one conversation topic to another, no segue needed. Unfortu-nately before I have a chance to say no, my brain conjures an image of Flynn. His auburn curls falling over his forehead, the light dusting of freckles on his nose, the way he looked down at me with such concern and care in his hazel eyes.

"No. And I'm not here for that," I say, stopping my thoughts before they stray to the feel of Flynn's hands on my shoulders as he talked me down from my panic attack.

"There's someone though," Emily says, a knowing smirk curling her lips. "Don't think I didn't see that."

"There's no one, Em. I'm here for Sadie. Nothing else. I've got this amazing job and I'm going to work my ass off and prove to Dallas and Sadie and everyone else that I'm better, that I can do this, that I'm here for Sadie and *nothing* else."

"You're allowed to have some fun, Abi. Don't forget that." A high-pitched screech comes through the phone speaker. "Shit. Cody just fell off his bike. Talk soon. Love you. Bye."

She ends the call before I have a chance to respond and I return to my dinner, thinking about what she said.

I don't know what expression crossed my face when Flynn came to mind. But whatever it was, it doesn't mean anything. He's just a pretty face with an even prettier smile.

I'm here for Sadie and nothing is going to stop me making up the past three years to her.

6

———

FLYNN

"DO you ever cry because you're happy?"

"What?" Dallas stops where he's connecting the rippers to the back of the tractor.

"Do you ever cry because you're happy?" I repeat. It's been over a week since Abigail started and I can't get her tears out of my mind.

"Umm, not really, no."

"Does Katie?"

"That woman cries at the drop of a hat, over anything. She's always crying, so I hope it's not always because she's sad."

This is true. Katie has always been a crier. She cries when she's happy, sad, laughing, shocked, angry. She's always crying. I find this somewhat reassuring. Maybe Abigail wasn't lying to me.

"Why do you ask?" Dallas is studying me, his hands propped on his hips.

"Oh, no reason really," I say, avoiding eye contact and attaching the final hydraulic hose. "Thanks for the assist."

"You sure?"

I glance up at him. "Sure." I force my face into a smile and hope he buys it. He watches me for another moment, then lets it go.

"Catch you later then."

"Sure thing, boss." I climb into the tractor and put it into gear, pulling onto the track that will take me out to the paddocks I'm ripping up today in preparation for planting over the next couple of weeks.

I don't know why I keep thinking about Abigail. Yeah, sure, she's gorgeous, but surely that's not the only reason she's stuck in my head. It can't be. But I can't figure out why she's there.

I haven't seen her in the days since she started. I haven't seen her in real life, I mean. I've seen her plenty inside my head. I'm a little nervous about seeing her again, in case this raging crush I have on her is completely obvious.

But also, the best way over a crush is to just get through it, and the best way to do that is to spend more time with her. It's like exposure therapy.

I spend time with her, the novelty of her being here will wear off and the crush will fade away. It's my tried-and-true method.

Works like a charm, especially when the other person gets sick of me first and makes their opinion of me perfectly clear. Hard to fall for someone when they're outright mean to me.

Plan in place, I focus on my work. Unfortunately, driving

around a paddock working up the ground up to get it ready for planting our annual crops doesn't distract my mind enough. It's constantly drifting back to thoughts of Abigail and the way her skin felt under my thumb and how I wish she'd turned her head the slightest amount in that moment and rested her cheek against my palm.

I refocus, but over the hours I drive that tractor back and forth, my mind always wanders back to Abigail. The way her ass looked in that dress with those shiny black high heels, the scent of her hair, the tears filling her eyes when I found her in her office.

As usual, the ripping takes longer than I expected and it's well past lunchtime when I finally make it back. I park the tractor outside the implement shed across from the barn and use my bike to get to the main house. I contemplate ducking home to change into a slightly less dusty shirt, but no one's going to care.

I kick my boots off on the front porch and make my way inside.

The old-style villa has always been like my second home, and since these days I can't go to the place that feels like my actual home because someone else lives there, this is as good as it's going to get.

I follow the sound of voices to the kitchen.

"I know, Mum," Olivia is saying as I step into the room. "I'm trying." She falls into her seat and drops her head into her hands.

"Hey, Flynn," Violet says, handing me a plate of food the

moment she lays eyes on me. I don't even know where she pulled it from.

I let out a small groan, one that's nearly muffled by the growling of my stomach. "I love you, Vi." She pats my cheek and shoos me to the table where I flop down across from Olivia.

"I know you're trying," Violet says, returning to their previous conversation. "I just don't like her being down there by herself all the time. Then going home where she's alone. It's just a lot of time alone."

"I know, but I can't force her to come here. I invite her every day, for lunch and dinner. Maybe she's just overwhelmed but as she gets to know us, she'll start coming up."

They must be talking about Abigail. There's no one else Violet would worry about being alone.

Well, there's me.

But since I'm in the room during the conversation and am not a she, it's safe to say they aren't talking about me this time.

Violet purses her lips but doesn't say anything else, so Olivia turns her focus on me.

"Ripping all done?"

"Yep," I say through a mouthful of food.

She pulls a face. "You're so gross."

Swallowing, I laugh. "Only to you, darlin'." I blow her a kiss and she pretends to gag.

I finish my sandwich and the coffee Violet set down in front of me, then spot two cooling racks of muffins resting on the bench top.

"Can I?" I ask Violet, indicating the muffins.

"Since when do you ask?" Olivia says behind me. I poke my

tongue out at her and she returns the gesture. Because we're mature like that.

"Take a few," Violet says, handing me an old ice cream container.

I grab several and drop them into the container, an idea forming in my mind as I snap the lid closed.

"Leave some for the rest of us," Olivia snipes and I roll my eyes at her, ruffling her hair as I head back out the door.

"Thanks for lunch, Vi," I call, already halfway down the hall.

I rest the container on the fuel tank of my bike as I head through the farm. It's faster to go around the road, because I don't have to deal with gates, but riding along the dry gravel road isn't half as nice as riding through the lush green paddocks. I take my time, balancing the container of muffins and absorbing the scenery, reminding myself why I love it here so much.

I've never wanted to be anywhere else. Nearly all of my childhood memories were on this farm, even though we didn't live here. Dad worked side by side with Olivia's dad, Henry, until he encouraged my dad to start a contracting business. Then, my dad went from farm to farm carrying out whatever tractor work they required. In his quiet times, he always came back to Wildflower Ridge to work with Henry again.

I never went to any of those other farms with Dad. Only Wildflower Ridge. On the days I couldn't be with dad and I wasn't forced into a classroom, I'd spend the days with Mum and Violet and Olivia. My brother Hunter and Olivia's sister Willow would disappear off together, leaving us younger siblings behind, but that was fine by us because we got to lick all the bowls when our mums were baking, which they did a lot. Apparently it's a miracle Violet can bake these days, because she couldn't at all when she first moved to Kauri Creek.

It made perfect sense to me that when I left school, I'd work at Wildflower Ridge. I didn't even have to ask Henry for a job, just confirm I wanted one.

I'd already been working here most of my life, even if it wasn't in any formal capacity. As I got older, the jobs came with more responsibility and Henry started transferring money into my bank account regularly. It wasn't much, but it was still nice. I wonder if he did the same for Katie when she moved here and started working alongside me and Olivia. Almost certainly.

As the end of school approached, Henry pulled me aside one afternoon and told me a job was here for me whenever I wanted it. He knew I had zero intentions of going to university, but he also encouraged me to do what I really wanted to do, not just fall into the job here.

Lucky for both of us what I really wanted was a job here at Wildflower Ridge.

I crest the final hill and the function centre comes into view. It's an old barn that once upon a time Violet and Henry got married in.

It's been Olivia's dream since we were kids to refurbish it and run it as an events centre. She worked her butt off to get it exactly how she wanted it, and now it's a stunning, and sought after, venue.

Unfortunately it had barely been finished when Henry passed and Olivia had to redirect her focus to managing the property overall.

That's where Abigail comes in. It's her job now to make Olivia's dreams come true. And even though most people think I'm fickle and irresponsible, and while they're mostly right, I'm going to do everything I can to help the family that was there for me when I lost my own.

I TAKE A DEEP BREATH, readjust my hands under the box and brace my core as I lift it off the ground.

God damn, this box is heavy. Who knew wooden platters could weigh so much?

I shuffle a few steps and pause to readjust my grip. It's such an awkward size to lift and I'm not wearing the most practical shoes for the task. They're gorgeous, but not very sensible right now. I'm going to need to keep a pair of flats in the office for days like today.

"Here, let me," a voice says and I feel hands brush against mine as the weight is lifted out of my arms.

I look up, across the top of the box, meeting Flynn's hazel eyes. They're a shimmering blend of golden brown, bronze and mossy green. "I've got it," I say, my voice coming out snappier than I intended. I try to take the box back, but he whisks it away out of my reach.

"Where do you want it?" he asks, striding across the brick-paved floor of the main reception room.

I sigh, brushing the dust off my black wide-leg pants and pink top—another poor choice for this task—and follow him out of the storeroom. I thought I'd just have a quick look through the space to familiarise myself with what we have on hand, and where it's located. But while Olivia had mentioned it needed a tidy up, it's a far bigger mess than I anticipated. The space obviously had an organising system once upon a time, but it looks like nothing has been stored properly after the last few events and the labels are not matching up with the items.

I'm glad I realised now and not right before an event.

"Over there." I wave to a table I have set up where I'm sorting and cleaning everything I'm pulling out of the storeroom. Then I head back inside and grab the next box, bracing myself for the lift.

"I've got it." Flynn approaches me again, his hands out to take the box, an easy smile on his face.

"I'm fine," I say, again. "I can manage."

"I have no doubt you can, but I'm happy to help."

He smiles again, looking so laid back and relaxed. I feel my brows draw down and my lips tighten. I can do this. I have to prove to Olivia and Dallas that I'm capable. I can't do that with Flynn swooping in to save me all the time.

"I don't need help."

"Okay." He holds up his hands in an 'I surrender' gesture. "Do you need muffins though?"

"Muffins?" I eye him. He's looking way too pleased with himself.

"Yep," he says, popping the 'p'. "The best you'll get in Kauri Creek."

"That's a bold claim," I say, setting down the box I was carrying and trying not show how much effort it took to carry it across the short distance. I don't want to eat muffins with Flynn, but my stomach is beginning to get annoyed with me.

"Well, Violet made them, using my mum's recipe. It actually doesn't get better. Come on."

Flynn grabs an ice cream container off the shelf by the door and waves for me to follow him.

"But, I'm working," I say to his back as he disappears out the door.

"Come on, Abigail," he calls and even though I should be focussing on my job, I follow him.

He's waiting for me at the corner of the barn, and when I catch up he heads around the side, towards the wedding lawn and lake. He collapses onto the bench seat in the gazebo, slouching to the side so he can kick his boots up on the seat across the corner.

I perch across from him, chewing on my lip as I take in his lanky frame spread halfway across the gazebo.

Flynn snaps the lid off the container and pulls out a muffin. They do look delicious, huge and golden with a crust of cinnamon sugar baked into the top.

While he's focussed on unwrapping the muffin I let my eyes linger, taking him in properly for the first time.

His auburn hair flares redder, with little flashes of gold, when he tilts his head and the sun hits it. Right now his hazel eyes are closed in bliss as he chews his first mouthful, but I'm never going to forget the concern in them from that first day we met ... both times.

His body is long and lean and he wears his worn-out jeans, t-shirt and heavy brown jacket like they were made specifically for him.

"Here." Flynn holds out the container, but I have no chance of reaching it unless I stand. "Come over here," he says. "The view of the pond is better." He smirks, like he's laughing about me calling it a pond.

Those muffins really do look good, so I step across the gazebo and lower myself down next to him, gingerly taking a muffin from the container he's still holding.

The pond is pretty and all, but sitting across from him wasn't exactly a hardship. I kick that stray thought out of my head the second it crosses my mind. Absolutely not.

I can feel his attention on me while I turn my focus to unwrapping the muffin. I can't just take a massive bite like he did, especially with him watching me like this, so I break off a portion and pop it in my mouth.

I actually groan. Out loud. In front of this virtual stranger who is my work colleague. That's so embarrassing.

"Oh my god. That's so good," I say, wanting to hit myself in the head as the words tumble out.

Flynn positively beams at my reaction. "Told you," he says, settling back against the seat and looking out across the pond/lake again.

"Who did you say made them?"

"Violet. She's an amazing cook. You should come up for lunch. Muffins like this almost daily."

"You said something about your mum?" I ask, not sure why I'm heading down this line of questioning, but something in the way he phrased it is niggling my brain.

"Yeah. It's my mum's recipe. One of her favourites. She's the one who taught Violet to bake."

"Your mum and Violet are friends?"

"They were. Best friends." He shifts, dropping his feet back to the floor, the easy confidence I was admiring in him just a moment ago evaporating.

His shoulder brushes mine. I don't even know how we got this close. I shiver. I feel like I've stuck my foot in it. I take another bite of muffin to avoid saying something else, and study how our thighs align while we sit side by side on this bench. I can't help but compare his filthy jeans and worn workbooks to my dress pants and high heels.

Flynn lets out a big sigh and slumps back. "My parents died when I was fourteen," he says, his voice low and quiet in the still afternoon.

Oh. I was getting the feeling his mum wasn't around anymore, but I wasn't expecting both parents, and not when he was so young.

I have no words. None that are going to mean anything anyway, so I reach out and squeeze his hand. His head jerks up at the contact.

"Thank you for telling me," I say.

The corner of his mouth curls. "It's not exactly a secret."

"Can I ask what happened?"

"Car accident," he says, his voice rough and detached.

"They went out for their usual date night. Someone crashed into them."

I squeeze his hand again and his fingers flex around mine, then slowly relax. I wait for a moment, then extricate my fingers when I realise he's no longer holding them and I'm just sitting here clinging onto him.

Flynn sucks in another deep breath. "Violet and Henry were like my surrogate parents after that."

"They took you in?"

"No. My brother was eighteen and we wanted to stay together." He rolls his eyes, like he can't imagine why they'd wanted that. "He was my official guardian, but he only got that because of Violet and Henry vouching for him. And they helped feed us, and did all the parent-type things they could." He sighs as he slouches further into his seat. His shoulder brushes mine again and I try to ignore the goosebumps that travel down my arm at the contact.

It's not to do with Flynn. It's to do with the fact that it's a fresh afternoon and we're sitting outside in the shade.

"You're cold," Flynn says, obviously paying attention to those goosebumps. He takes in my short-sleeved top. "Sorry. I didn't think when I made you come out here."

"It's fine," I say. "But I should get back to work." I point awkwardly over my shoulder at the building.

"Do you want a hand sorting out that storeroom?" he asks, fiddling with the paper case from his muffin.

"I'm fine," I say. "I'm sure you have other things to do."

He shrugs. "If you want help, I can help."

"I don't need help," I say, tone sharpening without my

consent. What's with him not thinking I can do anything myself?

"I know you don't need help, Abigail, but if you *want* it, I can help you. You don't have to work down here alone all the time. My job is to do whatever needs to be done, and if that storeroom needs to be cleaned out, you're allowed to ask for help. No one's going to think less of you for it."

I ignore the way my name rolls off his tongue and instead focus on the end of his little speech. He might think no one is going to think less of me for it, but he doesn't know. He doesn't know how much I have to prove myself. I can't let anyone think I'm avoiding my responsibilities, especially with the way they're all so close here. They'll definitely talk to each other about me, and if Flynn or Olivia thinks I'm slacking off, Dallas is going to find out.

I won't let that happen. I won't let him hear things like that about me.

"Thank you for offering, but I really am okay," I say, pushing to my feet. "Thanks for the muffin."

Flynn frowns, then holds the container. "Take the rest. But you know where to find more when those run out. If you want I can come pick you up so you don't have to walk in there alone."

I wrap my fingers around the container, careful not to touch his, and it takes a moment for me to realise what he's talking about. Lunch at Violet's.

So they're definitely talking about me.

Olivia asks me every day if I'm heading up to the house for lunch. Dallas has asked me too. Apparently this means something to them.

The thought of it terrifies me—walking into that house, finally meeting Katie, making small talk with co-workers I have nothing in common with. I just want to do my job, reconnect with Sadie and spend my free hours at the cute little house in town. But Sadie is a part of this place, of this family, and I'm going to have to try harder.

"Okay." My voice comes out in a whisper. "Yes, please."

He grins, his eyes sparking with delight as I agree. "I'll come by tomorrow and pick you up then."

"What time?"

He rubs his hand through his hair. "I have no clue," he says with a laugh. "I'll try and text you with an update."

I bite my lip. That is not how I roll. I need a schedule, but I'm going to have to deal with it. "Okay. See you tomorrow. Thank you for these." I hold up the container between us.

"See you tomorrow, Abigail."

8

———

FLYNN

I FEEL like I'm spending way too much time standing outside this building, staring up at the sign and running my hands through my hair, like I'm *nervous*.

I brush some dirt off the leg of my jeans, which does nothing because they're filthy. I've been working on a farm for several hours, and even with every laundry trick in the book, these jeans will never truly be clean again.

They're my favourite and I try not to think about why I chose to wear them this morning when I knew I'd be seeing Abigail.

I take a deep breath, shove the thoughts of this silly little crush to the back of my mind and step through the door.

The main function room is quiet and still. It's so gorgeous in here, all rustic timber and brickwork. It's stunning when it's all done up with flowers and ribbons for weddings, but I like it the most when it's quiet like this.

I pause just inside the door. Abigail's car is outside, so she can't be too far away, but there doesn't seem to be any movement inside. I'm about to go back outside in case she's out on the wedding lawn or beside the lake, when I hear music playing quietly. She must be upstairs in the office.

Obviously. That would make sense.

I take the stairs two at a time and lean on the doorframe at the top. Abigail looks up, a professional smile plastered on her face. When she sees it's me, the smile melts away.

"Oh, hey Flynn," she says, turning back to the papers spread across her desk.

"Heya, Abigail. How's it going?"

"It's fine. Really busy," she says.

"You ready to go?"

"Go?" she asks, staring at me with a confused look on her face, as if she doesn't know why I'm here.

"Lunch at Violet's," I say. I know where she's going with this and I'm not having it.

Abigail gestures at the paper spread over the desk. "I can't go to lunch," she says.

"Yeah, you can. You need to eat. It'll fortify you for your afternoon of doing whatever it is you need to do with all that paper."

Abigail narrows her eyes, like I've offended her. "I have a mountain of planning to do and a client meeting this afternoon. I don't have time for lunch."

"What time is the client coming?"

"I'm not exactly sure. They're going to text me when they're in town."

"Well that'll give you enough warning to get back here then."

"I'm not coming."

"You're nervous," I say, ignoring her last comment, because if I know anything it's that I can be very persuasive. It's all part of my charm: annoying people into compliance.

"I'm not. I'm just busy."

"You're anxious."

It's pretty obvious, and I can understand why. These people are my family, but they're strangers to her, all except Dallas—her ex and father of her estranged daughter. Not to mention Katie, Dallas's new girlfriend. Katie's one of my best friends, and I know she wants the best for Abigail, because it means the best for Sadie, but Abigail doesn't know that. She doesn't know Katie isn't going to be bitchy and resentful of her arrival.

"Fine. Yes. Happy now?" I shrug and Abigail huffs out a breath before continuing. "I know they're all really nice, and they're your family, but it's still terrifying. The fact you're all so close makes it worse somehow."

I chuckle. "I get that. But you still need to eat and the sooner we go, the sooner you can get back to your paperwork."

"Why are you so judgemental about the paperwork? It's important."

"Oh, I know. I'm not judgemental. It's just something I'll never understand. Things on paper never make sense to me. Plus, you know what else is important? Food. Come on."

She lets out a little growly noise and a smile tugs at my mouth. She pushes to her feet and grabs her phone off the table.

"Fine. Let's go." She's in full business mode and I can't deny how hot it is when she's like this.

"Awesome. I'm starving." I spin and head back down the stairs, listening to the sound of her shoes on the timber stairs as she follows me. I lead her outside and swing my leg over my bike.

"What the hell is this?" She stares at me.

"A motorbike." I grin at her. "Mode of transportation. Your ride to lunch."

"No."

"It's this or walking and Abigail, those shoes wouldn't make it. Do it for the shoes." I laugh, gesturing at the pair of sexy as fuck high heels on her feet, and I see a spark of humour in her eyes before it vanishes again.

"No."

"Come on. We need to get back to the paperwork." I pull a disgusted face.

"Yeah, I'll do that now," she snaps and spins to head back inside.

"Nope." I reach out and snag her wrist before she gets too far away from me. I tug her towards me and she stumbles a little, ending up way closer than I anticipated. "Sorry," I murmur. "You need to get on the bike. It'll be fun."

"I just ... it's ..." She gestures at the bike, then at herself, then back at me. I wait until she processes whatever it is she's trying to say. She gives up and says nothing, just giving a defeated little shrug.

"You'll be safe," I say, an embarrassing thread of hope

shining in my voice. "Come on, Abigail. I'll look after you. I promise."

She takes a deep breath, glances back over her shoulder—no doubt desperately trying to come up with an excuse I'll let her get away with—then takes a step towards the bike.

"I am not suitably dressed for this," she mutters as she delicately places a hand on my shoulder and awkwardly swings her leg over the bike.

"You really do need to get some jeans and boots," I say twisting to face her. "But this," I gesture at her sitting astride my bike, "It's a good look."

Her cheeks flush and I grin, then direct her where to put her feet, warning her to be careful of the exhaust.

"Where do I hold on?" she asks, voice soft with a slight quiver giving away her nerves.

"You hold on to me," I say, stamping down on the kickstart. The bike flares to life and Abigail lets out a startled sound. Her fingers dig into my shoulders as her body slides forward, pressing into mine.

I did not think this through.

"Wrap your arms around my waist," I say and when I feel her forearms band around my torso I realise just how much I didn't think this through.

Abigail in that skirt is hot.

Abigail in those heels is hot.

Abigail on my bike is hot.

Abigail on my bike in the skirt and heels ... way hotter.

Abigail on my bike in the skirt and heels with her body pressed into mine so I can feel the swell of her breasts and her arms wrapped around me, palms splayed across my chest and stomach ... the hottest thing that's happened to me in my life.

I feel a little dizzy at her proximity, at the heat of her, at the way she smells, at the feel of her breath against my neck as she clings to me.

"You good?" I ask in a hoarse, raspy voice.

Abigail nods and I feel the movement against my shoulder. "Yeah," she whispers, then steels her tone. "Let's do this."

"Atta girl."

9

———

ABI

I START the bike ride with my eyes squeezed shut, clinging onto Flynn like I'm going to fly away if I lessen my grip at all. I quell the shaking in my hands by pressing them against Flynn's stomach, my fingers clutching at his shirt and listen to the sound of my heart galloping in my chest.

I'm expecting him to rev the bike and speed through the farm, but the pace he sets is sedate and after a few moments where I try to get my breathing under control, I pry my eyelids open.

Flynn must feel the moment my grip on him relaxes slightly —I'm still hanging onto him for dear life—because he takes a hand off the handlebars and pats my arm where it's wrapped around his middle. "See, you're all good. I've got you."

I've got you. Somehow it feels like more than just in this moment. Since I got here Flynn's had my back, even when I don't want it. He gives my arm a soft squeeze, then returns his hand to the handlebars, which I have to admit, I'm relieved by.

We follow the road around to the main part of the farm, where the house is, and I'm just a tiny bit disappointed we didn't get to go through the farm. I was looking forward to seeing just how beautiful it is.

"We aren't going through the farm?" I ask.

"So you've managed to open your eyes, huh?" he asks, and I can hear the humour in his voice.

"Yes, but that doesn't answer my question." It comes out grumbly and I hope he doesn't think I'm feeling bitchy about this.

"There's a lot of gates to open if we go through the farm. You're not exactly dressed in appropriate bike gear, or farming footwear. I'm just trying to preserve the shoes."

"You're really taken with my shoes."

"You always have great shoes. I'm assuming it's because you like them. I'll take you down the farm sometime when I'm not worried about what you're wearing. I don't want to ruin your nice stuff, or have you get hurt."

I glance down and realise the way I'm sitting on the bike, and pressing against Flynn's back, has made my skirt ride up. My bare thighs slot in against the backs of Flynn's denim-clad ones. The expanse of exposed skin, the way my green suede heels are propped on the little pegs Flynn showed me, and the way this position forces my knees apart is downright pornographic.

I let out a groan and my head falls forward, coming to rest on Flynn's shoulder.

"What's wrong?" he asks, immediately on high alert.

"I just realised what I look like on this bike, dressed like this. I look like some bike guy's wet dream."

He slows to a stop in the middle of the Wildflower Ridge driveway, resting one foot on the ground to hold us and the bike upright. He twists his body, turning to face me as much as he can.

His gaze trails over me, eyes darkening as they linger on the hem of my skirt, hitched somewhere around the underside of my ass instead of near my knees. His tongue slips out and swipes along his lower lip and something in me twinges at the sight of it. The scruff on his jaw makes me want to reach out and feel the roughness against my fingertips.

He drags his gaze upwards until it locks with mine. "I'm not going to deny you look incredible right now, but it wouldn't matter what you were wearing, you're probably always going to be some bike guy's wet dream. You're hot as fuck. You know that."

It's more than just a twinge this time. White-hot lightning strikes through my body at his rough voice. If I physically could right now, I'd be pressing my thighs together, trying to quell the sudden ache there.

It's not even him telling me I'm hot, or that I look incredible. It's the way he says "some bike guy", like he knows exactly which bike guy would be dreaming about me.

It's him.

He's the one who'd be dreaming about me.

He abruptly turns back to the bike and finishes the slow drive up to the house. He pulls up outside, beside the ute I know belongs to Dallas, and flicks down the bike stand with one deft twist of his foot. It's super-hot considering what he's doing. I bet he doesn't even think twice about it.

"Careful hopping off," Flynn says gruffly. "The exhaust will be hot."

I swing my leg over the back of the bike and slide to the ground, tottering a bit on my heels. Flynn's big, calloused hand lands on my leg to steady me. It should be fine. It should just be a simple, casual touch to prevent me tripping over my own feet.

But my skirt is still riding too high and instead of landing on the fabric, his hand connects with my bare thigh.

His palm is hot and firm, just slightly rough from the physical farm work he does daily. If he's affected by the feel of my skin, he doesn't show it and as soon as I'm steady on my feet, his hand is gone, leaving behind an invisible but searing palm print.

He swings his leg over the bike and strides up the porch steps to the front door. His jeans tighten around his ass and thighs as he moves. I shouldn't be staring at his ass, but my mind is still a haze of heat against the soft skin of my thigh, and a certain bike guy's wet dreams and the way Flynn's tongue dragged across his bottom lip.

Fucking hell. Nope. Nope. Nope.

Co-worker, co-worker, co-worker, I force myself to chant in my head. I can't think about him like this.

Sadie. I need to think about Sadie. I take a breath and refocus on Dallas's big black ute. Sadie is why I'm here, not to get the hots for a farm worker several years younger than me.

Nope, not going there.

I square my shoulders and follow Flynn up the porch steps. He kicks his boots off at the door.

"Your shoes will be fine," he says, pushing the door open.

I take one look at the gorgeous hardwood floors and bend to unbuckle my shoes. I don't care if Flynn says they're fine. I don't need my every step heard by everyone inside this house.

He watches me and when I stand barefoot in front of him, he leads me into the house.

"Look what the cat dragged in," Flynn announces to the room as we step into a large, airy kitchen. And here I was hoping he'd let me slip in quietly.

Olivia is across the room, heaping food onto a plate. Violet's sitting at the table, a mug in hand while she laughs at something Dallas is saying. A stunning blonde who I know is Katie sits beside him, shovelling pasta into her mouth. Even with a mouth full of food, she looks gorgeous. Her gaze snaps to me at Flynn's words and she swallows before her face splits into a huge grin.

"I hope you're not referring to yourself as the cat in this situation," she says to Flynn, then turns her focus to me. "Hey. Grab a plate."

I appreciate her easy acceptance of my being here. She's not making a big deal about it, neither going over the top excited about my arrival, or surly because I'm here.

Violet moves to stand, but Flynn pushes her back into her seat with a gentle hand on her shoulder.

"I got it," he says, heading for Olivia. I trail along behind him, greeting Dallas on the way, and when I reach my boss, she hands me a plate that Flynn piles high with a deliciously creamy pasta filled with chicken and bacon and mushrooms.

"How's it all going?" Olivia asks, sliding into a seat at the table and gesturing for me to sit across from her. Flynn sits beside Olivia and immediately falls into Dallas and Violet's conversation.

"It's good," I say. "I have a meeting with the Barclay-MacDonald wedding group this afternoon. Way to throw me in the deep end."

Olivia laughs. "That's why I needed you to start so soon. I didn't want to have to deal with it." Her face turns serious. "Everything going alright?"

"Yeah, it's great. Everything's under control."

"And for this weekend?"

That's right. My first event. Thankfully it's a small wedding and the couple don't seem to be nearly as high maintenance as the Barclay-MacDonald couple.

"It'll be your first event this weekend, yeah?" Katie asks and I nod. "I'm sure it'll go great," she says, her voice warm and kind.

"I hope so." My voice sounds thicker than usual and I hope no one notices. I force a smile and turn my focus to my food, hoping Olivia will drop the conversation.

She does, turning to Katie and asking her about Aurora, who I think is one of the horses Sadie introduced me to the other day.

The women beside me chat about the horses for a few moments while I continue to shovel food into my mouth.

"Oh, Abi ... Abigail ..." Katie trails off when she trips over my name. I'm sure Dallas has only referred to me as Abi. That's what he always called me, but Olivia and Flynn always call me Abigail. So far that's all I've been known as here.

"Abi is fine," I say, trying to smile in a way that doesn't look like I'm about to jump off the edge.

"Abi." She smiles. "Sadie and I are going riding on Sunday.

Do you want to come with us?" She takes a breath but before I have a chance to respond, she's talking again. "You don't have to. If it's weird. But if you do want to, you're more than welcome to join us. We have a horse you can ride, obviously. I don't know how confident you are, but he's a real sweetheart. And we can go anytime, like after you've done what you need to do at the event centre."

"Katie Kat," Flynn says, his eyes sparkling with humour. "Stop talking and let her respond."

Everyone at the table laughs and I realise now everyone is waiting for my response.

"Yeah, I'd like that," I say, hoping that come Sunday I can actually go through with it.

10

FLYNN

I HAVE to smother my smile when Abigail accepts Katie's offer to go riding.

I covertly watch Abigail from the corner of my eye while we eat lunch and she makes slightly awkward small talk with us. Everyone is welcoming, of course.

I didn't expect anything less from them. Everyone wants Abigail here, for Sadie's sake, and also for Olivia's, because we all know she needs more hands.

When Abigail compliments Violet on her muffins, Violet regales us of her history of baking fails and as Abigail laughs along with everyone else, her head tipped back and her eyes bright, I feel like I can finally relax.

It's then that I remember what my big, stupid mouth said to Abigail on my bike.

I can't believe I told her she was hot as fuck and my wet dream fantasy.

Good one, Flynn. Way to make things fucking awkward.

It's true though. She looked so fucking good perched on my bike, her bare legs pressing against mine and her arms around me, palms splayed across my body.

I've got to put a stop to the thoughts in my head about this woman. Since I can't rid myself of them fully just yet, I push them to the back corner of my brain and refocus on the room.

Abigail has finished eating and is fiddling with the end of her fork. Everyone else is still chatting away like they have all afternoon. Which they kind of do, there's nothing pressing on the schedule today.

"Right, I better get back to it," I say, pushing back from the table. I snag Abigail's plate along with my own and stack them in the dishwasher. "I'll give you a ride back," I say to her.

Olivia opens her mouth, to protest and suggest Abigail hangs out a little longer, but I can see the tension creeping back into Abigail's shoulders as she glances at the clock on the wall more and more often, so I cut Olivia off.

"Some of us have work to get back to." I ruffle Olivia's hair and she bats my hand away.

"Yeah, work," she mutters, her eyes briefing closing, and her shoulders slumping slightly. "Yay."

I bend down and wrap an arm around her in the briefest hug. "You got this, babe," I whisper in her ear, low enough so no one else can hear. Then I stand and gesture to Abigail to follow me as I stride from the room.

Olivia is doing her damn best, but the girl never got a chance to grieve her dad passing away before she got thrust into full-time running of the farm. Sure, Violet is still technically in charge. She's the owner of the place, but she doesn't have the same understanding of the farm's operations as Olivia does. The plan was always for Olivia to take over eventually, but Henry was supposed to be around for years yet.

I know Olivia loves this place with all her heart, and she's surrounded by people who love it just as much, but I understand sometimes you just need a break. With the first wedding since Henry's passing happening this weekend, she's probably feeling an extra layer of pressure.

I get outside and slip my feet back into my boots, then swing my leg over my bike, fiddling with the handlebars while Abigail puts her shoes back on. She approaches the bike with a fraction more confidence than last time, but still takes a deep breath before sliding her leg over the seat, her hand coming to rest on my shoulder to steady herself.

I have to close my eyes at the contact, and squeeze them tighter when her body settles against my back, her arms snaking around my stomach.

"Good to go?" I grit out, willing myself not to get hard when she sighs and presses her cheek against my shoulder.

She takes a shaky breath, but agrees, and we head back to the events centre. I spend every second of that ride thinking about horrible, boring things, like responsibilities, and absolutely not thinking about Abigail's soft hands and long fingers, with fingernails perfectly painted. Today they're a dusky pink colour and I definitely don't think about what that colour would look like tangled in my hair, or running over my bare skin.

I don't think about the way her bare thigh felt under my palm, or the way she trusted me by getting on the bike in the first place.

Instead, I think about tractor maintenance and how I need to get the power harrow ready to go for next week.

I park my bike outside the events centre and switch off the engine while Abigail carefully climbs off. When she's clear, I swing my leg over, coming to stand beside her.

"Thank you," she says, looking up at me with nervous eyes. "That was … less scary than I expected." She gives me a small smile.

"We all want you here, Abigail." I hover over her name for a brief second, wondering if, when she told Katie she could call her Abi, she meant I could as well. She doesn't correct it though and I refocus on my point. "We want you here, for Olivia's sake, for Sadie … and aside from them, I like having you here."

"That's sweet of you," she mumbles, looking away as she blushes.

I want to tell her there is nothing sweet about the places my brain goes to when I think of her.

Abigail blows out a breath, fluttering the strands of hair hanging around her face. I reach a hand up, slowly, giving her the chance to move if she wants to. She doesn't. She stays frozen under my gaze as I run my fingers through her hair, smoothing out the tangles caused by the ride.

My fingers reach the end of her hair and my eyes lock with hers. I reach up, without thinking, without taking my eyes off hers, and slide my fingers through her hair again.

She lets out a tiny gasp as the pads of my fingertips brush her scalp. Her hair is like silk and my fingers slip through the dark strands like I'm trailing them through water.

The anxiety leaves her eyes and instead I see a flash of something darker, hotter. She catches her plush lower lip between her teeth and it drags my attention away from her intense gaze.

God, I want to kiss that mouth. I want to kiss her. I want to know what her skin feels like. I want to slide my hands up her legs, beneath the skirt she's wearing today. I want to explore every inch of her.

My dick throbs and the spell breaks. Holy shit. I cannot be thinking things like this about Abigail. I just can't.

She's my boss's ex.

She's Sadie's mum.

We work together.

I clear my throat and take a step backwards.

It takes her a moment to catch up, to realise I've ruined the moment, then that heated look fades from her gaze and she looks at me with something akin to horror on her face.

"Right, well. Good luck with your meeting. I'll see you around," I stammer. "I'll be here on Friday to help you set up. Let me know if you need anything before then."

"Okay," she says, her voice barely a whisper. "Bye, Flynn."

She doesn't move, she just stands there, staring at me with captivating eyes. I spin on my heel and swing my leg back over my bike. I need to get out of here before I do something reckless and so, so stupid.

I stomp on the kickstart and the bike flares to life. The vibration of the machine under me steadies me somewhat, until I glance back up at Abigail who's watching me, one arm crossed over her chest, the other elbow propped on it while her hand rests against her throat, those dusky pink nails dragging across the delicate skin there.

Nope, nope, nope. Not thinking about that.

I release the clutch and twist the throttle. The bike shoots forward and as I race away from Abigail, I will the ache in my pants away.

I wish I didn't have to. I wish I could turn around and go straight back to her, wrap my arms around her, slide my hands along her skin, drag my lips across her throat where her fingers were stroking.

But I can't.

Because Abigail doesn't need more on her plate. Her priority is Sadie, and I love that kid with all my heart, so there's no way I'm getting in the way of her reconnecting with her mum.

I shove all thoughts of Abigail away and think about my plans for the afternoon. That power harrow needs a service.

But first I might go take care of something at home. Then maybe when the pressure in my dick is gone, I'll be able to focus on reality again.

11

———

ABI

THE WEDDING WENT off without a hitch.

Well, as far as I'm aware. But I haven't had any irate brides, grooms or family members on the phone screaming at me about it all going wrong, so I'm happy.

I'm smiling and humming as I do a quick inventory of the state of the venue on Sunday morning. This wedding was a venue hire, rather than a full wedding package, which means the couple and their families are responsible for just about everything. And they've done a good job. The function room is cleared up and while I'll do a proper check through tomorrow to make sure everything is in order, I don't think I'll have to worry too much.

I breathe a sigh of relief.

First event done. Now it's time for my next challenge—riding with Sadie and Katie.

I've spent more time with Sadie since our first meeting. I love how quickly Dallas has included me in Sadie's life, and appreciate it more than I could ever express to him. It took us a little bit of time for the initial meeting to take place because I was busy finding a house to rent and moving, and Dallas needed some time to adjust to the idea of me being around again—which I totally understand. But after the first meeting on my first day at Wildflower Ridge, Dallas hasn't been keeping me from her at all.

I've seen Sadie several days after school, and yesterday her and Dallas stopped by to see if I needed any help.

I had just finished setting everything up for the wedding when Sadie skipped into the big old barn in her pink sparkly gumboots and a skirt designed for twirling. She stopped when she saw me, her shy smile creeping over her face.

"Hi, Sadie," I said. "I heard you're going riding tomorrow. Do you mind if I come along?"

The shy smile dissolved, replaced with a bright, beaming one. "Yes!" she nearly squealed. "You can ride Paddy." She paused, turned to Dallas and said, "You're not coming, are you?"

I burst out laughing at her tone while Dallas rolled his eyes at me. "Nah, Sadie girl. I'll leave it to you and Katie to give Abi the grand tour."

"Can we show her where you nearly died?"

My breath caught at her words, but I managed to refrain from shrieking at him. "Died?" I whispered instead.

Dallas shook his head. "I cut my arm. But I was alone and couldn't ride my bike. Katie had to come and find me. It was all fine." He glanced around the room then, taking in the mostly set up venue. "Do you need any help here?"

It was my turn to shake my head. "Pretty much all done.

Flynn gave me a hand." I hoped the heat I felt in my cheeks wasn't obvious to Dallas. I should be used to that heat now, because it crawls across my skin every time I think of Flynn, but somehow I'm not. And unfortunately, I seem to be thinking of Flynn rather a lot. I forced the images of him out of my head and refocused on Dallas. "The groom's sister will be here any moment to get everything else set up. Thanks though."

"Alright," Dallas replied. "We'll leave you to it. Come on, Sadie."

"Bye," Sadie said, following her dad out of the barn. "Don't forget to bring a carrot for Paddy."

And now, with the wedding over and my tasks for this morning finished, it's time to go riding with my daughter.

I close up the function barn, climb into my car and head for the main farm entrance and the real barn. I pull up beside a bright blue ute and grab the carrot off my passenger seat. I tuck it into the back pocket of my jeans as I head towards the horse paddock, keeping an eye out for Sadie and Katie to arrive.

There's no sign of them yet, so I lean against the fence. A pretty roan horse ambles over to greet me. She starts snuffling at my clothes, obviously looking for treats.

"Are you Paddy?" I ask, stroking the horse's soft muzzle. I don't think it is. I'm sure Sadie introduced me to this horse on Monday and its name wasn't Paddy. What it is, I couldn't say, but I'm sure Paddy isn't right.

"No, that's Aurora." Flynn leans on the fence beside me. Aurora turns her attention to him. "You should feel extremely honoured. That horse doesn't approach just anyone."

"She had no problem with Sadie."

"Yeah, because Katie and Sadie spend pretty much all their time with her. But when she first arrived, she was in a bad way, and scared of everyone. I think you're the first person she's approached without you having gotten close to her first." He shoots me a smile, then his eyes trail down my body.

Heat sears across me, not just my cheeks this time, but down my throat, across my chest and lower. His look shouldn't do this to me. But he shouldn't be looking at me like that right now either. Or ever really I suppose.

I'm wearing old jeans and a pair of boots I bought on Friday afternoon at the farm supply store in town. The jeans fit me like a glove. I chose to wear them today specifically for the confidence boost they always give me, because being beside Katie all day is going to make me feel inadequate enough.

Flynn's mouth quirks when he notices the boots and he reaches out his foot to tap it against mine. "Nice boots," he says.

"I figured none of my heels were suitable for riding."

"Probably true." His eyes flash, darkening for a moment before returning to their usual clear hazel. A twinge in my belly makes me desperate to know what thought just crossed his mind. Was it anything to do with how I looked on his bike in high heels and a skirt most definitely not designed for motorbike seats? "I, uh, better get back to it." He gestures over his shoulder to where the tractor is parked near the giant shed. "Have fun on your ride."

"Thanks," I say, hoping my smile comes across more confident than it feels.

He strides back to his tractor. I watch him go, leaning back against the fence and letting myself have this one moment to admire him from behind. He reaches up and grabs a handrail attached to the tractor, swinging himself up the steps. The twinge in my belly hits again as his jeans tighten around his ass. I have got to stop ogling him.

Aurora must agree, because at that moment she snakes her nose through the fence, snagging the carrot from my pocket.

"Hey!" I spin around and she tosses her head. "Sorry girl," I murmur, dropping my voice to a gentle, soothing tone. "That carrot wasn't for you." Aurora crunches down on the vegetable. "What am I going to give Paddy now?" The tractor rumbles to life and heads out towards the paddocks, a bale of silage trailing behind on the bale feeder. I watch it go, then return my attention to the horse.

A few minutes later, I'm still scolding Aurora for her thieving tendencies when Sadie and Katie arrive.

I recount the story, minus the lusting after Flynn part—because that is exactly what I was doing, as much as I don't want to admit it—and Sadie giggles. Katie laughs too, but the look of joy on her face when she hears Aurora approached me first definitely outweighs the humour she finds in Aurora stealing my carrot.

"Now I don't have anything to give Paddy," I say to Sadie in mock despair.

"It's okay," Sadie says, then pulls four carrots out of her jacket pocket. "I brought lots."

"Sadie!" Katie stares at the carrots. "No wonder we keep running out so fast." Sadie giggles, staring up at us with the most innocent expression. That kid could get away with murder with a face like that. "Go grab the lead ropes," Katie says.

"Okay." Sadie dumps the carrots into my hands then turns and races towards the barn.

Katie releases a long breath and shakes her head as she watches Sadie go. "That kid's hysterical."

"She's incredible," I whisper.

"She sure is." Katie turns to me. "It's why she's my favourite human."

I furrow my brow. "Isn't Dallas your favourite human?"

"Him?" Katie shakes her head and laughs. "Absolutely not. He's a pain in the ass. Sadie's got him by a country mile."

But I can see it in her face—it's clear as day—exactly how much she loves Dallas.

"You're living together?" I blurt. I was trying to ignore the urge to ask when she referenced them running out of carrots.

That pulls Katie up short. "Not officially." Her relaxed posture from a moment ago has vanished and now she's rigid and stiff.

"I'm not judging, or have any issue with it," I say, trying not to sound judgemental. "I just didn't realise. Not that it's my place to have an issue. I'm going to shut up now."

Katie shoots me a smile, like she understands the rambling and what I'm trying to say. "I know it seems fast. It feels fast, even for me. But I do love him, and being here makes me happy. Being around them makes me happy."

I smile, but even I can tell it's watery around the edges. I can't believe I gave that all up. It didn't feel like I had a choice at the time, and I'm a better person now. A stronger one.

"You make them happy too," I say. "I'm really glad they have you."

"And we're really glad you're here too." She sniffs and I realise her lashes are lined with tears. "Right, let's get these horses ready. Where's Sadie?"

"Here." My daughter skids to a stop beside us, holding up three lead ropes and halters.

"You ready for this?" Katie asks, the tears that welled in her eyes subsiding.

"Sure am," I reply and share a grin with her.

Katie. My ex's new girlfriend. My child's stepmum.

I meant what I said.

I am really glad they have her.

12

———

ABI

PADDY IS an elderly bay gelding with a wide stripe of white down his face and four white socks, all the same height, so it looks like he's stood in a puddle of white paint up to his fetlocks.

Unfortunately right now they're more green and brown than white, but Sadie is helping me wash them, while explaining to me that when horses have baths they don't get into an actual bath and just get hosed off.

She sounds disappointed horse bathtubs aren't a real thing.

Once Paddy's feet are looking a bit closer to their actual colour, Sadie returns to grooming Scout. The horse looks far too big for her, but it's obviously extremely gentle and Sadie is completely confident around her, while still showing the respect and care needed around a horse of any size.

She's more cautious around Aurora, but still gives the roan mare plenty of pats.

I move on from Paddy's legs and brush out his tail. He lets

out a contented snuffling sound as he relaxes one of his hind legs.

"He's loving all this attention," Katie says with a smile. "He almost made it to retirement before Dallas agreed to learn to ride."

"But ... he knew how to ride," I say, unsure if I should be bringing this up. "I mean, he wasn't great, but he could ride."

Katie draws in a deep breath, then exhales, glancing at Sadie and suddenly it clicks. Sadie's accident, all those years ago, the one which saw us both falling off a horse and Sadie being seriously injured. She's had no lasting complications from the accident, but that doesn't mean it didn't affect Dallas and me.

Ultimately, it was the accident that ended our relationship.

Katie must see my expression shift. "Are you okay?"

"Yeah," I breathe. "I had no idea. Dallas lost his nerve?"

Katie nods. "He found it again, eventually." She eyes me for a moment. "You're still okay around horses though?"

I nod. "Yeah, weird that it affected him like that, but I've never had the fear of horses come up." Fear of other things, for sure, but never horses. Sadie's accident wasn't the horse's fault, it was just an accident. Logically I know it wasn't my fault either, but try telling that to my anxiety. It's not something I need to get into right now though, especially because I'm pretty sure Katie knows my history almost as much as Dallas does.

Once the horses are thoroughly groomed, we tack them up. Sadie shows me where Paddy's gear is, gives me an explanation of the type of bit he uses, then asks me to carry Scout's saddle since she's too small to lift it.

"You grab the bridles and I'll take the saddles," I say, hefting them into my arms. Katie already has Aurora's and is gently laying it over her back. The mare stands quietly and Katie's grin is contagious.

She notices me watching. "I'm still waiting for her to freak out on me, but she's doing so good."

"Flynn said she'd had a hard time."

Katie nods. "She has. But she's doing better now." She rubs the mare gently on the forehead.

We finish tacking up, with Sadie keeping up constant chatter despite neither Katie or I responding. We're both lost somewhere in our heads.

Once the three horses are ready to go we lead them out into the sunshine. It's a glorious day and it makes the sky look bluer, the grass greener and life in general brighter.

It probably helps that things are going so well so far, though like Katie keeps waiting for Aurora to freak out, I keep waiting for this perfect life to come crashing down around me.

I never thought reconnecting with Sadie would go this smoothly. I thought she'd be standoffish and shy, which I wouldn't blame her for. I thought she might hate me, but she shows no signs of that. I thought Dallas would be more resistant, I thought his partner might be worse. This job could have been the worst thing ever, but so far, I love it, and I haven't even got to the really good stuff yet. My boss could have been a bitch, the guy I have to work with an asshole. But none of that has happened. Olivia's a generous boss and Flynn's biggest flaw is how hot he is, because it's so, so distracting.

I even love the house I live in. I never thought I'd find something so charming in a place like Kauri Creek.

Sadie leads Scout to the mounting block, then scrambles onto it.

"Woah, Lady Sadie," Katie calls out, then taps a finger to her head three times.

Sadie's hand flies to her head and a gasp slips through her lips. "I left it in the barn."

"Go grab it then," Katie says, and I hold out my hand to take Scout's reins.

Sadie thrusts the leather straps into my hands, then races back to the barn. Katie swings into Aurora's saddle, the mare barely registering the movement.

"I'm no expert," I say, "but I feel like you don't need to worry too much about Aurora freaking out on you.

Katie laughs. "Yeah, Olivia keeps telling me I need to work on my trust issues."

"Trust issues?"

"Yeah, like trusting that the world isn't a totally shitty place all the time."

Oh. I study her, sitting comfortably astride this stunning horse, her long blonde hair braided down her back, smile on her face as she watches Sadie appear in the barn doorway. I know the man she's in love with, and the place she calls home, the people she calls her family. It's hard to believe Katie could ever believe the world is a shitty place.

"Let's go, Lady Sadie," Katie calls.

"Coming," Sadie shouts back and plonks her helmet on her

head. She races across the gravel yard trying to secure the chin strap as she goes.

In a moment so fast I barely register it happening, Sadie trips over her own feet and flies through the air. She hits the ground, sliding to a stop in the small, fine gravel, her unfastened helmet skidding away.

My breath stops.

All I can hear is the thundering of my heart in my ears. My vision blurs and I think for a moment we're experiencing an earthquake as the world around me tilts.

Time slows down and speeds up and everything I've eaten today rises.

I might faint. I might vomit. I might stand here frozen, unable to move as I stare at the tiny body on the ground.

Then Katie's boots hit the gravel and a second later she's kneeling on the ground beside my daughter.

My daughter, who lets out a piercing wail and starts to cry as Katie helps her sit up. There's blood spilling down her chin and she holds her palms up to Katie. I can see the red from here.

Katie checks Sadie over as I stand frozen, my fingers locked around the two sets of reins. Aurora doesn't seem fazed by the commotion or Katie's quick dismount and takes a couple of steps towards the pair on the ground, as if seeing for herself that Sadie is okay. The mare snuffles at Katie's shoulder.

"She's okay." I hear Katie say the words, but they sound muffled, like I'm underwater. It kind of feels like I'm underwater actually, like I don't quite have full control of my body and my lungs are burning because I can't breathe.

Breathing. That's important.

I open my mouth and suck down some air, then release it in a shuddering exhale. I take several more breaths, forcing myself to slow each one down, even though my body's natural inclination is to gasp in rapid intakes of oxygen.

Katie is helping Sadie to her feet now, after carefully inspecting each inch of her. "Let's get you cleaned up. Do you still want to go riding after?"

Sadie's eyes are huge, round and filled with tears. Her cheeks are wet and blotchy, but the blood on her chin is already drying. I don't know where she's bleeding from. Did she graze her chin when she hit the ground? Or is the blood coming from her mouth?

The little girl stands with her palms face up in front of her and shakes her head, never taking her blue eyes off Katie.

"Okay," Katie says. "Can you wait real quick while I get the horses back in their paddocks?"

Sadie's lip wobbles, but she nods and sniffs.

"I'll take care of it." My voice is so rough it takes me a moment to realise that it was actually me saying the words.

Katie glances at me, as if remembering I'm still here. I understand why she forgot I was, it's not like I did anything when my daughter hurt herself.

"You sure?" Katie asks, her voice soft.

"Yep, you take care of Sadie. I'll put these guys away." I gesture to the horses, then reach out for Aurora's reins. "I hope you feel better soon, Sadie," I say, the words sticking in my throat.

She sniffs again, then wipes her tears away on her sleeve. Katie puts a hand on her back and turns her for home. I watch them go, then lead the horses back to the barn where I strip them of their gear and lie to myself that I didn't just completely screw everything up.

13

FLYNN

THE TRACTOR RUMBLES beneath me as I guide it back to its parking spot beside the implement shed. I switch off the ignition and appreciate the moment of silence that follows. It's a strange thing, because even though the world isn't quiet, in the seconds following turning a tractor off it always feels like it is, before my hearing adjusts to a normal noise level again.

I glance across at the barn. No sign of Abigail, Sadie and Katie. I'm surprised because I didn't see them out on the farm. I'd have thought we would cross paths on my way back in from feeding out to the Herefords. Maybe they went somewhere else, though I can't think where they could have gone that I wouldn't see them.

I climb out of the cab, dropping to the gravel with a satisfying thud. My farm duties are done for the day and now I have most of the morning and an entire afternoon to do whatever it is I want. The problem is, I don't know *what* I want to do.

I should go home and clean. The bathroom is in dire need of

it and I need to repair a dodgy piece of timber on the front porch steps. But my bike is sitting right there and because I'm never going to pick housework and chores over a ride, I stride over to it and wheel it towards my ute.

A quick ride and I'll come back and be responsible.

Movement near the paddock catches my eye. Aurora and Scout are just inside the gate of their paddock. Someone with a head of dark hair is between them.

There's only one person here with hair that dark.

Abigail.

I watch as she slips the halters off both horses and gives them a final pat before she heads back into the barn. I glance at the next paddock over. Paddy isn't where he should be.

What is going on here?

I kick down the bike stand and once it's stable, head straight for the barn. Did Katie and Sadie not show up? But if that was the case, I don't think Abigail would have taken the horses out of the paddock. She seemed content to wait when I was here earlier.

I stride across the yard and pause in the barn door. Paddy, Henry's old gelding, is tethered to the railing we get the horses ready at. Abigail is leaning against him, her arms wrapped around his neck and her face pressed into his mane. Her fingers are knotted in his thick, dark mane and she lets out a low keening sound, almost like an injured animal.

"Abigail?" I ask, taking a tentative step forward.

She jerks violently, spinning away from the horse towards me.

Tears streak down her cheeks and at the sight of me she lets out a broken sob.

"Abigail." I race towards her, instinctively wrapping my arms around her and pulling her into my chest. "Shit. What happened?"

Abigail doesn't speak, she just shakes her head and presses her face into my worn-out old t-shirt. I should start wearing something a little nicer if I'm going to have hot women pressing themselves against me. Fucking hell Flynn, now is not the time for *those* thoughts.

Abigail's arm is wrapped around my waist, her other hand gripping my shirt, fingers tight in the fabric like they were in Paddy's mane when I first walked in here.

I hold her close while she cries, one hand cradling her head, and I wait, murmuring soft words against her hair.

Her sobs peter out and when they do, I can feel the moment she realises how wrapped up in me she is. Her whole body tenses and she tries to pull away.

I don't let go. "What happened?" I say softly against her temple.

Abigail sighs and softens against me again. I want to melt into her. I want to take away all this pain. She shakes her head against my chest.

"Why aren't you riding?"

"Sadie tripped over," Abigail whispers. "Katie took her home."

"Is Sadie okay?"

"I think so," Abigail says, leaning back in my arms to look up at me. She isn't trying to run away this time, so I release my hold a little to allow the movement. "A few grazes, but Katie didn't seem too worried."

I don't understand why she's this upset. Sadie trips at least once a week and Abigail doesn't even seem particularly concerned about Sadie's safety. If it's just a few grazes and Katie isn't worried, then I don't understand *this* reaction.

Abigail's vivid green eyes are staring up at me, still filled with tears. I manage to keep my mouth shut, to stop myself asking why she's this upset. It's a fight, but I manage it.

"I—I froze," Abigail whispers. "Sadie went down and I just … I panicked. I don't know what happened."

"You had another panic attack?" I ask and while I ask it like a question, it isn't really one.

"Yeah … I guess I did." She tips her head forward, her forehead coming to rest on my collarbone. "I haven't had one in so long."

My arms tighten around her. I don't mean to do it, but I can't help it.

"Oh," she whispers. "Except for my first day here, I suppose." She lifts her head again, a sheepish look on her face.

"You used to have them more often?"

Abigail nods. "After Sadie had her accident—do you know about that?" I nod and she continues. "After that, I'd have one whenever I was supposed to be looking after Sadie. It got to the point Dallas couldn't leave us alone together. I … I kind of lost all reason. The anxiety spiralled into every aspect of my life. That's why I left them."

I hold my breath as she speaks. I can't believe she's telling me all this. Abigail seems to keep things close to her chest. She doesn't like accepting help, and here she is, still wrapped in my arms, spilling her heart to me. As her voice breaks over her last words I resist the urge to pull her even closer, to tell her it's all okay now. I'm saved from having to say anything at all, because she's still talking.

"I moved back to my parents' place and went to therapy. A *lot* of therapy. I started taking medication. It took a year just to figure out which one was best for me and then another six months to fine-tune the dosage." She pauses for a long moment. "I thought I was ready. My therapist thought I was ready. I've worked so hard. Everything was going well."

I smooth her hair back as she looks up at me again, her expression wary. I tuck the dark, silky locks behind her ear. "You are ready, Abigail," I whisper. "Everything is going well. It's a blip. You've got this. I know you do."

She bites her lip and I slide my hand into her hair to keep myself from using my thumb to tug it free. Fisting her hair seems like the safer option, even though it's also dangerous. I'm playing with fire where this woman is concerned.

"I'm sorry I cried all over your shirt," she says, dragging a hand down my chest, trailing her fingers over the wet spot over my pec.

"It's fine." My voice is so gruff she glances back up at me. I have to let her go; I have to step away. The situation is becoming dire because I do *not* want her to realise the effect she's having on me. I tilt my head back and stare at the rafters before taking a deep breath and telling my dick to calm the fuck down. She's crying for god's sake. I squeeze my arms tight around her for a final time, then force myself to let go and step back.

"So, no ride then?" I ask, willing my voice to come out normal. I step towards Paddy to give him a pat, and hide the bulge in my jeans.

"No riding."

"Do you have other plans?"

"I might go finish tidying up from last night. Save me doing it tomorrow."

"I have another suggestion." What am I doing? I'm supposed to be getting away from her. This idea is a Flynn-special for its level of stupidity too, but if I leave Abigail alone, she's just going to stew on what happened. She'll probably cry again. I can't have that.

"Oh, yeah? What's that?" Abigail steps up beside me and unties Paddy's lead rope. I cross my fingers that she doesn't look down.

"How do you feel about a ride of a different kind?" Fucking hell could I have made that sound any more sleazy? "My bike, I mean." I can feel heat rushing up my throat, which means my face is about to turn bright red. Spectacular. "We could take my bike for a spin. You're dressed more appropriately today."

And now I'm thinking about her on my bike in a tight skirt and sky-high heels and miles of bare thigh and her hot body pressed against my back.

Fuck, fuck, fuck. This is not helping the boner situation.

Abigail's mouth curls into a wicked smile. She's laughing at me and I can't even be mad because I totally deserve it.

"You don't have anything else to do?"

"Nothing," I mutter, trying to think of the most unsexy

thing ever but my brain is still stuttering over images of the other day.

"I—I don't know ..." She trails off and I glance at her. "I should go clean up."

"You weren't going to be doing the cleanup today if you went riding with Katie and Sadie."

She purses her lips and I mentally slap myself. She's trying to get out of it and I shouldn't be pushing the issue.

"It's okay," I say, stepping away. I shoot her a smile but it's not my usual. I bet she can tell too. "Maybe another time, if you want." I spin to walk away but her hand catches my wrist.

"Wait, Flynn. Yes. Please. Let's go riding."

I study her, searching for any hint that she's just humouring me. I get it. There is no discernible reason a woman like her would want to hang around a guy like me.

"You sure?" I ask eventually.

"I'm sure. I need to get out of my head, so let's go freak me out about something else."

"You know I'm not going to let anything happen to you right? I'll look after you."

"I know you will, Flynn. That's why I'm coming with you."

14

———

ABI

I RETURN A WELL-GROOMED Paddy to his paddock. He looks at me with the same confusion Aurora and Scout did when I'd put them away without a ride. I give him several pats and feed him the last of the carrots Sadie brought.

"Good boy, Paddy. Another time."

I hang the lead ropes back in the tack room and force myself to forget all the things I told Flynn in here earlier. I can't believe I let my mouth run away with itself like that.

I also can't believe I let Flynn hold me for that long.

His initial hug was a surprise, but when his strong arms banded around my back, pulling me into his solid chest, any resolve, any fight, I'd usually have put up crumbled. I let myself have that moment of weakness, but when I finally managed to stop crying I should have stepped away.

I shouldn't have leaned closer.

I shouldn't have let him trail his fingers through my hair.

And most of all, I shouldn't have enjoyed that entire experience so much.

Not even when he eventually released me and immediately turned to Paddy. It took me a moment to realise why, but when I did, it stupidly increased my enjoyment of the moment ten-fold. Knowing I got him hard, even crying on his shirt, sent a pang of longing through me so intense I nearly threw myself on him then and there.

Instead I watched his thick fingers work their way through Paddy's mane and pat the gentle old horse on the neck.

I shake thoughts of Flynn, his body and the things I do to his body, out of my brain as I prepare myself to cross over to where he's loading his motorbike onto the back of the blue ute I parked beside.

"Where are we going?" I ask, pausing beside him and resting my hands on my hips.

"I'm taking you to my favourite place," he says, sending me a cheeky smile. "It'll give us more space."

"More space?"

"Yup. We'll need it."

He doesn't elaborate, just strides around the ute to finish strapping down the bike. When that's done, he disappears inside the shed and returns a moment later, blowing dust off a motorbike helmet. He shoots me another grin and my stomach turns over. I can't figure out if it's because I'm terrified of what I've got myself in for, or because that is just what Flynn's smile does to me now.

We climb into the ute and head out the driveway. Flynn pauses at the driveway entrance and sends a text.

"Everything okay?" I ask.

"Yep, just letting Vi know where we're going."

"I'm starting to have regrets," I say. I add in a smile but it's wavering.

"You'll be fine." He reaches over and pats my knee. The gesture is supposed to be funny, but the spike of electricity that shoots up my thigh is anything but.

Flynn's eyes land on his hand and he must realise he's left it lingering because he yanks it back like I've burned him.

He accelerates out of the driveway, tyres skidding in the gravel.

We don't travel far. It's further away from town than Wildflower Ridge, and we pull off the road, stopping at a roadside gate. Flynn unbuckles his seatbelt and moves to get out of the ute.

"I can get it," I say, rushing to get out before he does. I close the gate again once he's driven the ute through, then climb back in beside him. "I'm not completely useless you know."

"I know." He sighs. "Sorry. I'm so used to doing it myself."

We drive slowly across the paddock. We're heading for a ridge line and as we crest over the top I can't help the gasp that slips from my lips.

"This is gorgeous," I say, taking in the long expanse of wild coastline spread out in front of us. "I didn't know Wildflower Ridge reached the coast."

"It doesn't." Flynn rubs the back of his neck, looking like he really doesn't want to elaborate.

"Are we allowed to be here?"

"Well, no one's ever told me I can't be here."

"Flynn!" I spin to face him in the seat. He's still driving, slowly making his way down the slope to where the paddock ends and the beach begins.

"It's Constellation Station," he says. "The Sheridan's are our neighbours. They were friends with my parents. I was friends with their sons when I was a kid. We used to come out here all the time. I don't know if they know I still do, though the tyre tracks through the paddock are a bit of a giveaway."

"What if we get caught?"

"George and Clarissa won't have an issue. It'll only be Max who has a problem and frankly, I give zero shits about any opinion Max Sheridan has. Katie and Olivia call him Max fuck-ing-bastard Sheridan for a reason." His hands clench on the steering wheel for a moment, his knuckles flashing white, before he unclenches them and parks the ute. "Come on, Abigail."

"You know you can call me Abi, right?" The words tumble out of my mouth before I have a moment to think them through. I kind of like how he always calls me Abigail. I like that he didn't just assume he can call me Abi because Dallas does. It makes sense that Katie calls me that, because that's how Dallas would have told her about me.

"I wasn't sure, to be honest," he says. His hand tangles in his hair and I flash back to how it felt in my own. God, I have got to stop these runaway thoughts. "I didn't want to assume."

A smile tugs at my lips and I let it unfurl. "I appreciate the thought, but Abi is fine."

"Is it what you prefer though?"

"Maybe a bit of both," I shoot back. "Depending on the occasion."

His eyes flash with something dark and lustful and the tension spooling in my belly tightens a little more. "I can do that, Abigail."

I might melt right here in the front seat of his ute.

Then, in a flash, smouldering Flynn is gone and the usual easy-going, flirty Flynn is back. "Come on, Abi. We haven't got all day."

He jumps out of the ute before I have a chance to refute his argument, but when I reach the back tailgate where he's already releasing the straps securing the bike in place I can't help myself.

"We actually do have all day," I say.

He gives me an appraising look. "I mean, yes. But also I wasn't sure how long you'd be able to tolerate me so I figured I should get on with it."

"Get on with what?" That uneasy feeling I had earlier, the one that feels like I don't know what I've gotten myself into, kills any of the residual lust in my system.

Flynn hands me the helmet. "It's time to teach you how to ride."

15

FLYNN

ABIGAIL—ABI—TRIES to argue. Of course she does. I wasn't expecting anything else.

For a woman who's determined to prove how capable she is, she really doesn't like to get out of her comfort zone. She tries to argue, but I just smile and nod and let her think she's making a point.

If she really doesn't want to ride the bike herself I won't make her. It'd be a pretty hard thing to force her to do, but I hope once I've managed to get her out of her head, she won't be so resistant to the idea.

I just want her to let go, to have some fun, and to trust me. I don't know which one I want the most, but when I think about her trusting me I get this weird fuzzy feeling inside my chest.

I tell it to piss off, then help Abi fasten her helmet before pulling my own on. She eyes it with suspicion.

I swing my leg over the bike and kickstart it. A sense of calm settles over me with the familiar sound and vibration. Abi doesn't come any closer.

"Abi," I say, gesturing for her to come forward. She takes a tentative step.

"Why do you need the helmet?"

"Because I'm not an idiot and I'd like to keep whatever brains I already have."

"You don't wear one on the farm."

"I know and I should. But the beach can be unpredictable, and I tend to be a bit looser when I'm riding out here."

"Looser?"

"Abi." I reach for her, my fingers encircling her wrist. "Abigail. I'm going to look after you, I promise." I want to ask but I'm not sure if the next question is pushing too hard.

I throw caution to the wind because I have to know. I need to. "Do you trust me?"

She takes a deep breath and steps even closer. Her hand comes to rest on the face guard of my helmet, her fingertips barely brushing the skin across my cheekbone.

I hate this fucking helmet. If it wasn't there, she'd be cupping my face with her hand. I'd feel her entire palm against my skin.

"Yes, Flynn," she whispers. "I trust you."

"Is your anxiety being a problem about this?" I ask, hoping it doesn't cause her to shut down.

"Not my actual anxiety, no. I'm just generally scared about it." She laughs nervously.

"I'll take it slow," I promise.

She taps her fingers against the side of my helmet, then

slides onto the bike behind me. The helmets make it less intimate, but I hope she's going to let me really get going and when we're going that fast, it's always safer to have something protecting your head. Plus, it's a weirdly hot look for Abi to be wearing my spare helmet. I'm beginning to think this woman could wear or do *anything* and I'd find it hot.

I really need to get a grip.

Her thighs fit in behind mine and her arms snake around my torso. I give her hand a quick squeeze, then release the clutch on the bike and let it roll forward.

Abi clings on tight as we make our way down the sand. The dry, soft stuff is the hardest to get through, but once we get down below the high tide mark it's solid footing for miles. I turn and head down the beach, pacing myself. I want Abi to enjoy this, I want her to relax. I don't want to scare her, or push her too hard.

Her grip slowly loosens until she's barely holding onto me. That's when I slowly begin to increase the speed. At first she tenses when I accelerate, but when she realises I'm not taking off at warp speed, she relaxes again.

We travel down the beach, the sea salt scent in my nose, the breeze on my face, the sound of crashing waves thundering along the shore beside us.

This. This is it. Perfection.

My happy place.

The only way this could be any better was if the woman riding behind me was one I actually had a chance of falling in love with.

Well, I could probably love Abi without too much trouble.

It's her loving me back that'll be the problem. I'm not the kind of guy a woman like Abigail Fletcher falls for.

As we race along the sand, I slowly increase the speed and Abi's grip on me gradually decreases. Eventually she removes one hand from where it's pressed against my stomach and holds it out beside us, hovering just past my shoulder. When nothing drastic happens, she raises it in the air.

I whoop and laugh and she echoes the noise, her joy cutting right through my chest.

I slow the bike, rolling to a stop and twist back to see her. Her eyes are sparkling, a wide smile stretched across her face. "You ready to drive now?"

Her laughter cuts off with five simple words. Rather than immediately dismissing the idea though, I can see her thinking about it. "I don't think I can."

"You're wrong," I say. "You can do anything." I shouldn't feel those words in my chest the way I do.

She looks doubtful, but when I gesture for her to climb off the bike she does. I stand beside her and pull my helmet off, hanging it on the handlebars, then help Abi with hers.

"Look," I say, turning to face her. I get distracted by a lock of hair, set askew by the helmet. My fingers automatically find it and smooth it back into place. I refocus on her face and find her staring up at me with her lip caught between her teeth. God, I need to focus. "You can do this. I wouldn't offer to let you ride my bike if I didn't think you could. If any of the others knew I was offering they'd want me to get my head checked."

"Yeah, because me driving that thing is a ridiculous notion."

"No, because I usually don't let anyone ride my bike."

Abi raises her eyebrow at me. "Yeah, like I'm going to believe you're going to let me ride it if you won't let anyone else."

"Maybe I trust you more. You've met my best friends, right?"

"Have I?" Abi's voice is quiet. Quieter than I thought this moment was.

"Yeah. Katie and Olivia."

"They're your best friends?"

I quirk an eyebrow. "Will you ever believe anything I say without me having to argue the point?"

Her cheeks turn pink. "Sorry," she mumbles. "I just didn't realise."

"It's okay."

The breeze picks up and whips Abi's hair across her face. I capture it between my fingers and tuck it back behind her ear. I need to stop touching her, being close to her.

Because every time I am, I want more.

More of her.

More of my fingers on her skin.

More of her body pressed against mine.

More of her opening up to me, sharing herself with me, letting me in.

"You actually think I can do this?" Abi asks, eyeing the bike like it might bite her.

"I do, and I'll be right there with you the entire time."

Abi lets out a long, heavy exhale. "Okay."

"Okay?"

"Against my better judgement, yes."

My hands fall to her shoulders and squeeze, then break free from the contact.

Apparently it doesn't matter how much I try to avoid touching her I *can't*.

I'm naturally touchy by nature, even with Olivia and Katie. It's always been hugs and arms wrapped around shoulders and smoothing hair.

But with Olivia and Katie it's never felt the way it does with Abi.

"Right, on you get." I hand Abi her helmet and refasten the strap once she has it on. She swings a leg over the bike and straddles the seat. "Kick start is here," I say, indicating the little lever tucked against the side of the motor. "It can take a bit to get the hang of it, so I'll deal with that for now. Clutch, brake, throttle, gear shift," I say, pointing to each part of the bike. "It's pretty much like driving a manual car with the clutch and throttle, but it's hand controls instead of feet."

"That's a fabulous analogy, except I can't drive a manual."

My jaw drops. "Abigail. That's unacceptable. Driving lessons coming right up."

"Yeah, sure. Right after I manage this," she mutters, but the corner of her mouth is tipped up and her eyes are filled with humour.

I pull my helmet on and slide onto the bike behind her. I did *not* think this through, but what else is new?

"Just move this leg a bit," I say, sliding my hand along her denim-clad thigh—fuck, these jeans are a work of art—and lifting it so it's out of the way of the kickstart. I stamp down on it and the engine flares to life. I use my left foot to hook the bike into gear, then lean forward and place my hands over hers on the handlebar grips. I try to keep my hips back as far as possible, well away from Abi's delicious ass. It feels like I'm about to face plant into her shoulder, but at least my dick isn't pressed up against her.

"Now, just ease off the clutch," I say, squeezing my left hand over hers, "and slowly twist the throttle towards you." I squeeze my right hand.

Abi takes a deep breath, then does as instructed. As expected, the bike jolts and stalls.

"Shit," she gasps.

"All good," I say. "That's pretty normal for a first go. And a tenth. It takes practise to get the feel just right."

I drop my right hand to her thigh again, lifting her foot out of the way so I can restart the bike.

We go again, and again, and again. Each time the bike stalls, Abi gets a little more frustrated with herself.

"Hey," I say after I restart the bike again. I've lost count of our attempts. My hand is still on her leg and I give her a squeeze then rub my palm over the muscle. "You've got this. Take a breath. There's no rush, there's no pressure."

"You sure you don't want to admit I'm a failure yet?" she mutters, then lets out a deep groan and slumps forward, her head coming to rest against the handlebars.

"You're not a failure. At all. Come on, try again. Just a little more gas this time."

"I'm worried if I give it more gas then it'll take off and I won't be able to stop then." But she sits up again and settles her hands into position. I place mine over hers.

I hope my hands aren't too rough. They're not soft and delicate like hers. They're calloused and chapped, always sporting a healing cut or scratch from where I've nicked myself on something, most of the time I'm not even sure what.

"More gas," I remind her as she begins to loosen her grip on the clutch. I put a little pressure on her right hand and she twists the throttle.

The bike shoots forward and Abi squeals and twists the throttle even further towards us. It's a natural feeling to twist the throttle when you're riding, but unfortunately it's also the natural thing to do when you're panicking as well.

I manage to wrestle the control away from her and slow the bike enough for Abi to get her wits about herself again.

Then she slams on the brakes and the bike stalls. Again.

And in the chaos, I've slipped forward, so now I'm pressed right up against Abi's back, from shoulders to hips. Immediately my cock starts to thicken and I shove myself back on the seat.

I clear my throat. "Almost had it," I say, grateful she can't see my wicked blush.

"I give up," Abi moans. "No more."

"Give me five more tries."

"One."

"Three." I drop my hand to her leg again, the movement now completely natural, but unfortunately repetition hasn't dulled the affect the touch has on me.

"Fine. Three."

It only takes her two.

16

———

ABI

I CAN'T BELIEVE I actually did it.

A hysterical laugh bubbles out of me as we ride down the beach, my hands gripping the handlebars like the world will end if I loosen my grip.

We might still both die with me clinging on this tight, but I'm driving a motorbike. Riding a motorbike? What's the correct term? I was riding it when I was behind Flynn, but now I'm in control.

As much as it terrifies me, the feeling is amazing.

I did this. I learned it and now I can drive a motorbike.

Another laugh bubbles up and Flynn squeezes my hips, where his hands now rest. I'm not sure if it's better or worse than when he held them over my own and helped me control the bike, but once I got more confident in maintaining the speed, he slipped one hand, then the other, off mine and placed them carefully onto my body.

He's not sitting pressed up against me like I do to him and I find myself wishing he was. There was a moment or two when I was learning to start that he slipped forward, his hot, hard body coming into contact with mine, but each time he immediately shoved himself backwards again.

My mind wanders back to earlier in the barn when I know I made him hard and I wonder if that's what he's trying to avoid. With him pressed up against my back, there's no way I wouldn't feel it.

I need to stop thinking about Flynn like that. He's got no interest in a woman like me, despite what his body is saying. I'm barely holding it together. I cling to control like a life preserver and I'm lost at sea.

Flynn is young and carefree. No responsibilities beyond his job. He doesn't want to be slowed down by me and my issues.

"Go faster," he shouts over the noise of the bike and the thundering of the ocean. He places his left hand over mine again, hooking his foot around mine and as I accelerate, he somehow smoothly changes gear.

I want to have the casual confidence he does on this bike. I hope he lets me ride it again. It's a similar feeling to riding horses, and while I can do that, I'm not very good at it. I can walk, trot and canter, jump the tiniest obstacles, but anything that requires actual skill is outside my abilities.

This though, it's all of the adrenaline and feelings of freedom without having to maintain a horse. I'm not sure my property manager would be super impressed with a horse being kept in my back yard.

But a motorbike ...

I'm getting ahead of myself. I refocus on the moment. The

salt air is fresh on my face, the breakers crashing to our right, the thrumming bike beneath me, and behind me ... Flynn.

His hands are gentle on the curve of my hips, his fingers resting on the crease between pelvis and leg and his thumbs brush the top of my ass. I'm surprised he's not holding on for dear life, but his soft, confident touch is reassuring.

It's also a fucking turn on.

"I don't know how to slow down," I call back to him when we eventually approach the spot where we parked the ute.

I can hear Flynn laughing, but he guides me through the process of slowing down, changing down gears and eventually stopping.

Somehow, even with his input, I still manage to stall the engine and it causes Flynn to slide forward again.

Before he can shift back, my hand lands on his thigh and he freezes.

He's touched me in the same place over and over today. Every time he had to restart the bike he'd drag his palm along the back of my thigh to get me to move my foot out of the way. I don't know if he realises I was well aware of where to put my leg, but I didn't want him to stop.

Flynn's got both feet on the sand, holding the stalled bike upright and I'm perched uselessly on the front, my feet on the pegs. If he wasn't there, I'd be sprawled across the beach, probably trapped under this machine. I squeeze Flynn's leg and lean back into his chest, resting my head against his shoulder.

Heat pools between my legs as his hands come to rest on my hips again.

I raise my free hand and grasp at the chin strap of the

helmet. I need two hands, but I refuse to let him go, and I don't know why. I should let him go, but right now, I can't.

Flynn's hands knock my fumbling one out of the way and the tips of his fingers brush against my throat as he deftly undoes the strap, then pulls the helmet off and drops it in the sand beside us.

I want to protest ... because *sand* and I know he'll be finding pesky grains in the lining for eternity, but when Flynn's helmet hits the ground beside mine a moment later, and his hands return to my waist, I forget all about the sand.

I drop my head back to his shoulder and tilt it so my forehead connects with the side of his neck.

A strangled breath escapes him and he tries to shift backwards, away from me.

I grip his thigh tighter, my fingertips grasping the solid muscle and instead of moving away, Flynn lets out a guttural moan and slides forward.

His hips fit against my ass and there's no mistaking the hard cock digging into me.

This is ... this is not what we should be doing. But he feels so *right* against me. We fit together perfectly.

I press my forehead into his neck and my free hand reaches behind me to tangle in his thick red hair. His lips brush against my temple as his hands drift higher and the rest of the world fades away.

I twist back, my lips finding the smooth, hot skin of his neck. I brush my mouth against any part of him I can reach, then lick a stripe all the way to the hinge of his jaw. He groans as my teeth nip at the soft skin, lips tingling with the slight rasp of stubble.

"Fuck," he hisses, his hands brushing against my breasts, once, twice, before settling over them with a firm grip.

I make a noise that should be embarrassing, but just makes Flynn curse again in that sexy-as-fuck husky voice.

One of his hands stays on my tits, alternating between cupping each breast and toying with the low neckline of my loose t-shirt, as if he's unsure he if he should slip his hand inside. His other hand finds my chin. He grasps it between his fingers and tilts my head, manoeuvring me into position so I'm looking up into his face.

His hazel eyes are dark and drenched with lust, but that's all I see before his lips come down on mine.

I gasp and Flynn takes the opportunity to slide his tongue into my mouth.

Holy fucking hell.

This man can kiss.

Even twisted the way I am, this is the best kiss of my life. Flynn's lips leave mine and I whimper. I actually whimper, but his hand drops from my face to my thigh and trails up the inner seam of my jeans, coming to rest on the juncture between leg and hip, his fingers tantalisingly close to exactly where I want them.

It's like the touch of our lips has freed any inhibitions he had, because his hand plunges inside my shirt, shoving aside the sports bra I wore today. I hate that I came prepared for horse riding and not whatever it is I'm currently doing with Flynn.

Whatever it is, it's definitely a terrible idea, but before we come to our senses I'm going to extract every drop of pleasure I can from this unhinged moment. We've already crossed a line we shouldn't have. We may as well make the most of it while we're here.

I tilt my hips. It has a two-fold affect, pushing my ass back into Flynn's cock, and dragging his fingers closer to my pussy.

Flynn lets out a muffled grunt and bites my neck, immediately soothing the sting with lips and tongue. He gets my intention though and presses his hand between my legs so I can grind down on him, while he thrusts his hips against me from behind.

God, the pressure is intense. The friction making me lightheaded.

I need at Flynn's dick. I drag my hand higher on his thigh, reaching for the button on his jeans. I fumble awkwardly behind me, but as my hand brushes over the impressive thickness in his pants, Flynn freezes.

Both his hands are on me, one in my shirt, one between my legs, and his lips are still pressed against my skin, but in a flash, all points of contact are gone.

Flynn throws himself off the bike and strides several metres down the beach, his hands in his hair, before he spins back to face me.

"Holy fucking shit," he gasps, cheeks flushed, eyes wild, dick still straining at his jeans. "I'm so fucking sorry."

I DON'T KNOW what I'm doing.

All sense has left my head. Fuck, the way I was pawing at Abi like a horny teenage boy.

I mean, I feel like a horny teenage boy.

I tug at my hair, tilting my head back and cursing at the sky. What was I thinking?

Aside from the fact that Abi is hot as fuck, and the confidence she found when she figured out the bike controls was even hotter, apparently I wasn't thinking at all. The intensity of my attraction to her went to my head ... the wrong head.

I return my gaze to her and regret it immediately.

Wild green eyes, her dark hair blowing in the sea breeze, cheeks flushed a delicious rosy pink, she's still astride the bike, panting softly, one foot now on the ground helping support it. At least somewhere in that haze of madness I managed to kick the stand down so when I leapt off the bike I didn't leave her with the entire weight of it.

Abi's hands are pressed against her throat as she watches me and I want to race back to her and replace those hands with my own. Or my mouth. The sounds she made as I dragged my tongue over her skin were indescribable.

"Flynn," she says, voice barely audible over the crashing of the waves and thundering of my heart.

I don't know what idea was stupider: that I let that happen in the first place, or that I stopped it. Because damn, I doubt I'm ever getting an experience like that again.

I don't even know how it started. I think it was Abi's hand on my leg, refusing to let me go, my chest pressing against her back, and when my dick—my still hard dick—came in contact with her ass, I lost all reason.

Abi climbs off the bike and approaches me, the same way someone would approach a spooked horse. "Flynn," she says again. "Breathe."

Why's she telling me to breathe?

Oh.

Because I've stopped.

That thundering in my ears isn't just the ocean.

I suck down a lungful of air.

"I'm sorry," I croak. I think I'm repeating myself.

"Why are you sorry?" Abi asks, her eyes uncertain and her steps towards me tentative.

"I shouldn't have done that. Touched you like ... that."

She pauses right in front of me and tips her chin up to look me directly in the face. I want to avoid her gaze. I want to shift away.

But at the same time, I want to close the distance between us again, to carry her back to my bike and lay her across it.

I want to strip those tight, tight jeans off her body and spread her out.

I want to savour her, get down on my knees in the sand and worship her.

"I started it," Abi says, lifting a hand between us, as if to touch my face, but she doesn't make contact and it hovers between us for a moment before she lowers it again. "And I wouldn't mind finishing it."

Oh god. I thought she'd be running for the hills by now, if not because I just groped her like a fumbling teenager, but because the second her hand touched my cock—through my pants—I flung myself halfway across the beach away from her. I'm super classy like that.

"Sadie," I blurt. I shake my head. "Dallas."

Oh, fuck. Dallas. Katie and Olivia. They're going to destroy me for this.

The flush in Abi's cheeks fades rapidly. "Dallas doesn't really get a say in my life anymore," she says. "I'm quite capable of making my own decisions." She has that flinty look in her eye, the one she gets when she thinks I'm implying she's not capable of handling things on her own.

"I know you are, but I'm a really, really bad one."

Abi laughs. "I don't know why you think that. You're one of the nicest guys I've ever met. Like an actual nice guy, not one of the ones who just *thinks* he's nice."

That may be true, but how nice I am doesn't come into it.

It's my attachment issues that are the problem, and my complication isn't my avoidance of attachment.

I already feel a pull to Abi. I want to be around her all the time. I want to learn every little detail about her, and I know that if any more happens between us, that feeling is only going to intensify.

It'll build and build, then one day she'll be done with me and want to get as far away from me as possible.

Except here, she can't get away from me because we work together, and she doesn't have an option of getting away from me, because of Sadie.

So long as Sadie's at Wildflower Ridge, Abi is going to be around.

My heart has taken a beating more than once over the years when people have left me, especially my parents and Katie when she left Kauri Creek for a few years. But to have to see Abi every day and know she's done with me, that she doesn't want me back ... I don't think my heart would recover when she chooses to leave me.

"It's too complicated," I mutter, turning my head away from her.

"Complicated?"

"Yeah." I sigh and step around her. I can't explain all of this.

"What's complicated about a bit of fun between two consenting adults?" Abi calls after me as I trudge back to the bike and flick up the stand, hefting its weight and preparing to drag it back across the soft sand at the top of the beach.

"Your daughter, our jobs, your ex being my boss, me." I point to the helmets sitting in the sand. "Can you bring those?"

Abi huffs out a frustrated breath, and I get it. I'm frustrated too. The ache in my balls still hasn't gone away. I'm beginning to wonder if it ever will.

"None of that has to be complicated," Abi says, grabbing the helmets and following me up the beach. "We keep what happens between us, well, between us. We keep it separate from work. We keep it away from Sadie."

I waver. She makes it sound so simple. A bit of fun between friends. Mutual pleasure. Some shared orgasms.

My dick would appreciate it, I'm sure.

I don't respond as I struggle to push the bike through the sand. Should have just ridden it, but apparently I felt like punishing myself.

By the time I reach my ute I'm breathing hard. I'm grateful that the task of getting across the sand without ending up squished under my bike kept my focus for a few minutes. It gave me a moment of space.

I load the bike onto the tray of my ute, and strap it down, then turn to face Abi who's standing beside the vehicle, looking a little lost. "You missed explaining away one of the complications," I say and my tone is bitter.

"Which one?" Abi asks.

"Me."

She narrows her eyes. "You don't want to?"

I groan and rub a hand through my hair. "Of course I want to. Isn't that much obvious?" I snap. I don't mean to, but I need this whole thing to be over. I need to go back to yesterday when we were friendly workmates and I just had a pointless crush on Abi. I never expected she'd reciprocate my attraction. Somehow we're going to have to go back to how things were before, but now I know the feel of her body under my hands, the taste of her skin and the breathy little sounds she makes when she's turned on … I don't know how I'm ever going to do it.

"I don't know," Abi says, her tone cutting. "You seem to be throwing everything in as an excuse. If you don't want me, just tell me."

"That's not it. Fuck." I slam the tailgate closed, then take the helmets from Abi and toss them into the backseat. "I don't know how to do this." I gesture between us.

"It's just sex." Abi shrugs. "There's only one thing that should be hard." She smirks and *fuuuck*. It might kill me. Always in control Abi making dick jokes.

"I've never done it," I blurt out.

"The friends with benefits thing?" She looks thoughtful. "Huh. More a one and done type of guy?" Her eyes widen. "I'm not judging. You can have sex with whoever you choose, as often as you choose."

Oh great, I'm going to have to spell it out for her. My neck heats and I know I'm going to be blushing hard in about three seconds flat.

"No, Abigail." I nearly growl her name. "I've never done the friends with benefits thing. I've never done the one night stand thing. I've never done the sex thing at all."

18

———

ABI

THE RIDE back to Wildflower Ridge is a quiet one.

After Flynn dropped the bombshell that he's a virgin—which is the only thing I can assume he meant by his "I've never done the sex thing at all" statement—he didn't explain further, just pushed past me and slid into the driver's seat. He turned on the ignition, then waited for me to climb in beside him.

As we pull into the driveway to Wildflower Ridge, I try to broach the silence. "Flynn," I say, even though I'm not sure what I'm going to follow it up with.

"Just don't. Please." He grips the steering wheel so tight his knuckles go white. He's completely rigid in his seat, shoulders tense, jaw tight. "I need to not talk right now, and later I might go fall in a hole. A really fucking big hole."

"I'm sorry. I shouldn't have pushed. You don't want to and that's enough of an answer."

I'm intensely disappointed, but that's my own issue.

I've been disappointed since he broke off our make out session, the ache between my thighs still present.

I was so desperate for him I felt like begging him to get me off. I wanted to promise him anything in the world if he'd let us finish what we started.

Even mentioning Sadie didn't deter me. All I could think about was his hands on my body and if a grinding session on his dirt bike could feel that good, how good could the rest of it be?

I probably should be thinking more of Sadie, because if something went wrong between Flynn and I, it would make things super awkward on the farm, and they're already bad enough.

But I don't want to think about all my failures right now.

I want to go back to that moment where I felt fully surrounded by Flynn. His solid chest against my back, his hands on me—and not in a gentle or friendly way—and his erection rubbing against my ass. I can't stop thinking about it.

In that moment, nothing else mattered except his hard body and how it made mine feel. His hands made my blood sing and while our bodies were pressed together, I was completely out of my head and completely in that moment.

I'm not ready to let that feeling go, but I can't push him any more than I already have.

"Can we just pretend today never happened?" he asks and when I glance over at him, he's looking at me with pleading eyes. His usual carefree grin is nowhere to be seen. There's no teasing in his expression now.

"I can't." My voice gets stuck in my throat and Flynn slams his eyes closed and groans. "Because I learned to drive a motorbike today and that's the coolest thing I've done in forever."

A smile tugs at Flynn's mouth as he slowly cracks his eyes open again, as though waiting for some awful punchline. "That was pretty cool," he admits. "You can remember that part."

I open the ute door and unbuckle my seatbelt. "Thank you, Flynn. I had a great time. I don't intend to forget a second of it. *Any* of it."

He tips his head back and groans. "Abigail."

I ignore the way he drags out my name and the shiver that runs down my spine. "See you tomorrow, Flynn," I call back to him as I jump out of the ute and scurry to my car.

As soon as I leave the farm, my brain kickstarts the replay of those moments on the beach—Flynn's hands on my body, him massaging my tits and his fingers between my thighs, his mouth on mine and that delicious hard bulge I felt in his pants.

There's no way I'm going to forget that. Not even if I wanted to.

I have to force myself to drive slowly back into town. I want to race. I want to be back there already, because I've got a long afternoon planned with the curtains closed and the memory of our tryst on the beach firmly at the front of my mind.

I THINK Flynn is avoiding me.

Since I started at Wildflower Ridge he's been everywhere, always willing to lend a hand and getting in my space, even when I didn't want him to.

Now, I do want him in my space and he's like an elusive little butterfly, always just out of reach.

It's not like I never see him. He's around. He calls into the function venue at least every couple of days. I see him on the occasions I head up to Violet's house for lunch, which I try to do at least weekly, sometimes more often. I can even drive myself up there without Flynn or Dallas dragging me out of my office and forcing me to go, like the first few times.

I even once saw Flynn at the tiny supermarket in town on a Tuesday night. He was wearing a bright green hoodie, shorts and sneakers. I almost didn't recognise him out of his farming clothes, but once I did, I couldn't stop staring. That hoodie looked made for hugging. He didn't hug me though, just waved from his spot in the checkout line. By the time I'd grabbed my few essentials and paid for them, he was gone. I had to give myself a severe lecture about the level of disappointment I felt after that interaction, but I still went home and got off to thoughts of his hands on my body.

Every time I see Flynn, he's friendly and chatty with his trademark grin. It's like nothing happened between us. Meanwhile, I only have to think of Flynn, or that moment on the beach and I feel like I'm going to spontaneously combust.

But he asked me to forget it, and while I can't actually do that, I can pretend like I have when he's around.

I've spent years feeling like I'm constantly trapped in my head, between my anxiety and the massive depression I slid into after I left my family. While I have those issues mostly under control these days, the overthinking and second guessing has never left.

Until that moment on the beach with Flynn.

First it was the motorbike and the feeling of freedom racing along the beach, then learning to drive it and the sense of accomplishment for doing something so far outside my comfort zone I thought I might vomit the first time Flynn mentioned it.

Then he put his hands on me and there were no thoughts in my head, except for the man wrapped around me.

It's probably selfish, but I want that again. I need that again.

I just don't know how to get it without pushing Flynn too hard, without hurting him. I don't want him to feel used and as much as friends with benefits sounds like the perfect solution to me, I'm not going to risk the friends part.

I've screwed up enough relationships in my life already. I'm not willing to risk any more.

19

———

FLYNN

I NEED TO SEE ABI. I can't avoid her anymore.

I've tried to keep our interactions limited for the past few weeks and while I feel like a douchebag doing it, I needed to put some space between us so I could try to get over the crush I have on her.

I still kick myself for turning her down, but I know in the end it's for the best, because if we'd taken things any further, I'd have blown it all up in my face. I feel like I'm doing that anyway and it sucks.

I like Abi. I want her to be happy here and Sadie needs her, so I'm fighting all my natural instincts, which are to spend as much time with Abi as possible because I constantly want to be around her.

Instead I'm keeping my distance, because it's better for everyone. It really, really is.

But the look on Abi's face when I duck in and out of her

office without lingering tugs at my heart. She almost looks … disappointed.

I shake that thought out of my head. She's probably relieved. A bit of space from the beach make out and she'll have realised it was a mistake for us to go there.

I kick dirt off my boots and head towards the door to the function centre.

We're hosting a massive wedding tomorrow, the biggest we've had here at Wildflower Ridge and Olivia will kill me if I don't help out, even if it means close proximity to Abi. I can't exactly tell Olivia why I want to limit contact.

I smooth my hair—a pointless exercise, and irrelevant, but my hand does it anyway—and step through the door.

What the fuck?

Tables are set up all over the room and laid out across every one are roses. So many roses, in the deepest red and crispest white. They're gorgeous, but no more than the woman standing in the middle of it all, her hand tangled in her hair as she stares down at the flowers before her.

She takes a breath, frees her hand from the spill of her dark hair and picks up a flower.

"Let's do this," she mutters, then under her breath starts singing 'Every Rose Has Its Thorn'. I cross my arms and lean against the doorframe, waiting for her to glance up and notice me. She doesn't, instead her voice and enthusiasm rises as she gets into the chorus of the song.

"Need a hand?" I call across the room when it's clear she still has no idea I'm standing here.

She shrieks and presses her hand to her chest, the other one still clutching a rose stem. "Holy shit."

I grin. "I'd apologise, but it was funny, so I'm not going to."

She stares at me incredulously, then giggles. She slaps a hand over her mouth, cutting off the sound immediately, but I still heard it. I can still see her cheeks turn pink above the edge of her palm, still pressed over her mouth.

Oh my god. The distance hasn't helped.

One look at that blush and I'm back on the beach, her face pressed against my neck, her cheeks that same delicious rosy colour.

"What the hell is going on in here?" I ask, stepping into the room, careful not to knock any of the tables.

Letting out a groan, Abigail slumps into a chair beside the closest table. "They were supposed to come prepared." She drops her head into her hands. "Wildflower Ridge's biggest event ever and I've fucked it up already."

"Did you order them to come prepared?" I ask, stepping closer and dropping into a crouch when I'm in front of her. She looks one second away from a full-fledged meltdown, not that I'd blame her with the sheer number of flowers currently in this room.

"Yeah, prepared, fully arranged in vases, the whole shebang. But it doesn't matter, because they aren't."

"So, it's not your fault."

"Not sure the bride and groom are going to see it that way. You've heard what they're like."

"Super loaded, super fussy."

She shoots a finger gun in my direction. "Got it in one."

A phone chimes and Abi looks at me. I shake my head. "Not mine." I pull it out of my pocket and show her the blank screen. Because apparently being near her has made me awkward as fuck. Go me.

Abi glances around the room. "I've no idea where I've left mine." She gives a defeated little shrug. "They'll call if it's important."

The phone starts to ring. Abi groans. "Fuck."

I follow the sound and find Abi's phone on the edge of a table, peeking out from under a pile of flowers. "It's Emily."

"Oh, well she can wait." She runs a hand through her hair and slumps in the chair. "I was worried it was the bride or someone equally as terrifying."

"The bride's terrifying?"

"Not really. I just really don't want to screw up her wedding day. It's a lot of pressure."

"I can only imagine. You sure Emily can wait?"

"Yeah, she's my friend. Probably just wants to chat. I'll call her back later."

I hand Abi the phone, then stand beside her. I don't know what to do with my hands. Since when were they so *awkward*.

Abi glances at the screen and taps a few times, then tips her head back, eyes closed. I refuse to let my gaze linger on the way her eyelashes fan over her cheeks or the plump curve of her bottom lip.

"Maybe it is important, what your friend wants," I blurt out. "Since she texted and called."

"She didn't text," Abigail says, not opening her eyes. "That was Olivia, asking me to go up for lunch so I can update her on progress."

"Oh, well I can give you a ride." Yay, something that'll actually help me feel useful.

"I can't go," she whispers, turning tumultuous eyes on me. There are so many feelings in them but it's clear the most prevalent is anxiety. "I'll have to tell her about this mess, and I just ... *can't*. Plus, I have to get these flowers sorted. I don't have time."

"You'll get it done," I say. I'll stay all night and do them for her if I have to.

"And admitting to my boss that I've screwed up her biggest event?"

"She's not going to blame you."

"I'm still not telling her, Flynn." She pushes out of her seat. "Please don't tell her either. Please."

God, what am I supposed to say to that pleading face. I want to tell her that Olivia will help her, not blame her. But Abi doesn't seem willing to hear that. Her breathing stutters and she spins away. Fuck, is she about to have another panic attack?

"I won't tell her." The words race out of me. I don't know if it's the right choice, but it's not like Abi will have to do it all on her own. I'll be here with her, learning flower arranging, to help her get this done.

Abi turns back to me, the relief on her face evident, though her eyes are a touch glassy.

I usher her from the building. "But we are going to lunch. Come on."

20

———

ABI

FLYNN ISN'T TAKING no for an answer.

I'm making him lie to his best friend and employer, so I don't feel like I can argue anymore anyway. I tuck my phone into my back pocket, take another look at the mess waiting for me, and follow Flynn outside.

I can't believe the roses came like this. I ordered them to come ready in their vases so all I had to do was place them onto the tables. Now, I have what feels like a billion beautiful roses and twenty-four vases that I somehow have to arrange into wedding-worthy displays. I also have to set up everything else and I have no idea how I'm going to get it all done. I'm sure the logical course of action would be to ask for help ... but I'm not ready to give up yet. As generous as Olivia and Violet seem, I don't know how they'll react to such a monumentally epic fail. I'm also not sure what they can do because I vaguely remember there's some farm thing that needs to happen this afternoon that involves all hands. Violet's picking Sadie up from school and looking after her until Dallas is done for the day.

Then there's Flynn, finally right here in front of me and I want to *eat* him. He looks delectable in his usual jeans and faded t-shirt. It's a deep blue today and it sets off his hair and eyes. The t-shirt is so old it looks like it'll fall apart if a strong gust of wind hits it, but I kind of love how Flynn doesn't give a shit. The worn, comfortable vibe suits him.

I freeze when I step outside and find Flynn already swinging his leg over the back of his bike. Memories from the beach come rushing back. Heat prickles at my skin as I flush and a bolt of lust jolts through my core.

Then I remember the day he first got me on the bike, in my ridiculous skirt. At least I'm wearing jeans today.

My eyes connect with Flynn's and by the colour in his cheeks and the way his pupils are blown wide, I can guess he's thinking about the same things I am.

I need to be professional here. He asked me to forget, to pretend it didn't happen. He's my friend and I don't want him to feel weird around me. I don't want him to think I'm some horny little hussy just after a good time with him. I mean, I am, but I also want to keep this little baby friendship intact. I need to, because in Kauri Creek, Flynn is currently the only friend I have.

There's Dallas, I suppose, but it feels like we have too much history for our relationship to ever feel like it's on equal footing again.

I know Flynn's loyalties lie with the other people at Wildflower Ridge, they're his family after all, but I like what we have. I like spending time with him.

Most importantly, I just like him.

I've missed him since that day on the beach.

I haven't encountered many people like Flynn in recent years. The ones I've spent time with have all been jaded and bitter about life, or too serious and uptight. But Flynn is none of those things.

He's sunshine and freedom, like riding down a beach on the back of a dirt bike. He's smiles and jokes and constant positive energy, even though he'd be well within his rights to feel sorry for himself with what life's thrown his way.

I slide onto the bike behind him, careful to limit contact between our bodies. I'm wearing a sweatshirt and I slip my hands into the sleeves before carefully grasping Flynn's hips. Shielding my hands with my sweatshirt was a completely pointless exercise because I can still feel the heat of him burning through my fingertips.

"You ready to go?" Flynn twists his head around to check I'm situated, before starting the bike.

"Yep, all good," I say, trying to sound casual but failing. I sound like I've spent the last five minutes choking. Oh, that's not an image I need in my head right now.

Flynn's hand lands on my thigh, just above my knee. One simple touch and I want to swoon. "You don't feel like you're holding on," he says as his hand slides higher. Right before he reaches the swell of my ass, he applies pressure and tugs me forward.

I don't realise what he's doing until it's too late and my chest is pressed up against his back, legs bracketing his.

"Better," Flynn says. "Now, hold on properly."

I sigh, but wrap my arms around him, leaning my head against his shoulder. "Let's go," I say.

Flynn pats my arm where it rests across his stomach. "Don't worry, Rosie. The flowers will get done. I promise."

Rosie ... That's new. I've noticed Flynn loves a nickname though, calling everyone on the farm some cute version of their name. I guess this flower disaster just got me mine.

I squeeze my arms around him a little tighter. I appreciate his optimism, I just don't see how it's actually going to happen.

LUNCH IS THE USUAL, chaotic affair. Violet's made scones and there's sandwich fillings spread across the table, including the delicious bread from the local cafe and bakery, Sugar. That place is my favourite in Kauri Creek. I've been finding myself in there on too many mornings to grab a coffee. But spending a few minutes sitting in the bright, airy space admiring the rows of delicious treats lined up within the cabinet is no hardship. There's pastries and slices, filled rolls and sandwiches, and of course the quintessential Kiwi pies and sausage rolls.

Then there's the cupcakes and, on the odd occasion, small cakes. They're like little works of art with swirled frosting and shimmery accents. Colours that would be right at home in the world of My Little Pony. I haven't actually eaten one yet because my coffee stops are all early morning and it doesn't seem like the right time to be eating a cupcake like that.

"I love this bread so much," I say to Violet as she passes a wooden chopping board down the table to me. I take a couple of slices and pass it along to Flynn, who's fallen into the seat beside me.

Dallas is nowhere to be seen, but Katie and Olivia are across from us, their mouths full of food.

"It's from Sugar," Violet says. "Have you been there yet?"

I snort. "Almost every day. It's kind of embarrassing actually."

"Nah, that's accurate. I go there every time I go to town," Katie says after swallowing her mouthful. "It's the best place in Kauri Creek, second only to Wildflower Ridge." She shoots Olivia a wink. Olivia rolls her eyes. "Those cupcakes they do now are to die for."

"Cupcakes?" Flynn asks, interest suddenly piqued. He'd tuned out for a little bit there.

"Yeah. Like these incredible lemon ones. And the chocolate ones." She makes a humming noise. "So good. Were they your mum's? They definitely weren't grandma's."

I blink as my brain takes a moment to catch up. Whose mum? Are we talking about Katie's grandma? Why would they be her cupcakes?

Flynn shrugs beside me. "Don't know. I don't remember her doing cupcakes but maybe." He focuses on making his sandwich, effectively removing himself from the conversation I'm still not following.

Violet must see it, because she fills in the gaps. "Flynn's

mum used to own Sugar." She shoots a look in Flynn's direction, sympathy and sadness all wrapped up in one brief glance, then she returns her focus to me. "After she passed, Katie's grandma took it over. She used a lot of Isla's recipes, that were then passed onto the current owner."

"Oh, that's pretty cool," I say. "To carry it on like that." I glance at Flynn, but he's still fully focussed on the food in front of him, his movements stiff and jerky.

A phone chimes and interrupts the awkward moment we're descending into. Olivia pulls hers out of her pocket and gasps.

"Oh my gosh. Look at this." She holds the phone out to Katie who squeals.

"What is it?" Flynn asks, sandwich halfway to his mouth.

"Puppies." Olivia hands him the phone. "I have an alert set up for any that come available."

Flynn places his food back on his plate and holds the phone in his left hand, angling it in my direction so I can see as well, but I still have to lean into him to get a good view. His free hand comes down on my knee and I jerk in surprise. He gives a soft squeeze, then brings the phone a little closer to me, leaving his hand in place. I don't know what's going on with us, but this doesn't seem like the time or place to question it.

Flynn flicks through the pictures. There's five Border Collie puppies, their little black and white faces utterly adorable.

"Oh, this one," I say with a small laugh. The puppy is clearly posing for the camera, the look on its face filled with confidence and cheekiness. A lopsided white stripe runs down its face, ending with a tiny nose that's half pink and half black.

Flynn doesn't say anything, just scrolls down the screen to

read the information. He's quiet for a long moment, studying the words, then flicking through the pictures again.

Olivia and Katie are chatting about the puppies and if Olivia should get one. Katie is tossing up the pros and cons, as if convincing herself she doesn't need one.

"Can you send me that?" Flynn asks quietly once he's finished scrolling and hands the phone back to Olivia. He runs his hand over my knee, gives it a squeeze and lets go. I immediately miss the reassuring weight of his palm.

Olivia blinks at him. "You're going to get a puppy?" She sounds gobsmacked.

Katie snorts. "Flynny, if you get a puppy you'll have," she gasps dramatically, "*responsibilities*."

The girls giggle and Flynn laughs too, but he's a second behind.

"No more impromptu surf trips," Olivia says.

"Poop," Katie adds. "So much poop."

"I can handle a bit of dog shit," Flynn mumbles. "But you're right." He smiles, but I don't buy it. "A dog does sound like a bit much responsibility. Wouldn't want to mess with a good thing."

"What's the good thing?" Katie asks, a teasing lilt to her tone.

"My life, Katie Kat. Right now, it's pretty damn perfect."

21

———

FLYNN

PRETTY DAMN PERFECT except my two best friends think I can't even look after a puppy.

I pick up my sandwich and take a huge bite.

Thankfully that seems to be the end of the discussion about my lack of responsibilities, and about puppies.

It's a ridiculous notion, me being responsible for another life. I can't even make a relationship with a person work. But a dog running around with me all day sounds great.

I love Katie and Olivia. We've been best friends for years, but now Katie is with Dallas and Olivia has stepped up to fill Henry's really big shoes, things aren't the same. They're busy and they're moving forward with their lives.

Meanwhile, I'm still in the same place I've always been.

Olivia turns the conversation towards the wedding and I feel Abi stiffen beside me.

"It's all going to plan," Abi says, lying through her teeth. She plasters on a completely fake smile. I don't know how I know it's fake, but I think it's something to do with the way the corners of her eyes aren't crinkling.

"I'm so sorry I can't help this afternoon," Olivia says, but Abi waves her off.

"It's fine. I can get most of it done today and you'll be around if anything comes up tomorrow. It's completely under control."

Ha. Yeah, right. Let's not forget the piles of roses strewn about the old barn that she has to deal with this afternoon.

It makes me a little uneasy to keep the information quiet, mostly because I usually blurt out whatever's on my mind.

But Abi asked me not to say anything about the flowers, and it's not like Olivia can actually do anything to help anyway. She's fully booked this afternoon otherwise she'd be down there already.

I finish my sandwich, then move onto the scones. Abi nibbles at her sandwich and as soon as she's done she turns to me.

She opens her mouth, but when she notices the two scones still on my plate, she closes it again.

"You ready to go?" I ask her, since she's going to be polite about me still stuffing my face with food.

"When you are," she says, but I don't miss her glancing at the clock on the kitchen wall.

"Let's go then. Thanks Vi. See you two losers later. Some of us have work to do." I scoop my scones into one hand, ruffle Katie's hair with the other and usher Abi out of the room in front of me.

We're both quiet as we the climb on the bike and we head

back down to the function venue, but at least this time when Abi slides on behind me she doesn't feel a thousand miles away. She slips into place behind me, her chest to my back, arms around my waist, head against my shoulder.

I didn't need to pull her closer to me earlier, but when she sat so far back to avoid touching me it felt wrong on all kinds of levels. I probably shouldn't have touched her, like I shouldn't have dropped my hand to her knee in the middle of Violet's kitchen, but I'm naturally affectionate, and with Abi the desire to touch her all the time is continuously at the forefront of my mind.

I still can't believe I turned her down for her friends with benefits idea.

"Thanks, Flynn," she says quietly as she climbs off the bike as I roll to a stop outside the function centre. "Lunch wasn't too bad after all."

"Of course not. I was there."

Abi rolls her eyes. I flick the bike stand down with my foot, then swing my leg over, coming to stand beside her.

"Show me what to do, Rosie," I say, my voice uncharacteristically serious. But I want it to be clear I'm not joking around with my offer.

Her brow furrows. "Rosie? Is that because I'm about to die under an avalanche of them?"

"That. And your choice of song."

She lets out a groan. "I was hoping you hadn't heard that."

I chuckle. "Was hard to miss," I say. What I don't tell her, is the nickname also relates to the delicious colour her cheeks turn when she's blushing. "Come on, these roses aren't going to prepare themselves." I sling an arm around her shoulders, like I would with Katie or Olivia in this moment. I realise my error when Abigail tenses under me. I'm about to remove my arm when she softens and leans into me. I lead her inside. "Show me what to do."

"You're going to stay?" She sounds so ... confused.

"Yeah, of course I am. You need help. Helping you is part of my job. Unless you'd rather I call Olivia down here."

"No!" She spins to face me, leaving my arm to fall limply at my side. "Don't tell Olivia."

"Guess you're stuck with me then." I shrug.

"Why do you make it sound like such a threat?"

I scrub my hand through my hair and stare down at her. "Because, sometimes you make it feel like one." She purses her lips, but I continue. "We're all on the same team here. It's not you against the rest of us. I know you tend to work alone over this side and that you like to be in control of everything, but you don't have to be ..." I drop my voice. "Around this place we're a team, a family. It sounds stupid, and totally corny, but it's true, and every person here wants you to succeed. Sometimes to do that, you need help. You're allowed to accept it. You're even allowed to ask for it."

The tension leaves her face, her pursed lips softening back into their natural pillowy state. I realise I must have stepped forward during my little speech, because she's right here in front of me, staring up with wide eyes and that mouth, all pink and delicious looking.

Back up, Flynn, I tell myself, as I force a step backwards. I can't get too close to this girl. This *woman*.

She isn't like any of the girls I've had my limited experience with. They were all young and stupid, like me.

Abigail is neither of those things. She's a full grown-up and while she's a little unsure on how this place works and where she fits, it won't take her long to catch up.

Then she won't need me anymore.

Who would need an aimless guy who couldn't even commit to a job promotion because he was too scared of the responsibilities?

I don't often let my mind wander in this direction. I didn't want the farm manager position, so I turned Henry down when he offered it to me almost a year ago. After I declined, he found Dallas to take on the role and that couldn't have worked out more perfectly.

So, I know that job wasn't meant for me. If I'd taken it we wouldn't have Dallas and Sadie here. Katie probably wouldn't have stuck around.

I'm happy with my choice. I like things the way they are, with me not being in charge.

But if that wasn't for me ... then what is?

22

—

ABI

WHAT FLYNN IS SAYING ISN'T stupid corny like he thinks it is. It's amazing.

They're a chosen family. They choose to be on this team together, and while Violet and Olivia are the owners of the property and officially the bosses, it doesn't feel like that. They're all as invested in this place—and each other—as the person beside them.

I love that.

I'm just not used to it. And definitely not used to being a part of something like that.

I'm an only child, but with the surprise arrival of Sadie, to a guy my parents didn't really approve of—for reasons I still can't figure out because Dallas is one of the best guys out there—our relationship fell apart.

When everything went wrong for me with Sadie and Dallas, I went grovelling back to my parents. I've got to hand it to them, they handled it well. They helped me out, got me into therapy, gave me a place to stay and supported me until I got back on my feet.

They've come to terms with being grandparents now, and I think they're hoping they can be a part of Sadie's life, once I get the relationship between me and her settled.

But even with their support, it's still been a solo venture for me. There is no team. There's no unwavering acceptance.

I clear my throat. "Okay," I say, my voice raspy. "I'm not used to it."

He gives me a quick, short nod, the corner of his mouth barely tilting up. I'm a little surprised by the reaction. I was expecting one of his big, easy smiles. I'm so used to seeing his features light up with those grins that to not get one now, when I'm agreeing with him on something so monumental, is jarring.

I pick up a rose from the table nearest me and twirl it. It's a stunning flower; the colour a deep, smooth red, the scent subtle and refined, the petals perfect.

I glance up at Flynn, holding the flower between us like an offering. "Will you help me? Pretty, pretty please?" I bat my eyelashes and give him a coy smile. I stop before pouting my lips though, because that seems like a step too far.

We've already blurred the lines between us and while Flynn's made it perfectly clear he doesn't want to go further, I can't deny that I do.

He's a wonderful human, and an incredibly good-looking guy.

I remember the first time I laid eyes on Flynn. He sped up on his bike, hair dishevelled and eyes worried after Olivia sent him an SOS text, because they couldn't find Katie. Flynn and I didn't speak that day, and I didn't think I'd ever see him again. I didn't think I'd end up working here, and when I took the job, Flynn hadn't crossed my mind.

Then, on my first day, when he found me mid-panic attack, there was no space in my mind to appreciate him. I was too worried he'd tell Dallas I'm not fit to be around Sadie, and too panicked about coming face-to-face with my daughter—a daughter who didn't even remember me.

But as far as I can tell, Flynn hasn't told anyone about that day and the state he found me in.

And now he's standing in front of me, staring down at me with clear hazel eyes, and he looks like a dream.

A really, really, excellent dream.

He watches me for another moment, his face expressionless. I shouldn't have spoken to him like that. I shouldn't have been silly and flirty. I've got a job to do and things to prove and making Flynn uncomfortable by flirting with him isn't the way to do it.

I want to turn away from him, but his gaze has me trapped. I'm still holding the flower between us, but my hand is dropping. I suck my bottom lip in and sink my teeth into it. I need to extract myself from his allure and get to work.

Flynn's fingers brush mine as he takes the flower, his tense expression from a moment ago softening. "Of course, I'll help you," he says. "Anything you need, Abigail. Just show me what to do."

His touch on my hand is electric, but the sparks tingling up my arm snap me out of my stupor.

"Right, well we've got a bunch of flowers to deal with," I say, clearing my throat and smoothing my hands down my front. I try to ignore the way Flynn tracks the movement, his eyes lingering on my hips, but my heart rate picks up just a little.

I cannot be so affected by this guy. Sure he's a lot of fun and pretty to look at, he has sinful hands and a mouth he knows how to use, but that doesn't mean my body should be reacting to him like this. I have got to focus.

I pick up a pair of shears, ready to show Flynn how to prepare the flowers so we can create the table centrepieces that were supposed to come fully formed, not as a collection of parts.

"Shall we start with a playlist?" he says, pulling his phone out of his back pocket and interrupting my train of thought. "As beautiful as your rendition of 'Every Rose Has Its Thorn' was, I think we can do better."

My face flames. I can't believe he heard me singing earlier. Absolutely mortifying.

Flynn smirks at me, and even though it's at my expense, it's a much better look on him than that sombre, slightly lost expression he was wearing a moment ago.

"Songs about roses," he mutters as he taps away at his screen, then he looks back at me. "What've you got?"

"What do you mean?" I'm supposed to be showing him what to do, but now I'm not quite sure what we're talking about.

"Songs about roses. Give me your picks. There's obviously Poison, and that Outkast one. Oh, definitely need some Guns N Roses." He taps away, and I realise he's actually making us a playlist of songs about roses. "What else?"

"That Miley Cyrus one. I know it isn't roses, but..."

"Love it. Yes. Added. What else?"

My mind blanks. Like goes utterly vacant. "I have no idea," I admit.

He frowns down at his screen, looking a little like a petulant child who isn't getting what he wants, especially with his wind-blown curls falling in his face. "This is a very sad playlist," he says.

I hate the almost defeat in his voice. Like he's about to give up on this ridiculous playlist idea. For some reason I can't stomach the thought of that, so I grab my phone and search for songs about roses.

The look on his face when I start throwing in contributions makes this completely pointless exercise worth it. His eyes sparkle as he looks at me, the disappointed twist of his lips curving into a brilliant smile as he realises I've committed to the game.

"Okay," he says after I've shot a bunch of songs at him from a very helpful webpage. "That should be enough. I haven't even heard of most of these. They better be good."

"Can we get to work now?" I ask, trying to hide how much I actually enjoyed creating a stupid playlist. It was fun. That inane process of suggesting songs to Flynn to make a playlist we don't need filled me with a weird fizzy feeling. I'm not used to it. I'm so used to being serious all the damn time. And Flynn's right. I don't always have to be in control of every little thing.

"Sure can," he says, his smile bright and I have to look away, reminding myself of the piles of roses we have to deal with, before I get trapped in his magnetic pull again.

I also remind myself of the dozens of reasons Flynn is off

limits, including me not having time or space for a man in my life. Just this job and Sadie. Sadie needs to be my focus.

And the biggest reason, is that Flynn has already said no. I'm okay with that. I just wish he hadn't.

I pick up another rose and show Flynn what to do with it. He listens with rapt attention and while I thought for a moment he wouldn't take this seriously and would be more of a hindrance than a help, he seems determined to get it right, taking extreme care when cutting stems and stripping leaves.

I watch him for a moment as he gets settled into the task to ensure he's doing it correctly and when I'm sure he is, I let my eyes linger on his hands. Big, strong, calloused and capable. Hands that set my body on fire.

Apparently it doesn't matter how much I tell myself I can't look at Flynn like *that*, my brain doesn't listen, because all I want is for Flynn to be handling me the same way he's handling these flowers.

23

FLYNN

WATCHING Abi work is a turn on I wasn't expecting. Everything about her is a turn on, but I wasn't expecting watching her work to be this much of one.

She's so confident in what she's doing, so in control. Like she knows exactly what she's trying to achieve and more importantly, knows exactly how to get there.

She showed me how to prepare the flowers—trimming the stems, removing the leaves—then started arranging them into a collection of short, square vases.

I couldn't take my eyes off her hands while she was demonstrating what she wants me to do and when I picked up the shears and my first rose, I desperately wanted her to do that cringey movie thing where she takes my hands in hers to help me get it right.

She apparently has too much faith in my abilities, because she didn't touch me at all.

She's arranged all the flowers I had trimmed for her and is

now stripping leaves off stems I haven't got to yet. I'm working too slow, but I don't want to rush this. I don't want to let her down.

I know most people think I'm reckless and foolish and have zero regard for responsibility, but that's not always true. If someone is depending on me I do everything in my power to get it right. I just can't always do that though. Sometimes, despite my best efforts, everything goes wrong anyway.

But not for Abi. I'm refusing to let her down. She's doing a great job, I know she is. I'm not letting this useless florist mess things up for Abi.

Not that Olivia would hold this chaos against Abi. Olivia isn't a tough boss. Sure she wants things done right, but she's never an asshole about it. Abi doesn't know that about her yet though, and there's a lot at stake for her. It needs to go well.

So, I don't rush. I methodically trim stems to exactly the right length and I don't allow myself to be distracted by Abi's confident fingers working alongside my own.

I've plugged my phone into the sound system, playing our ridiculous flower-themed playlist. I don't know half the songs, but I find myself humming along to the ones I do. Occasionally Abi will start singing under her breath, and when Poison comes on, I glance down at her as I bust out the lyrics, her cheeks flushing the most delicious shade of pink. After a few nudges of my elbow, Abi starts to sing too and before long we're screaming the lyrics at each other and giggling.

It's a refreshing change to see Abi like this, rather than the almost uptight version I get most of the time. The more time I spend with her, the more little glimpses I'm getting of her fun side. And I love it.

Life isn't supposed to be taken too seriously. It's supposed to be fun and right now, giggling and singing along to rose-themed songs, her dark hair tumbling down her back and eyes sparkling with amusement, she's never looked more beautiful.

And that's saying something, because Abigail Fletcher is a stunning woman at any time.

We work through the sun setting and dinnertime, and finally, the flowers are done. There's a line-up of vases along one table, the flowers arranged perfectly. You'd never know they were cobbled together by a farmhand and an event planner.

"It's time to eat, right?" I ask, rubbing a hand across my stomach which gave up growling at me a long time ago.

Abi purses her lips. "Yeah, go grab dinner. Thank you for your help," she says. "I really appreciate it."

"Anytime, Rosie. Let's go." I hold out my arm, expecting she'll waltz up beside me and slip hers through it. She doesn't though.

"Oh, I have more I need to do." She gestures around the room.

"It's after eight. You need food and sleep before tomorrow. It's going to be a big day."

Immediately I know I've said the wrong thing. She straightens, pushing her shoulders back and standing tall. She's wearing jeans, a loose sweatshirt and sneakers. It's far more relaxed than her usual outfits.

She's still intimidating as fuck though.

Impressive.

Gorgeous.

Maybe a little pissed off at me.

"I know what I need, and right now it's to finish my job. Thanks for your help, Flynn. I appreciate it but you can go have your dinner now."

I've been dismissed and it stings. I feel like we've taken some steps towards repairing the friendship we had been slowly building before I groped her on the beach that day, then steadfastly avoided her. But maybe she doesn't want that anymore.

I'm about to argue with her, to say that if she has more to do then I'll stay and help her, because it's my job too, but before I can form any words, my stomach grumbles loudly.

I really do need to eat something.

"Bye, Flynn," she says, turning away and busying herself with a stack of tablecloths she's pulled from a side table.

Alright then. I guess I'm leaving.

"See you later, Abigail," I say.

I turn and stomp away, swinging my leg over my bike and being just a touch too aggressive on the kickstart.

I'm pissed off now too, but mostly because her dismissal hurts. Clearly she's one of the people who thinks I'm irresponsible, who thinks I can't be responsible for a puppy or someone's wedding. Maybe she just wanted to get rid of me.

I speed home, bypassing the main house and heading straight for my place. Once upon a time the long, low building was the shearer's quarters. But back around the time my dad was working on the farm, they were converted into two tiny one-bedroom flats. Each has a simple bathroom and minuscule kitchen, a basic bedroom and enough space in the main room for a couch and TV.

It's nothing fancy, but it's enough for me. I don't need any more space and it seems stupid for me to rent something in town when I can live here, with the accommodation included as part of my salary. So, I'm not *always* reckless and irresponsible.

I wheel my bike into the small lean-to shed beside my flat and prop it on its stand. Then I kick my boots off and head inside.

It's remarkably quiet in here. Almost lonely.

I sigh and flop onto the couch. I need to make something to eat. I'm not in the mood for people, so I'm avoiding going down to the main house for Violet and Olivia's leftovers. I know I'm always welcome, and there's always food for me, but I don't want to talk to Olivia. I don't want to have to choose whether I say something about Abi's situation down at the function centre.

So it's easier for me to avoid them all.

I lie back on the couch and stare at the ceiling.

My parents lived here when they first got married, before Hunter and I came along. By the time we arrived, they were living in their own home in town and Dad drove out to the farm every day to work. Hunter and I still own the house, but use it as a rental. Neither of us wanted to sell it, but neither of us wanted to live in it after I turned eighteen either. Hunter moved into a dingy apartment above the mechanic's workshop where he works. I moved here to this slightly less dingy flat.

My eyes trace over the floral design my mum painted around the edges of the ceiling, something Henry refused to let be painted over, even after they moved out. It's something I'm grateful for now—a tiny, whimsical piece of my mother.

"What am I supposed to do now, Mum?" I mumble.

I know she's not here anymore, but I can still hear her voice, feel her warm hand smooth the hair back from my forehead. I imagine her hand would feel a lot smaller against my face now that it did when I was fourteen.

Words echo through my mind, in her voice. "You already know what to do, Flynny," she says.

I sigh and push myself to my feet.

The voice that sounds like my mum is right. I know exactly what to do, so I open my fridge and hope I have something I can turn into a meal.

24

ABI

GUILT LINGERS after Flynn leaves for the night.

I organise place settings and clean up the mess from the roses as I stew on how we left things.

I didn't miss the way he called me Abigail right before he left either, after I've gotten used to him calling me Abi, and he spent the afternoon calling me Rosie.

I hurt him when I dismissed his help like that, when I snapped at him about knowing what I need to do.

I do, but he wasn't coming from a place of nastiness or controlling. He was trying to help me, look out for me.

I'm reminded again that I'm not used to being part of a team. I'm used to being alone, to having only myself to rely on.

And while Flynn might come across as unreliable, I don't think that's really the case. I think if I truly needed him, he'd be there for me in a flash.

I sigh and drag another table into position, wincing as the steel legs scrape across the cobbled floor.

Then suddenly the sound stops and the other end of the table is lifted.

"Where's it going?" Flynn asks.

"Wh-what are you doing here?" I ask.

"I wasn't leaving you here to do it all on your own, Rosie. We're a team, remember?"

I sigh, not in annoyance with him, but in relief that he's here. He came back to help me.

"Over here," I say, taking a few more steps, then eyeing up the other tables scattered around the room. "Yep, here," I say, depositing my end back on the ground.

He gently places his end down, then turns and immediately strides back to the door, leaving me slack mouthed and confused, my hair falling from its ponytail. Is he leaving again? Why'd he come back if it was only to move a single table?

"I've got dinner," he says, picking up two plastic containers from the long bench seat running along the wall just inside the door.

He hands one to me, along with a paper towel. "Sorry, I don't have actual napkins." He drops his gaze to the box in his hands. "It's also not much. But it's something."

"Thank you, Flynn," I say. I feel like I'm always thanking this man. I feel like I already owe him so much. And after I was so rude to him, he went and made me dinner. I don't deserve a friend like him.

I lower myself to sit on the bench and stretch my legs out in front of me. It's a relief to sit for a few minutes.

I wasn't expecting to be under so much pressure because I'd ordered the flower arrangements to come fully formed. I never would have coped without Flynn, and I was a bitch to him regardless.

Then he turned up to feed me.

I pry the lid off the container. Inside is a thick parcel wrapped in tinfoil, a pot of yoghurt, a banana and a couple of slightly melted chocolate biscuits. There's also a spoon for the yoghurt.

I slide the tinfoil package out of the container and unwrap it to find a toasted sandwich, but not a basic one like I usually make. Flynn has used thick bread and the cheese is still warm enough to ooze out the sides. There's relish and bacon and a fried egg.

"Oh my god, this looks amazing," I say, fighting the urge to groan. "Smells amazing too."

Flynn lowers himself to sit beside me and opens his own container. His mouth is curled into a soft smile as he watches me take an enormous bite.

This time I can't stop the moan from slipping past my lips. Lunch at the main house feels like weeks ago.

Flynn's eyes are on my mouth as I chew, and his expression looks like he's at war with himself.

"Do I have food on my face?" I ask after I swallow.

He shakes his head, his curls dancing with the movement. "No," he murmurs, still watching my mouth.

I wipe my face despite his assurances because the way he's looking at me is like he wants to say something, but isn't sure how. At my movement he startles, snapping his gaze away and taking a bite that's almost half the sandwich.

We eat in silence, and once we're done, Flynn helps me

arrange the tables and chairs. Then we spread tablecloths and place our flower arrangements in the centre of each one. I lay out cutlery while Flynn unpacks wine and water glasses. Plates are stacked ready for the buffet, the boxes of alcohol that were delivered this afternoon are stored in the cooler after the bar fridge is stocked.

We work side by side and together we smash out every task I had on my list for today.

Finally, when Flynn has walked around every table and straightened every knife with perfect precision, he turns to me. "What's next?" His hair is dishevelled, his eyes tired and his posture is drooping. The poor guy did a full morning of physical farm labour before spending all afternoon and night helping me.

"Nothing," I say. "We're all done."

"Are you messing with me?" he says.

"Nope, we're done. Well, until tomorrow." I give him a grin. "We did it."

"Fuck yes we did. Of course we did. Why do you sound like it's a miracle?"

I laugh, the sound a little delirious now I'm coming down from the adrenaline high I've been running off since lunchtime. "Because it feels like one."

I head for the stairs at the back of the room and Flynn follows me into my office. I need to grab my bag, then I'm heading home for a shower and some sleep. I collapse onto the couch in the office and let out a groan as I realise my mistake. Maybe I'll just be sleeping here tonight. I tilt my head back and close my eyes.

"God, I'm tired," I mutter.

"Don't get mad at me for saying this," Flynn says, and I crack my eyes open watch him squirm as he stands in front of me. "But I don't think you should drive home tonight."

"I don't have the energy to be mad," I say. "Might just sleep here."

He crosses his arms over his chest and stares down at me. "No."

"Stop trying to tell me what to do, Flynn," I mutter, trying to glare at him but failing because it feels like too much work. Instead I close my eyes again and let myself sink further into the couch.

He lets out a huffing noise, loud enough to make me peel my eyelids open again. "I'm not. I'm suggesting you let people help you so you can be here for your daughter in the way she needs."

This time I pull off the glare. How dare he? I want to launch myself off this couch and smack him right in the face for insinuating I'm not doing right by Sadie.

He sighs. "I didn't mean it like that. We want to help you. And look at you. It's not safe for you to drive home, so I'm not letting you." He runs a hand through his hair, then drops his arms by his sides, a plea on his face. He looks as exhausted as I feel. "Because I care what happens to you."

"Fine, I won't drive." I reach for the blanket slung over the back of the couch, not wanting his words to affect me the way they do. He cares, I already know he does. It shouldn't make my heart all giddy like this.

"You can go stay in the main house for the night."

"No!" I actually manage to get off the couch this time. "Then Olivia will want to know why I'm still here so late when I should have been set up hours ago. Please, she can't know."

Flynn's jaw is tight as he stares down at me, a little furrow between his brows as he thinks. "There's one other option."

"I'll take it."

"You stay at my place," he says, his hand finding its way back to his hair.

"Yes, excellent. Great idea." Anything to avoid Olivia finding out.

"But," he continues, like he hasn't heard me. He closes his eyes as the next words spill out. "I don't have a spare bed."

Oh.

25

———

FLYNN

I CAN'T BELIEVE Abi took this option.

She's standing in the middle of my flat, taking in the simple space. She looks completely out of place with her glamour and elegance—even just wearing jeans and a sweatshirt.

Once she's finished assessing the space—my sparse kitchen, the simple couch and TV, the few photos I have of my friends and family hung haphazardly on the wall—she faces me, a touch of pink in her cheeks.

"Is it okay if I have a shower?"

I startle into action. I've been too distracted by the sight of her in my space. "Oh, yeah, of course. I'll grab you a towel." Thank fuck I did my washing yesterday. "It's right through here."

I lead her into the bathroom, scooping up the clothes I dropped on the floor last night and shoving them in the hamper as I go. I pull a towel from the cupboard and rummage through the drawers until I find a new toothbrush.

"Do you need anything else?" I ask. "Use whatever in the shower. I hope it's okay. The water takes a bit to get going and the pressure is shit. The mark one up from warm is the perfect temperature. Will you want more to eat afterwards?" Why can't I stop *talking*?

Abi gives me an indulgent smile when I finally keep my mouth closed for longer than a second. "I'm good, Flynn. Thank you."

"I'll leave you to it," I say, moving to pull the door closed as I step out of the room.

"There's one thing," Abi says and I pause. "Can I borrow some clothes?"

"Um, yeah, sure. Of course." My brain is glitching. Abi wants to wear my clothes. Well, wants to is probably too strong a choice of words. She needs to. "Sweats and a tee okay?"

"Perfect," she whispers. "Much better than jeans."

"Will find something for you."

"Just shove them through the door," she says and pulls her sweatshirt over her head, dropping it to the floor beside her. Her eyes return to me, gaze expectant.

Right. I'm standing here in the doorway when she wants to shower. In my house.

Then she wants to wear my clothes and sleep in my bed. Where I will also be sleeping.

I tap my hand on the doorframe a couple of times. "Let me know if you need anything." I pull the door shut and spin away, getting as far away from that bathroom door as possible.

I head into the bedroom and flop face first onto the mattress. I bury my groan in a pillow. What have I got myself into?

Would it really have been so wrong of me to let her drive home in the middle of the night on dark, remote backroads when she's clearly exhausted?

I couldn't let her drive, but I should have made her stay with Olivia. The main house has two spare bedrooms and multiple couches. Maybe I should go sleep down there. But how would I explain that away? That would be more complicated than Abi going there herself.

I groan again and press my hips into the mattress, trying desperately to smother my dick in the hope it deflates before she gets out of the shower. It's been half hard since she stepped through the front door.

When I have no luck smothering my cock into behaving, I shove off the bed and rifle through my drawers for something Abi can wear. My options are pretty limited, but I do have a pair of grey sweatpants that aren't too hideous and a huge grey t-shirt that I picked up as a freebie somewhere along the way. Those kind of freebies always come several sizes too big for me, but the fabric is soft, so it's still one of my favourites.

I knock on the bathroom door, then crack is open a sliver. "Clothes," I say, pushing the bundle through the tiniest gap I can. I'm not tempting fate or my willpower by opening this door any further than I absolutely have to.

"Thanks," Abi calls out before I jerk the door closed again.

Then I turn my attention to my bedroom. I'm not a total slob so it's not disgusting, but I am a single guy who works a lot and is more than a little lazy when it comes to housework.

I fold the pile of clothes I've dumped on the chair in the

corner and shove them back into drawers, then I strip the sheets off the bed and remake it with my spare set.

When everything is as tidy as it can be, I fall back on the couch, staring up at my mum's paintings again.

"I don't know what to do," I whisper to Mum, and like earlier, I hear her voice in my head, this time telling me I'll make the right choice.

The trouble is, I can't figure out what the right choice is.

Turning Abi down seems like the sensible one. I wasn't lying to her when I said it was complicated. Between Sadie, Dallas, Katie, Olivia and our jobs, complicated doesn't seem like a big enough word.

So yeah, keeping our relationship at the status quo is the sensible choice. Keeping our hot as fuck beach make out session a secret, also a sensible choice.

But sensible doesn't always mean it's the *right* choice.

And that's the thought running through my head when Abi opens the bathroom door and steps through in a rush of steam.

My eyes trail over her, admiring the way my clothes fit her. Or don't really fit her, because the t-shirt is oversized on her too, but the sweatpants are snug. I realise I'm staring at the curve of her hips and jerk my gaze away.

"All good?" I ask, like the complete fool I am.

"Yeah," Abi says softly as she steps across the room and lowers herself onto the couch beside me. She sits sideways, facing me, with one leg tucked up under her. Her cheeks are flushed that delicious rosy colour and her dark hair is piled messily on her head, the few loose tendrils damp and curling from the shower. "You're right about the pressure, but it still feels amazing being clean again."

I make a half-hearted grunting noise in agreement and immediately want to slap myself across the face. Instead I continue staring at the ceiling, willing my mother's spirit to give me some kind of clue.

"The flowers are a cute touch," Abi says, voice too cheery for my behaviour. Cool. I've made her uncomfortable.

"Yeah, my mum painted them when she lived here."

"Your mum lived here?"

"Yeah. Well, my dad did first. They lived here for six months after they got married. She painted the flowers, apparently trying to make this place nice, and Henry never let anyone paint over them, even after they moved out."

"I love that."

"Yeah, it's nice having that random little touch of her," I say. I don't tell her I ask the paintings questions. "You all done in the bathroom?" I push off the couch.

"Yeah, thanks."

"It's no worries, Rosie," I say, forcing a smile and trying not to think about all of my worries about this woman. "Bedroom is through here." I lead her through the only other door in the flat. "I'm going to go shower, but make yourself comfortable."

"Thanks, Flynn," Abi says, voice soft, then she turns back to the bed. "What side do you sleep on?"

"Side?"

"Yeah. I'll sleep on the other."

Oh. I laugh and it comes out more nervously than I was

expecting. "I don't sleep on a side. I tend to sleep right in the middle."

I'm so fucking smooth. Way to remind her I've never shared a bed with anyone. Well, there's been the occasional sleeping beside Olivia or Katie over the years. But that doesn't count and we never discussed what side we sleep on.

"Oh, well, can I sleep on that side?" Abi asks and points to the side furthest from the small window.

"Yeah, of course. Help yourself. Same with whatever foods in the pantry or fridge if you want something. I'll be back soon." Just after I finish trying to drown myself in the shower.

I spend way too long standing under the shower spray. I need to get to sleep, it's already way too late, but I can't make myself move. Not until the hot water runs out anyway. I towel off and pull on a pair of shorts. I wouldn't normally wear anything but underwear to sleep in. But I'm not doing that with Abi next to me.

By the time I slip into the bedroom, Abi is curled into a tight ball on her side of the bed and doesn't stir when I slide in next to her. I flick off the bedside lamp and settle in, willing sleep to come fast.

It doesn't. It doesn't come at all.

26

———

ABI

FLYNN CANNOT STOP MOVING. From the moment he slipped silently into bed beside me, he's been tossing and turning every thirty seconds. I can feel his restless heat across the bed—it's not a big one—and I want to roll over, reach out and smooth a hand down his spine. But I don't. Instead I lie still, faking sleep.

I pretended I was already asleep when he came to bed, because I feel like I've made him uncomfortable enough just by being here, let alone being in his bed.

I shouldn't have taken him up on his offer. I should have argued at his insistence that I couldn't drive home. Sure it would mean I would have gotten home and to bed a lot later than I had. Or I should have toughened up and admitted to Olivia what happened with the flowers. But turning up at her house in the middle of the night to confess, then beg for a bed, was too horrifying a thought to even contemplate. Way to show my boss I've got my shit together.

So I chose Flynn's other offer. His place.

It's kind of charming, despite clearly being incredibly old and a bit run down. You can tell they've tried to maintain it as much as possible, but there's only so much you can do with a building this old.

Flynn clearly isn't an interior decorator. His only contributions to the space are a collection of photos hung on the wall, including several of a man who looks exactly like Flynn and a stunning blonde woman. His parents, without a doubt. I didn't linger looking at the pictures, but my eyes did land on one of that gorgeous couple and two boys. The blond boy was slightly bigger than the other, taller and broader though still too young to be anything but a gangly teenager, and had a stern expression on his small face, his brow furrowed. The other boy had the opposite expression, a huge smile spread across his face under a tangle of wild red hair. Flynn, probably somewhere around age twelve. His parents were looking at each other in the photo, sharing a smile and the love between them was obvious, even from my quick glance.

Flynn lets out a low growling sound and a moment later the bed shifts as his feet touch the floor. He pads quietly from the room, leaving the bed feeling huge, empty and cold.

I lie still for several long moments, but Flynn doesn't return. I can't hear him in the bathroom. I can't hear him moving around at all.

Another moment passes and ignoring my better judgement, I slip out of bed and go searching for him.

In a home with three rooms, he isn't hard to find. I don't even have to go past the bedroom door.

Flynn is standing at the kitchen bench, hands braced on the edge, staring out the window to what I assume would be the hills beyond if it was daylight.

The glow of the moon through the window on the opposite side of the room traces his shoulders in soft light. He's only wearing a pair of loose shorts that sit deliciously low on his hips. So low I can make out the twin dips in his lower back. The long, lean muscles in his back flex and shift as his grip tightens on the bench top. He lets out a low groan.

"Flynn?" I whisper.

He startles and whirls around. "Shit," he says breathlessly.

"Sorry. Are you okay?"

"I'm fine," he mutters and turns back to the window.

"That's my line," I say and he huffs out a tiny laugh. "What are you doing?"

"I don't know." His voice is so low I barely hear him. He sighs heavily and I try not to be too distracted by his back muscles flexing again. He's clearly got something on his mind and I'm here ogling him. He spins around again, crossing his arms over his chest and again, my gaze lingers on long, lean muscles ... everywhere. "That's the problem, Rosie. I don't know what the fuck I'm doing."

I mirror his pose, folding my arms and leaning against the doorframe. There's a few metres between us, plus this simmering attraction that flares hotter as his eyes wander down my body, snagging on the hem of the t-shirt of his that I'm wearing. The space feels like miles, and also no distance at all.

The shirt smells like him, like grass and sunshine and a tinge of sea salt, and the fabric is so soft and worn I never want to take it off.

His eyes remain on the hem, his tongue slipping out to lick along his bottom lip and that's when I realise what he's staring at.

My bare legs, because I ditched his sweatpants before I crawled into bed. I have way more booty than this guy and they were too snug, and too warm, for me to comfortably sleep in.

"What exactly are you referring to?" I ask, voice husky.

"Everything." He drops his hands, bracing them on the bench again and holy shit. Biceps. Abs. Shoulders. Chest. Hip bones jutting out above the waistband of his shorts. I press my thighs together and he doesn't miss the tiny movement. "My whole life, Rosie. I don't know what I'm doing with any of it. But right now..." His eyes roam over me again and my knees feel weak. "Right now, my biggest issue is I don't know what the fuck to do about you."

"Me?"

"Yeah. I want you more than I've wanted anything in my entire life."

"You can have me."

"Maybe once."

"It can be more than once." I push off the door frame and step towards him.

"How come you're so into this? Into me?" He ruffles his hair, then smooths it down again. "It doesn't seem like your kind of thing. A fling with the reckless farmhand."

I study him, stopping halfway across the room. "Because you're hot as fuck too, Flynn. You're fun. I like you, and ..."

"And?"

"And that day on the beach, you got me out of my head. I don't know if you know this about me, but I spend a lot of time trapped in there." I smile sheepishly at him and am rewarded when his lip curls up into a half smirk.

He holds up a hand, his thumb and pointer finger millimetres apart. "Just a little." He chuckles. "So, you're just using me for your own gain?"

"If that's how you want to think about it. If it'll help you by thinking you're doing it to help out a friend."

He laughs. "You know me too well. I'd do anything to help a friend." His voice is low and husky. He stalks towards me. "I still don't know what I'm doing," he whispers as he stands over me in the near-dark.

"Just don't think too much about it," I whisper.

"I mean, I actually don't know what I'm doing ... with a woman."

"Mutually beneficial arrangement then. You can practise your skills while helping me get out of my head." I throw the last remnants of caution to the wind and close the gap between us with a final step. I press my body against his, my hands finding his hips, then I reach up on my tiptoes, ghosting my lips over his. "If nothing else, maybe it'll help you sleep tonight. You seem to be struggling." I swipe my tongue across his bottom lip, copying the movement he did himself earlier.

An instant later, his mouth slams down on mine.

He groans and I swallow it. His hands brace my waist and his tongue slips into my mouth. Fucking hell. My knees feel like jelly. My entire body feels like jelly.

He takes a step forward, hesitant at first, but his confidence grows as I follow his lead and let him guide me back until I'm pressed between him and the wall. He pushes his hips forward and the soft layers of fabric between us do nothing to hide how hard his cock is.

It's my turn to groan. His lips leave mine and trail kisses along my cheek to the hinge of my jaw, then drag down my throat. "Fuck, yes," I moan, lifting my hands to tangle them in his hair. "Don't you dare stop on me now," I mutter and Flynn's hot breath caresses my skin as he laughs.

"A sledgehammer to the head couldn't stop me." His voice is low and rough, almost growly and I shiver. "Cold, Rosie?"

"Fuck, no."

He pulls back and studies my face for a moment. His eyes are flaming with desire and want, but there's a trace of concern there too.

I reach up and capture his mouth again, licking my way inside. My hands find his back and I drag him closer, as I sling my leg around his hip.

The t-shirt rides up and it's one less layer of fabric between us as he rolls his hips against me his eyes fluttering shut at the sensation.

I drag my fingertips down his chest, across his abs to the waistband of his shorts. It's his turn to shiver as I run my nails along the edge of the fabric. Then I slip my hand inside and wrap it around the hot length of his dick.

Flynn moans, but goes rigid, so I freeze, his cock still in my hand.

"You okay, sweetheart?" I whisper against his mouth.

He takes a breath, drags his tongue along my lips and groans out a breathy, "Yes".

I shove his shorts down, freeing his dick, then drag my hand up and down, slowly pumping him as he relaxes back into the moment. His hands wander from my waist, skimming up to trail fingertips down my throat, cupping the full swell of my breast, thumb flicking over my nipple. God, if it feels that good through fabric what would is feel like with his hands on my bare skin?

His other hand presses against my hip and I twist against the pressure until my pussy connects with his thigh and I grind down. He lets out a surprised little grunt, then immediately catches on and uses that hand to help build my momentum, guiding my hips forward and back.

"Touch me," I whisper as pressure builds in my belly. I'm still lazily jerking him off and twist my hand over his head as I say the words. "Please, Flynn."

Flynn's movements stutter, then resume. His hand drags across my hip, down the outside of my thigh and back up the inside. He presses his forehead against mine, his gaze lowered between us, watching the progress of his hand. He bites his lip, then brushes his fingers against the damp fabric of my underwear.

My head falls back, hitting the wall with a dull thud. Flynn's gaze flicks to mine. "Don't stop," I gasp. "I want you to bury your fingers in my pussy."

"Fuck," he mutters as he presses his hand against me, twisting them in a tight circle. Then he hooks his fingers into the side of my underwear and shoves it aside.

His thick finger drags through me and it's all I can do to

keep myself standing. My hand has gone still on his cock, but I can't continue the attention I was giving it, especially not when Flynn slides inside me.

The moan I let out is guttural and raw. Flynn watches where his hand disappears under the hem of my shirt for a few moments, then his gaze lands on my face.

His cheeks are flushed, eyes burning and lips red and puffy from our kissing. His expression is so seeking I cup his cheek and whisper to him.

"More, sweetheart. It's so good, but I need more."

He immediately slides another finger into me, then presses his body against me, flattening me against the wall. His free hand tangles in my hair and he drags his mouth over my neck. "Fuck, you're incredible," he murmurs against my skin.

His hips take over where my hand left off when I got distracted by his touch and he thrusts against me, fucking into my hand.

We grind together, his fingers buried inside me, my hand wrapped around him.

My whole world is Flynn and the things he's doing to my body. Sensation builds and just when I think I can't bear it anymore Flynn tugs at my hair.

"Come for me, Rosie," he says, voice husky and a little desperate. My eyes flash to his. He looks utterly wrecked. Ruined. On the edge of the abyss. "Now, *please*."

At his plea, I fall over that edge and my orgasm rips through my body. A moment later, Flynn grunts and shudders, his cock jerking in my hand as he spills over.

He lets out a gusty breath, rests his head against my shoulder and groans. "Fuck me."

I laugh softly, my body still wrapped in the bliss of the afterglow. "Maybe another day," I say, ruffling his wild red curls.

27

———

FLYNN

SO APPARENTLY I have not one iota of good sense in my body.

I don't have it in me to care.

"I'm going to need another shirt," Abi says after long moments of me slumped against her.

Shirt. Ah yeah, because I came all over the one she's wearing, rutting against her like a horny teenager until I begged her to come on my hand because I knew I couldn't last another moment and didn't want to let her down by blowing my load before she'd got off. Class act, Flynn.

She doesn't seem to mind though. Apparently it was as hot for her as it was for me.

"Right, yes." I push myself away from her, reluctantly breaking the contact between us.

I don't know what I'm supposed to do in this situation, when I've got my co-worker and friend off against the wall. But I tuck myself away, grab a fresh shirt and hand it to Abi, who disappears into the bathroom to clean up my mess.

When she's done, I clean myself up and by the time I'm standing in the bedroom doorway trying to figure out what happens now, she's back in my bed.

"Come here, Flynn," she says, patting the sheets beside her. "I'm not going to bite. Not tonight anyway." She flashes me a wicked smirk. "We need to get to sleep."

She's right. Fuck. It was late enough when we got to my place, then my restlessness kept her awake and ended in *that*. She's got a huge day of work ahead.

I slowly cross the room, still unsure climbing into bed beside her is the right choice. "Maybe I should sleep on the couch. That way you're more likely to get some rest," I say, reaching for my pillow.

"Do you want to sleep on the couch?"

"Not particularly, no. It's not long enough."

"Then get in here with me," she says. She's sitting up on the mattress, hair mussed from where my hands have been tangling in it, cheeks still that edible rosy colour.

I hesitate for another second, then climb into bed.

I stretch out, pulling the duvet over me, then tilt my head to look up at Abi. "Ah, sorry it didn't last long," I say, feeling the heat in my cheeks.

"There's nothing wrong with fast and filthy, Flynn," she says, a sexy as fuck smirk on that incredible mouth. "And trust me when I say you know exactly what you're doing."

And I thought my face couldn't get any hotter.

Ugh. I'm such a loser.

What kind of twenty-four-year-old guy has such limited experience with sex? It's not that I've never been interested, but a one-night or casual thing never held any appeal and since people only see me as the good time guy, anything longer term hasn't been on the cards. I'm not long-term relationship material apparently. Plus there hasn't exactly been a large dating pool in the tiny town of Kauri Creek. Since it's the only place I've ever lived, meeting new people that see me as having relationship potential has been more than a little tricky.

"Hey." Abi slides down beside me in the bed, then grips my chin to turn it towards her. "There's nothing wrong with having limited experience. You're perfect, just the way you are." She presses her lips against mine for a brief moment. It doesn't feel like a thing fuck buddies should do. Sure, kissing in the heat of the moment with tongues and teeth makes sense, but soft, gentle brushes of lips in the dark after the fact is something else entirely.

Or I think it is.

What would I know?

Not much at all.

This whole thing with Abi feels like a lapse in judgement. The wrong choice. But as she curls into my side, splaying her hand across my abs and snuggling into my shoulder, nothing about it feels wrong at all.

THE BED SHIFTS and my eyes fly open, because I didn't move. Abi freezes halfway off the mattress.

"Sorry, I didn't mean to wake you," she whispers. "Go back to sleep."

"Why are you awake this early?" I ask, after a glance at my bedside alarm clock.

"Because I've got a whole wedding to pull off today and I have to go home first."

"Home?"

"Yeah. I need clothes. I wasn't expecting to stay, remember?"

"Right, yeah." I rub a hand over my face, then sit up. I'm generally an early riser because I like to get my work done before the day gets away from me, but this is pushing it for a Saturday, even for me. "How were you planning on getting back to your car?" I ask, peering at her as she slides her jeans up her legs. I kind of resent those pants from blocking my view.

Abi freezes. "Shit. You don't fancy a little drive do you? Otherwise I guess I'm walking."

I laugh. "Of course I'll drive you. Just give me a minute and I'll be with you."

"Sure. I'll just use the bathroom." She grabs the rest of her clothes and disappears into the other room.

I will my hard dick to go down and shove myself out of bed. I half-heartedly straighten the blankets, then find myself some clothes. Five minutes later, we're both climbing into my ute.

When I bypass the driveway towards the event centre and instead head straight for town, Abi gives me a sidelong glance.

"I want coffee, and food. I have neither in my house," I say. "I'll drop you at your place then I'll get us breakfast while you're doing what you need to. When we get back to the farm you'll be ready to go."

"Alright. Sounds good." She turns to the window and watches the paddocks roll by, before suddenly picking up her phone and tapping away.

The only sound between us the quiet music coming from the ute speakers. I'm busy wracking my brain for something to say to her—because what does one say after hooking up with their friend? But she speaks first.

"Flynn, were you serious about the puppy?"

"What?"

"The puppies Olivia showed you at lunch yesterday. Do you want to get one?"

I run a hand through my hair. I do want one. I want to feel less lonely, and a puppy seems like a good way to do that, but Olivia and Katie were right about me and responsibilities. I'm not very good at them. "Maybe. I like the idea of one, the reality might be a different story though."

She makes a small humming noise and a moment later my phone chimes with an incoming text. "That's the link. I think you should consider it."

"What?"

"I saw the way you looked at those puppies. There's no person in the world who I think would be a better puppy dad than you."

"Is that because I behave like a puppy most of the time myself?"

She laughs and I celebrate the sound. "Maybe." She shrugs.

"It just makes sense to me that you should have one. At least think about it."

"I did, but Katie and Liv are right."

She makes a tiny scoffing noise and I raise my eyebrows at her. "They don't think you can handle the responsibility of a puppy, but have no issue giving you plenty of responsibility with your job."

"I turned down the job with all the responsibility. Henry offered me the farm manager role and I said no."

"Just because you didn't want to manage the whole place, including the staff, doesn't make you irresponsible. You're not going to let a puppy down, Flynn. You never let me down."

There's still time. The thought flashes through my mind so fast I barely register it. "I don't know," I say, trailing off and hoping we can leave this conversation topic behind.

"Just think about it. Maybe go see them."

"Well, if I go and see them, I'll for sure be bringing one home, because did you see their faces?"

She laughs. "True, but I don't think that would be a bad thing."

28

———

ABI

I DON'T KNOW if I'm overstepping by pushing Flynn about the puppy. The look on his face when he saw the pictures of them, then the look that crossed it when Olivia and Katie shot him down is scratched into my brain though and I can't let it go.

Is encouraging him about the puppy really overstepping when I jerked him off and came all over his hand last night? Probably not.

I direct Flynn through the streets, still quiet and sleepy this early on a Saturday. The sun is just cresting the horizon and it's peaceful.

I don't know how peaceful things are between Flynn and I though. He seems ... conflicted.

I worry I pushed him too much and he regrets it, but there isn't much I can do about that right now.

"Left here," I say, pointing to my street. Flynn indicates and makes the turn, not saying a word. "This one with the blue door," I say and he jerks in surprise. It's then that I realise his hands are gripping the steering wheel like they did that day we made out on the beach. His knuckles are white and he's looking like if he lets go his whole world will fall apart.

"How long do you need?" he rasps, hands not leaving the steering wheel, not even to put the ute into park.

"You can come in for a bit if you want," I say, but Flynn shakes his head, jerking it roughly from side to side, his eyes fixed on my bright blue front door. "Um, maybe half an hour?"

"Okay. I'll see you back here."

I'm effectively dismissed and I climb out of the ute. The moment my door is closed, he's backing away.

So, I guess that answers my question about how he's feeling about last night. I shouldn't have been so flippant about his experience, or lack of it, or any of his other concerns about us hooking up. I just so desperately needed the escape from my brain, and it felt so good I don't even feel like I should regret it.

I don't want to regret it.

I sigh and shove my key into the lock. I flick Emily a message as I close the door behind me and dump my keys on the side table in the entryway.

I have a quick shower and by the time I'm out, Emily has replied. I pick up the phone and call her.

"Em, I think I fucked up," I say as soon as she answers.

"The farm hand guy? What's his name? Flynn?"

"What? How did you know?" I love that we don't have to beat around the bush with anything in our friendship. We've been through enough to know there isn't any judgement from either side. But I still don't understand how she could possibly know about Flynn.

"Because honey, you talk about him constantly. Way more than you talk about Dallas, almost as much as you talk about Sadie."

I sigh and slump onto my bed, then immediately jump up again, switching the phone to speaker and pulling on my clothes. "He's my only friend here," I say. "If I can even really call him a friend."

"Of course you can. You like him, you spend time with him. Apparently he likes to hang out with you. That's pretty much the definition of friends."

"Yeah, but like I said, I fucked up." I wrestle with the zipper on my dress. What I really need is another set of hands, but asking Flynn to do it when he gets back is out of the question, not when he can barely look at me.

"Why? Did you fuck him?" she asks and I can hear the cackle building in her voice. I groan and she unleashes her wicked laugh. "You did!"

"Not exactly."

"Did one or both of you come because of something you did to the other?"

"Yes."

"It counts, babe. But more importantly, how was it?"

"Really, really, really good."

"Was this the first time?"

I groan again and Emily lets out a shriek that's far too loud for this early in the morning. "We sort of made out on the beach a couple of weeks ago."

"Hot."

"It really, really was." My blood heats up just remembering that day.

"Was that the day he taught you to ride his bike? Didn't know that was a euphemism."

I laugh, the sound echoing around the room. "It wasn't. I really did learn to drive it ... then we made out on it."

"Maybe Simone needs a dirt bike ... That sounds super hot." Emily groans. "Right, sorry. Focussing. Why'd it take you so long between making out and getting off?"

"Because Flynn was worried about what would happen if we went further."

"And he's not worried now?"

"Oh, yeah, I'm pretty sure he's worried now. That's why I fucked up. I shouldn't have pushed him." I start in on my makeup while we talk and I can hear Emily making her morning coffee. I love this about our friendship, how seamlessly we fit each other into our lives. "He's acting weird this morning. I don't know how to fix it."

"You don't always need to be fixing things you know. Maybe he just needs a little time. Or a proper fucking."

"Em," I groan and she laughs.

"Just give him some time. He'll come around and either want to do it again, or he won't. Which is unlikely because, like, you own a mirror, right? But, more importantly, go you. I'm happy you're getting out of your head a little. A young, hot farm-hand is exactly what you need."

"Yeah, but what if he doesn't want to do it again?"

"Like I said, unlikely. But if he doesn't, I'm sure everything will be fine. From everything you've said about him, he's pretty laidback, right?"

"Right." Laidback is exactly the right word to describe Flynn. Laidback, fun, and really, really sweet.

"So even if he chooses not to take you to bed again, I don't think he'll freak out so much that your friendship can't recover."

I puff out a breath. "I suppose you're right. He hasn't done this kind of thing before. Maybe he's just adjusting."

"What kind of thing hasn't he done before?"

I hesitate. I could tell her that he hasn't done any of it before. But that's Flynn's business, not Emily's. And I don't want to tell her. I like that it's just between us. "The friends with benefits thing," I say instead.

"Oh, right, yeah well that can take some getting used to. He'll get there though." Her voice softens, all traces of vivacious humour gone. "It'll be okay, Abi. Don't let your head tell you otherwise. Flynn is your friend. Getting each other off isn't going to ruin that, okay?"

"Okay," I whisper, wishing my voice was stronger, that I believed it more.

"Now, don't you have a huge ass wedding to run today? Why are you freaking out on the phone to me?"

"I'd really rather you hadn't reminded me of that," I groan. Flynn had been a nice distraction from my job and all the things I have to stress about today.

"You'll smash it, Abs. I know you will. You always do. And if you need a pep talk, you know where to find me."

"That I do. Thanks Em."

"Love you, Abi. Go slay that wedding, then screw the guy. Winning all around."

I can't help laughing along with her.

I'm not sure I'll be doing either, but I'm not going to let the little voices in my head mess with me.

Not today anyway.

29

———

FLYNN

I SHOVE open the door to Sugar and slam straight into someone's solid back.

Who the fuck is standing right in the doorway with their back to it?

We both grunt at the impact and before I have the chance to curse the guy out for blocking the way, I have the foresight to glance up at him.

Oh. I've run headfirst into my brother.

I love Hunter—somewhere deep down inside he must love me too—but right now I am not in the headspace to deal with him. We have a strange relationship. We'd do anything for the other, he proved that when he gave up his chance at a life outside this town to stay home and look after me after our parents died.

But Hunter and I are not the same kind of person. He is … surly. And as much as his grumpy attitude to pretty much everything pisses me off, I can't even hate him for it, since he gave up all the good things in his life for me.

Ugh. I hate it sometimes. Would our relationship have been better if he hadn't become my legal guardian when he was eighteen? What guy fresh out of high school wants to suddenly be responsible for a fourteen-year-old shithead like I was? Like I still am.

"Hey," Hunter grunts at me before I have a chance to think what the heck to say to him.

"We have a new tenant," I blurt, which is not at all what I was expecting to say. I was hoping I'd just blank the fact that I just dropped Abigail off at my childhood home from my memory.

Hunter eyes me suspiciously. "Yes," he says eventually.

"You didn't tell me." I'm accusing him and I have no idea why.

"I thought you didn't want to know about the house," he says. Which is exactly why I don't understand why I sound so accusatory.

"You're right." I shake my head. "I don't. I was just surprised when I found out who lives there."

He's got that intense look on his face again, like he's trying to figure out what I'm on about. "Who does live there? The property manager doesn't tell me much about the tenants, just that we had a new one."

"She's the event manager at Wildflower Ridge," I say, rubbing at the back of my neck with one hand.

"Isn't that the mother of that kid?"

"Yes, she's Sadie's mum." I roll my eyes. How anyone can

dislike Sadie is beyond me, but Hunter can still find it in him to be grouchy in her presence. Not that it seems to bother Sadie, she appears to have taken it on as a personal challenge to cheer my big brother up. It hasn't worked yet.

Hunter narrows his eyes. "What's going on? Is she going to be an awful tenant? The property manager raved about her."

"No, no. She'll be a great tenant. I doubt she'll cause you any problems."

"And what about the problems she's causing you?"

My eyes jerk to his, meeting his steely glare. "Me? I have no problems with her." Damnit, I can feel my cheeks heating. My blush is about to arrive in full force. "I'm going to get a dog," I blurt to distract both of us from conversations about Abi. "I think. Maybe."

Hunter sighs, but accepts my change of topic. "Makes sense." It sounds like he'd rather nail his hand to the wall than consider a puppy. Ah, my big brother. So enthusiastic about life, so cheerful. Always such a delight.

"It does?"

He shrugs, pulls the cap from his head, runs his hand over his short hair and shoves the hat back into place.

"Hunter," Tilly Sheridan calls from behind the counter. "Here's your order."

Hunter turns away from me, grunts a 'thank you' at Tilly and grabs his food. "See you," he says to me, then shoves his way out of the door and into the street.

I want to chase after him to get him to finish our conversation, but Tilly is waiting for me, her eyes bright and smile wide.

"Hey, Flynn," she says.

I shoot another look out onto the street, but Hunter has already disappeared around the corner. I sigh and approach the counter. "Hey, Tilly."

I order coffee for both me and Abi, along with a couple of breakfast sandwiches. Tilly chats away as she makes the coffees, asking all about the farm and how everyone who lives there is doing.

Tilly's parents own Constellation Station, the neighbouring property. It's their place I trespass on every time I head down to the beach. We practically grew up together, despite her being a few years younger than me. Her parents were friends with mine and her brothers were my best friends during school.

I'm not friends with either of them now; Toby because he passed away—but after what I've recently learned about him, even if he were alive, I wouldn't call him a friend anymore. Max isn't a friend because he turned into a complete jerk somewhere along the line and took it out on Katie. We've never understood it. He took an instant dislike to her and it only grew over the years. He was one of the reasons it took Katie so long to come home again.

But I'm not holding any of that against Tilly. She's a total sweetheart. She has a kind word for everyone, a bright smile and a generally cheerful disposition.

"Here you go," she says, handing over the coffees and food.

"Thanks, Tilly." I pile the food in my arms. "Oh, hey. I meant to ask. Whose recipes are the cupcakes?"

Tilly's brow furrows for a moment, then clears. "Not your mum's," she says. "Sorry."

I wave her off. "That's okay. I didn't think so. Whoever makes them does an amazing job."

Her cheeks turn pink and she runs a fingertip along the edge of the counter. "Thanks," she whispers.

It's got to be her. I don't know if I should push it though. She seems uncomfortable about it. But as proved by my actions with Abi last night, I'm an idiot, so I ask anyway. "You make them?"

"Yeah." She gives a short nod, then her gaze flicks over my shoulder as the door opens and someone else steps into the cafe.

"They're delicious," I say. "Have a great day."

"You too, Flynn," she says, the shy smile still on her face, but a little glimmer of pride is shining through.

I'm out on the street, an armload full of food and balancing two coffee cups in my hands when I realise I now have to see Abi again.

30

———

ABI

I HEAR Flynn's ute in my driveway just as I'm finishing getting ready. I grab my bag—fully loaded with anything I could think of that I might need today—and head for the door, locking it behind me before Flynn even has a chance to get out of the ute.

I shove my bag into the backseat and climb into the front where there's a coffee sitting in the cup holder and a paper bag on the console between us. Flynn's already taking huge bites out of a toasted roll filled with bacon, eggs, cheese and spinach. There's aioli or some kind of sauce at the corner of his mouth and I want to lean over and lick it off.

"Breakfast," he says between mouthfuls, gesturing to the bag.

"That smells and looks amazing," I say.

"It is."

I laugh. "I can tell." Before I have a chance to stop myself, my hand is reaching out, swiping that stray bit of sauce off his mouth with my thumb.

He freezes as my skin connects with his. His eyes are wide and fixed on mine. I don't know what I'm doing. I'm supposed to be giving him space and time to get his head around everything. I'm not supposed to be pushing all his buttons.

But the way he's watching me ... it's like he wants to devour me instead of the sandwich in his hand.

Before I have the chance to pull my hand back—because this whole interaction is happening in a weird slow motion—Flynn turns his head and sucks my thumb into his mouth, licking the sauce off.

Okay, so maybe he doesn't need as much time as I thought.

As soon as I have the thought, Flynn's eyes fly wide, a look of panic on his features.

I pull my hand away, tangling my fingers in my lap and pressing my hands firmly into my thighs so I don't climb over and straddle him right here in the driveway.

At least I'm sure where I stand on the situation.

I want his hands on me again. I want his mouth on me. I want to explore every inch of his body, feel every part of him. I want to feel the hard cock I had in my hand last night in other places.

I have to rein in my thoughts. Today is not the day for thinking about sex. Today Flynn is my co-worker. He's going to help me pull off this wedding and another time ... Another time we'll get back to the sex stuff. If he wants.

I buckle my seatbelt and unwrap my sandwich, then glance at Flynn, who's sitting in the driver's seat, staring at the house.

"Are you okay?" I ask, unsure I want to hear the answer.

Flynn blinks, shakes his head and turns to me, plastering a

smile on his face. "Great," he says. "Let's go deal with this wedding, huh?"

SOMEHOW, Flynn and I make it through the day without me climbing him like a tree.

Fuck he's hot.

But also, I've been very, very busy. It's been all on from the moment we arrived back at the farm. Because of the flower mix-up and our late night, my day started a lot later than planned. But with Flynn's help, we managed to get everything set up in time for the wedding couple's family to arrive and add their touches.

The wedding itself went off without a hitch and the last guests have just driven out of the driveway, along with the bar and catering staff. I watch their taillights disappear over the hill and release a huge sigh of relief.

We did it. The Barclay wedding is over.

"Great job," Olivia says, coming to stand next to me as I stare out into the night. The sky is so clear tonight that I can see every one of the bazillion stars in the sky. It's like nothing I've ever seen before.

"You smashed it, Rosie," Flynn says, rushing around the corner after helping the bar staff pack everything into the outside chiller and scooping me into a hug, spinning me around once before realising I'm not alone. "Oh, hey Liv," he says. "Didn't Abi do great?"

Olivia stares at him for a moment, eyes wide and jaw

dropped, then shakes off the expression and looks at me and smiles. "She sure did. We're celebrating on Wednesday. Dinner at home, then line dancing at the hotel."

Flynn punches the air. "Yes! We're there."

Olivia gives him another look. "I hope you can make it," she says to me. Then she yawns. "Oh my god. I'm exhausted. I'm going to bed. You should too," she says. "I don't want to see you here tomorrow."

"But who's feeding the cows?" Flynn asks, a cheeky grin on his face.

"I was talking to Abi, you dumbass. You're still expected to turn up to work." She reaches up and ruffles Flynn's hair. He bats her hand away and tries to pin her arms by wrapping her in a giant hug.

I frown, not at their familiarity, but at Flynn having to work tomorrow. "Flynn's been a huge help to me," I say. "I couldn't have done this without him. Does he get some time off soon?"

Flynn and Olivia immediately stop messing around.

"Don't worry about it, Rosie," Flynn says. "I'm only feeding out tomorrow. I get the rest of the day off."

"Oh, okay. That's alright then."

Olivia is giving me the same look she was giving Flynn earlier when he picked me up and spun me in a circle. "Right. Well, I'm going to go. Do you want a ride, Flynn?"

He shakes his head. "Have my ute. See you tomorrow, Liv."

Olivia walks away, shooting us another look over her shoulder as she goes.

"She's super suspicious," I say to Flynn and even in the half-dark outside the barn, I can tell his face pales.

"About us?" He kicks his boot in the dirt. "Shit. How would she even know about last night?"

"I don't know. It might not have been about last night specifically. But when you spun me around her face was … something."

Flynn rubs his hand over the back of his neck. I've known him long enough now to know he does that when he's uncomfortable.

"It might be nothing," I say. "It's probably nothing. There's nothing for her to know." I wish I hadn't said anything. I hadn't meant to freak him out about it.

"Say nothing again." Flynn's tone is teasing and I'm relieved he's shaken off the worry and is back to his usual sunny self.

I roll my eyes at him, then turn serious. "Thank you for your help, Flynn. I really appreciate it. Couldn't have done it without you."

"Anytime, Abigail," he says, voice low and suddenly husky. "Do you need anything else done tonight?" I shake my head and he points over his shoulder, indicating the direction his ute is parked in. "I should get going then." He gives me a small smile that's a little shaky around the edges. He shuffles his feet, like he's not sure if he should leave or not.

This is my moment I guess. If I don't want him to go, or if I want to go with him, this is my chance.

I open my mouth, ready to ask him how he's feeling about last night. We've avoided it all day. There hasn't been anything more than friendly between us since he sucked aioli off my thumb this morning. But before I can throw myself at him again, I need to know where he stands.

Instead of words coming out when I open my mouth though, I yawn. It's huge and loud and the most unsexy thing I've potentially ever done.

"Are you okay to drive tonight?" Flynn asks. "Olivia would let you stay. You have a reason she can know about tonight."

I guess that answers my question about his opinion on last night. One time only apparently.

Then he yawns too. It's far more adorable than the one I just let out. "I'm absolutely beat. You must be too."

Maybe I'm reading into all this too much. Maybe he just needs some sleep. After two late nights in a row, I know I sure do. Or maybe he's worried because I mentioned Olivia being suspicious and he wants to keep a little distance so no one finds out.

That's probably for the best. While everyone at Wildflower Ridge has been welcoming, including Katie who was the one I was most worried about, their opinions of me might be skewed if they find out the things Flynn and I have done, and the things I really, really hope I get the chance to do with him.

I smile at him, trying to be reassuring, to convince him and myself that everything between us is fine. "Yeah, I am. Good-night, Flynn."

31

FLYNN

I FINISH BUTTONING my shirt and smooth my hair, then immediately mess it up again. Smoothed-down hair just doesn't look right on me.

I slip on my nicest pair of boots, the ones I keep for nights like this, grab my phone and wallet and head up the drive towards the main house.

The sun is just dipping behind the hills and everything is golden, the sky lighting up red and orange.

As the house comes into view, my breath catches at the sight of Abi's car parked beside Dallas and Olivia's utes.

Things between us have been completely normal since Saturday, not that I've seen Abi much. It wasn't even on purpose. But, even on Saturday things were fine between us, despite my actions trying to make everything super weird.

My head was spinning all day about Abi living in my house. Sure, I haven't lived there for years and I don't want to live there anytime soon, but to know she's in there ... it threw me, even more than the making out and hand jobs we'd given each other the night before. Is what I did to her even called a hand job?

I shake the thought off as I step up onto the porch. I've got to keep my head screwed on. Now is not the time to be thinking about giving Abi orgasms.

I'm the last one to arrive and when I step into the kitchen there's already noise and chaos everywhere. I barely have the chance to register the people in the room before there's a loud yelp in my direction.

"Flynn!" Sadie races across the room and leaps into my arms. "Hey, sprout," I say and she beams at me as she wraps her arms around me. She's like a little koala and I love it.

"Are you going dancing too?"

"Sure am," I reply. Sadie pouts. "What's that face for?"

"Dad said I can't go."

"Oh, well we're going to be out pretty late. But how about we teach you the steps and we can do our own dancing?"

"Okay! Now?"

"Um." I rub at the back of my neck. "Maybe tomorrow, after I've learned them myself."

"I thought you knew how to dance."

I do. But I can't remember line dancing steps. I can pull off a pretty stilted waltz and when it's just music and a dance floor with no required choreography I can hold my own. But I can't retain dance steps in my memory, no matter how many times I learn them.

"If you wait until tomorrow then we can all teach you," Katie interjects. "We'll go and learn tonight, then you'll get five teachers, instead of just Flynn."

"Does that mean I'll be the best? If I have more teachers?"

Katie laughs and tugs at one of Sadie's braids. "Sure, kid. Come eat your dinner."

Sadie wriggles out of my arms and drops to the floor, dashing back across to where Violet is placing a plate of food onto the table for her.

Once Sadie isn't occupying all of my attention I finally have a chance to take in everyone else. Violet; in her usual jeans and t-shirt, dark hair pulled back in a plait as she oversees the dishing up of food. Olivia; wearing light-wash jeans and a yellow button-up shirt that's tied at the waist. Her hair—the same colour as Violet's except without the traces of grey—is long and loose down her back.

Katie is wearing a denim miniskirt with knee-high boots and a low-cut, draped tank top thing. I don't exactly know what it's called, but it looks incredible on her. If she wasn't one of my best friends I'd definitely think she's hot. Dallas certainly does. I can tell by the way his gaze keeps snagging on her even while he's trying to pay attention to what Olivia is saying.

Then my eyes land on Abi and I nearly choke on my breath. She's wearing a white dress under a denim jacket, a pair of soft brown cowboy boots on her feet. The dress has a low neckline and her tits are full and lush under the fabric. The skirt swishes around her legs as she walks and there's some kind of stitching detail on it, but I can't tell from across the room.

Our eyes meet as my gaze travels back up her body and she gives me a wary smile, like she's not sure how I'm going to react to her being here. I grin and the wariness melts from her expression, leaving behind a burning stare.

Not thinking about giving Abi orgasms suddenly becomes really, really hard. Like something else that's hard. Nope, not thinking about hard things. It becomes difficult not to think about giving her orgasms when she's wearing that dress though.

"You getting a plate, Flynn?" Olivia calls across the room and I realise everyone else is sitting down at the huge timber table in the middle of the room. There's a formal dining room in this house too, but we never use it. Violet prefers to keep us in the comfort of her kitchen, and considering half my childhood memories happened sitting at this table I don't mind at all.

"Uh, yeah. Bathroom first," I stutter, then hustle out of the room. I head for the bathroom and spend several minutes glaring at myself in the mirror, willing my dick to go down.

Fucking Abi with my hand and her jerking me off on Friday night was incredibly hot, but I'm still not convinced a repeat is a good idea.

But I don't care anymore.

If Abi is up for it, I want more. I want to do it again. I want to do it tonight, while she's wearing that fucking dress. I groan and press down on my cock as the image of Abi straddling my lap, her tits spilling out over the neckline, comes to mind.

I consider a quick jerk to take the edge off, but I've already done that over thoughts of her today, and at this point I'd rather have the real thing. Besides, doing that in Olivia's bathroom feels weird.

I'm just going to have to suck it up and hope Abi's mind is going in the same direction mine is.

Then make it through hanging out with our friends without giving away how into her I am, because as much as they love me,

I know things will get weird if they find out Abi and I are messing around together. I don't want that for her.

I don't want them to think she's not taking her job, or her relationship with Sadie seriously. They'll think I'm being reckless and irresponsible, which I am, but I can't have them thinking the same things about Abi. Their opinions of me don't matter, their opinions of her do.

I take a deep breath and open the bathroom door. I can do this. I can get through the next few hours without drooling over her. I've made it this far, it'll be a piece of cake.

Then I step back into the kitchen and my eyes immediately land on her.

She's laughing at something Sadie is saying, warmth and love radiating out of her, and shit. It's not going to be as easy as I thought after all.

32

ABI

AS APPREHENSIVE AS I was about tonight—in that I tried to get out of it about seven hundred times, but Olivia wouldn't let me—I'm actually having a fantastic time.

First, I got to hang out with Sadie for dinner with the whole crew and as much as I sometimes think things feel awkward between Katie and I, or Dallas and I, the reality is that once we're in the same room, it just isn't.

I was expecting animosity or wariness in the least from Katie, but she's embraced my arrival fully. They go out of their way to include me in Sadie's life and while I haven't hung out with Sadie one-on-one yet, I almost feel like a part of the family. Almost.

I love the relationship I'm building with Sadie. She's sweet and funny, completely obsessed with horses and like all the adults around her, so very generous. But we're still learning each other, and I'm more than happy to take it at whatever pace suits Sadie and Dallas.

He mentioned me doing a school pick up this week and I can't wait. I've been careful not to push things, but picking my child up from school feels momentous. I wish I'd been doing it all along.

I push the melancholy thoughts out of my head, because tonight is for fun, not for rehashing all my mistakes.

After dinner, we piled into vehicles, Olivia claiming my passenger seat while forcing Flynn to ride with Dallas and Katie in his ute. Flynn pouted, loudly complaining about having to go with them, but when Olivia pointed out that if someone didn't go with them, they were likely to get distracted along the way and spend the night lost in each other instead of celebrating with the rest of us, he conceded. He shot me a look that let me know exactly what he thought about the situation though and I know he wished it was just me and him in my car.

But then we'd be the ones getting lost in each other, and I don't need those questions right now. From his reaction when he saw me, I'm pretty sure he's keen for a round two, but we haven't exactly had the chance to discuss it.

I lean against the tall table we've snagged at the Kauri Creek Hotel, the only reputable bar in the town, and tap my fingernails against the wooden surface, occasionally swiping at the condensation on my glass.

Dallas and Katie are on the dance floor, though the line dancing portion of the night hasn't actually started yet. Flynn and Olivia are out there too. I couldn't help the little pang of jealousy that shot through me when he'd held out a hand to her and whirled her away.

It's jealousy I have no right to. I'm fairly certain Flynn and

Olivia think of each other more as siblings than potential romantic partners, but even if they were into each other, Flynn and I are just friends. Hopefully friends who fuck, but that's still to be confirmed.

My eyes snag on them as the crowd shifts and they come back into view. Flynn's head is thrown back as he dances, baring his throat and I have to press my thighs together as a bolt of lust shoots through my belly. I want to bite his throat, lick my way down it, then keep going.

"Hey," a deep voice says beside me and I turn to look up at a dark-haired man. He has a deep shadow of stubble across his jaw, not a fully-fledged beard, but enough that he clearly hasn't spent time with a razor in the past couple of days, and his dark eyes drink me in. "I haven't seen you around here before," he continues.

"New to town," I say.

"Ah. You enjoying it?" His gaze roams over me again.

Before I have a chance to reply a body presses against my side and Flynn wraps his arm around my waist. Olivia steps up on my other side and stares at the man in front of me.

"Not on your life, Max," she says, steel in her voice. I didn't know Olivia could sound like that.

"Ollie," the guy, Max, says, but Olivia holds up a hand and silences him.

"Absolutely not."

Flynn turns me away from Max and leads me to the dance floor, Olivia following close behind after she throws the man an evil look.

"What the hell was that?" I ask, as the music fades out and

someone announces the line dancing will be starting in a moment. At least they can explain to me without having to shout over a driving bass.

"Max is ..." Flynn starts.

"He's a bastard," Olivia cuts in, face stony. "I know we can't actually tell you what to do or who you can spend your time with. But I beg you to please consider your choices when it comes to Max Sheridan."

I shoot a look between the two of them. Clearly they're taking this seriously. "Okay. I'll keep it in mind." I glance back to where Max was standing, but he's disappeared.

"Good," Flynn says and his hand squeezes my waist. How I didn't realise his hand was still on me I don't know, because now I know it's there all of my senses have zeroed on in the touch. "You gonna dance with me, Rosie?"

I want to do something else with him, but I can't exactly bring that up with Olivia standing right here. Flynn drops his hand from my waist and I suppress the whimper that threatens to escape at the loss of contact with him.

He lines up beside me while Olivia takes her place on my other side.

Someone stands on the small stage in the corner, walking us through the steps and after a couple of repetitions, the music kicks back up.

Thankfully I'm not the only one who can't keep up. Olivia stumbles along beside me, giggling every time she flubs a step. Flynn however looks like he was born to line dance. After watching him with Olivia earlier, it's not just line dancing he was born for. I'll have to hit him up about it later.

I catch sight of Dallas through the crowd. He and Katie found a spot across the room and while Katie's taken to the steps almost as well as Flynn, Dallas has not. Dancing has never been his thing. I was surprised when he so easily agreed to coming tonight, but as I watch him stumble along beside Katie, it makes perfect sense.

I've realised I've stopped dancing, too busy watching Dallas laughing, when Flynn's hand lands on my waist again. He gives a little tug, and I follow him without question as he leads me off the dance floor, towards a spot in the back corner of the room.

The lighting is dim back here, the music quieter, though not by much.

"You okay?" Flynn leans in close so I can hear him. I feel the soft brush of his breath against my ear and I recklessly lean into his body. He stiffens for a moment, but after glancing around the room, the tension leaks out of him.

"I'm fine," I say and he gives me a sceptical look. "I mean it. I'm good. Great actually."

"You're having fun?"

"Yes." I place my hand on his forearm, smoothing my palm up his skin. He tracks the movement.

"You were looking a little ... I don't know exactly, but like you were maybe sad?"

I shake my head, sliding my fingers as far as possible under the rolled sleeve of his dress shirt and just managing to brush my fingertips across his bicep. "Not sad. I was watching Dallas."

"Oh." Flynn straightens, extending the distance between us.

"He's so happy. It's been so long since I've seen him like

this. I love that he's made such an incredible life for him and Sadie. I couldn't be happier for them."

"Oh," Flynn says again. "I wasn't sure if you wanted another shot with him. It would have put me in a really awkward position."

"Because Katie's your best friend?" It makes sense. Not that I'd ever want to come between them. They're perfect for each other. A blind man could see it.

Flynn shrugs. "Well, there's that, but mostly because I want you for myself." His voice is a little breathless, tinged with hope, and the same feeling is clear in his eyes.

I dig my fingertips into the taut muscle of his forearm. "Suddenly all this noise is giving me a headache," I say, then reach up on my tiptoes to speak directly into Flynn's ear. "Would you be able to walk me home?"

I pull back just in time to see the request register and Flynn's expression goes from concerned and confused to salacious in one second.

He slips his hand into mine and tugs me along as he weaves through the crowd. He finds Olivia, taps on her shoulder to get her attention and leans in to speak to her.

I can't hear what he's saying, but her eyes flick to me, and down my arm to where my hand is still linked with Flynn's. She nods, then says something back to Flynn. He presses a kiss to her cheek, then turns back to me.

"Let's go."

33

—

ABI

I FOLLOW Flynn onto the street and we turn towards my place.

"What did Olivia say?" I ask as I shrug into my jacket, unsure if I really want to know the answer.

Flynn thinks for a moment. "She said if we think it's a good idea, then I should stay at your place tonight and catch a ride back out to the farm with you tomorrow."

I stumble to a stop. Flynn takes another couple of steps before realising I'm not beside him anymore. "What does she mean by that?" She has to know what's going on. Damn, that woman is perceptive.

Flynn just shrugs. "Said I deserved a sleep in. But if you don't want me to stay, I can head back to Katie's place tonight."

Katie's place. Because she doesn't officially live with Dallas and Sadie yet, even though she's there all the time. But she still has her house in town, and that's where everyone is supposed to be sleeping tonight before they head back to the farm early to get started on the day's work.

I want to laugh at his innocence. "She just gave you the perfect cover story so you don't have to leave," I say, resuming walking.

It's another few steps before Flynn speaks again. "If that's okay with you," he says.

"Of course it's okay," I say, turning into my street. One of the huge benefits of this town is how close everything is. I'm only two blocks from the main street. "I even have a spare bed."

I spin and walk backwards, watching the expressions play out on Flynn's face: relief, excitement, confusion, then devastation that makes my heart give a weird twist. I'd meant it as a joke, but based on his face, it's looking like he took it literally.

We reach my house and Flynn follows me onto the front porch. He stares at the blue front door like it wronged him somehow.

"You know what," he says as I rummage in my bag for my keys. "I probably should head back with the others. I have heaps of work to get through tomorrow."

I stop trying to unlock the door as Flynn takes a step backward.

"Flynn," I say, closing the distance between us before he can make it wider. "I was joking. I want you to stay ... I want you in my bed."

His breath catches and I reach a hand up to trace my fingertip along his eyebrow and down his cheek to drag across his bottom lip. He's frozen, eyes locked on mine as I trail my hand lower, skimming over his Adam's apple and down the length of his throat, inside the collar of his shirt to the dip in his collarbone. He swallows, but otherwise doesn't move.

My hand continues to drift lower until I hook the tips of my fingers inside the waist of his jeans and tug him to me. He takes a stumbling step forward, his body colliding with mine and pushing me back.

"I'm up for this," I say. "If you are."

My words break the trance he's in and he surges forward, mouth landing on mine with so much heat and force I almost collapse in a puddle on the floor. Flynn pushes me back again until my back hits the door, then he's cupping my face with his big hands, one sliding into my hair at the nape of my neck.

He licks across my lips and I open for him, going weak as his tongue drags against mine.

One of my hands is still tucked in the waistband of his jeans, and I wrap the other around his back, my keys digging into his shoulder.

Flynn breaks the kiss and presses his forehead against mine, panting into the space between us. His gaze drops, lingering on the exceptional cleavage I get with this bra and dress combo. "We need to go inside now," he rasps, then takes the keys from my hand.

I'm still a little dazed from that kiss, from the way his body against mine ignites me in a way I've never experienced before. He flicks through the different keys, picks the right one and slides it into the lock. Before I have a chance to explain to him how finicky the door is, he's turned the key, wiggled the handle in just the right way and shoves the door with enough force to get it to open smoothly. Something I still can't get right most days.

He holds the door open and ushers me inside.

That kiss really has slowed down my thought processes. How does Flynn have complete mastery of my complicated front door? He steps inside behind me, then flicks on the lights for the living area. He doesn't even hesitate to reach for the light switch, which I've always thought was in a really weird place.

"How do you ... you know my house?" I ask, the question sounding as dumb out loud as I was expecting it to.

Flynn rubs a hand across his neck, then runs it through his hair. "Yeah, just a little bit." The heat and lust in his eyes from a moment ago has faded and now he looks sheepish, and nervous. "I want to show you something." He turns and heads down the hall, like he knows this place inside out.

Stopping outside the hallway cupboard, where I keep my linens along with a whole array of miscellaneous stuff, he tugs the door open and steps inside, gesturing for me to slot into the tiny space between him and the doorframe.

I press into the space and his hands immediately fall to my waist, pulling me back against his front. He reaches out and traces his finger down the back of the doorframe where a list of names and dates are listed.

The one at the top reads Trent and beside it a date from decades ago. I lean forward and squint at the next one. Hunter. Eleven years ago. A few more dates with Hunter's name beside them. Below that is a mark for Isla, the date the same as Trent's. Right below that is another date from eleven years ago and beside that date, written in tiny flowing script is a single name.

Flynn.

The dates and height marks for Hunter and Flynn continue down the doorframe, one for each of them every year.

I'm stunned, my breath trapped in my chest, my heart pounding. "This was your house?"

"It still is," he says. He taps his finger against his name. "A few months after this I finally outgrew Mum, but we never got to record it." He sighs, then steps away from me, out of the tiny cupboard we'd wedged ourselves into. "I'm sorry I didn't tell you. That this place was mine, I mean."

"You didn't have to tell me. But now that morning you dropped me off here makes more sense." I close the cupboard and lean against the wall. He mirrors my pose opposite me. "I thought you were freaking out about what happened the night before."

He grins bashfully. "There was a little bit of freaking out about the night before. But mostly I was just shocked that you lived here, of all places."

"Why don't you live here? Or your brother?"

Flynn shrugs. "I wanted to be closer to the farm, to Olivia and Violet. It doesn't make sense for me to live here when I have everything I need out there. As for Hunter, who the fuck knows."

"You don't have to stay," I say. "Tonight, I mean. This has got to be weird for you."

"It is, but I also kind of love that you've made this your home. Want to give me the tour?"

I laugh. "I think you should be giving me the tour."

"Okay, no tour." He steps across the hall, right into my

space. I could get used to being pressed between Flynn's hot, hard body and whatever wall is close by. "What happens next?"

I'm about to toss back a flippant 'whatever you want', when I realise Flynn isn't asking to be flirty, he's asking because he really doesn't know.

"Let's get a drink," I say. "We'll take it from there."

34

FLYNN

ABI SLIPS out from where I have her boxed in against the wall —again.

She slides her hand into mine, and by this point I feel like I shouldn't be so affected every time she touches me.

But I am.

Maybe it's just what the touch from a gorgeous woman does to me.

Maybe it's only Abi's touch.

Maybe it's nerves because I have no idea what's going to happen tonight. As much as I try to fake confidence, tonight I'm struggling.

Especially being back in my childhood home. I hope that tiny factor isn't going to make this extreme levels of awkward. It's already bad enough.

Abi leads me into the open plan kitchen, dining and living area. "I don't have a lot of options sorry. Some Coke, white wine or gin."

I shake my head. "I don't need a drink," I say.

I step towards the doors that open out onto the back deck. My parents spent most of my childhood renovating this place. I love that pretty much everything is exactly the same as it was when I moved out six years ago, right after I turned eighteen and finished high school. By then I was legally no longer Hunter's responsibility, and I had my job at Wildflower Ridge to fall into.

I stare out into the night and exhale a long breath, then spin around to find Abi standing directly behind me. We both startle and a giggle slips from her lips. A moment later, we're both laughing and the tension that was curling up my spine releases.

"You're nervous," Abi says and it's not a question.

"Little bit," I say, pinching my fingers together. "I don't know the protocol here."

"Protocol might be a bit formal," she says, a smile curving her lips.

"You know what I mean," I grumble, but my mouth is tugging into a smile too.

"It's whatever we want it to be. Friends with full benefits, friends with hand jobs only, just friends. It's up to us, and we don't need to define everything right now. Things can evolve as we go. The most important thing is we're open and honest with each other. I don't want to push you into anything, and I don't want to lose the friendship we already have." She sighs. "Because you're my only one here, but ..." She trails off and toys with the ends of her hair.

"But?" I take a step towards her. The pull is too great and I can't stay away. My hands land on her waist and she sucks in a breath. It makes her chest swell, her tits rising under the edge of her dress.

And just like that my dick goes hard.

"But just the thought of you touching me has me wet and so turned on I can't think straight."

I thought my dick was already hard, but it gets harder. The pressure in my jeans makes me want to moan, and not in a good way. "Fucking hell, Rosie," I mutter. "You make my cock so hard I could cry."

"I could take care of that for you." The gleam in her eye is wicked as she slides her tongue across her bottom lip. Her hands find their way to the waistband of my jeans and after a brief pause to check if I'm going to stop her, she pops the button.

Her fingers work at the zipper, slowly dragging it down, and as that goes down, so does she.

"Wait," I blurt and she freezes, halfway to her knees. What the hell is my mouth thinking stopping her right now? "Come here." I pull her back to standing, cup her face in my palm and bring my lips down on hers.

She hesitates, then leans into the kiss, reaching up to slide her hands into my hair. The press of her fingertips against my scalp and the tug of my hair feels incredible.

"Don't you want to?" Abi murmurs against my mouth.

I take a few steps backwards, skirting around the coffee table in the centre of the room and dragging Abi with me. I drop onto the couch, leaving her standing before me.

"God, yes I want to. But I don't want it to be over in under a minute either." I run my hands up her legs, under her skirt and grip her thighs. "Get down here."

Abi climbs into my lap, my hands sliding to caress her gorgeous ass. My fingers brush lace and I want to make her get straight back up to get this dress off so I can see what she's wearing underneath.

Trailing her fingers up my neck, Abi leans in to whisper in my ear. "Just do what feels good for you, sweetheart."

I groan and pull her mouth back to mine. Our tongues brush and I lose myself in her. I know how to kiss, I've done that much before, so I lean into something I know I'm good at.

I drag my lips across her jaw and when she tips her head back, exposing the long column of her delicate throat I embrace the invitation. I press open mouthed kisses between her jaw and collarbone, alternating with tongue and teeth. Her breathy sounds, little moans and cries, encourage me. Surely she's not making those noises if it's bad.

One hand is still under her skirt, gripping the full curve of her ass and pulling her against me. My other hand is against her back, holding her steady. I drag it lower and my fingers brush the zipper of her dress.

"Yes," Abi moans against my temple as the fabric gives. The straps slide down her arms, exposing the soft pink lace bra she's wearing.

I don't have enough hands for all the places I want to touch her. I want one in her hair, one holding her to me, one cupping her ass, one caressing the incredible tits now right in front of my face and one sliding between her legs to relive the last time we were together.

"Lose the dress," I growl and Abi doesn't hesitate, tossing the garment across the room.

I lean back against the couch and drink in the sight of her. Miles of gorgeous skin dotted with occasional freckles and a few silvery stripes near her hips. I run a finger over them.

"Stretch marks," she murmurs.

"Fuck, you're beautiful," I say in response.

"Not the dirty talk I had in mind for tonight," she says, leaning in to press a soft kiss to my mouth. "But thank you."

"Dirty talk?"

"Mmhmm," she hums, grinding down into my lap. "I'm very good with instructions."

"Instructions?" I want to slap myself. Why have I suddenly lost the ability to talk?

She hums again. "Don't overthink it, sweetheart. Trust your instincts because they're very good." She moans as my grip on her ass tightens. "What do you want to do with me?"

I want to do everything. Absolutely everything with this incredible woman. But I'm going to have to pace myself.

I drop my hands from her body, letting them fall to the couch beside me. Abi goes still, her grinding on my lap slowing to a stop.

"Right now, I want to watch you," I say. "Keep going."

Her eyes darken with lust and she pulls her lower lip between her teeth, one hand lifting to bury itself into her hair. She lifts her hips and slowly presses back down.

She's wearing a matching set of lace underwear and the cowboy boots she never removed, while I'm still fully clothed and it's giving me a power trip.

But if this is what she wants, if I haven't misconstrued what she said ... I'm going to embrace it.

I rest my head against the couch and stretch my arms along the back of it, admiring the view before me. As much as I love watching the expression on Abi's face, my gaze keeps lingering on her body, on her soft waist and full hips and the way her tits look in that bra. It's partially see-through and I can make out the darker colour of her nipples. I want to touch them, cup the weight in my hands and watch her face shift as I suck them into my mouth.

Abi must notice where I'm focussing my attention because her hands come to her chest, teasing and playing with the edges of her bra. "What do you want, sweetheart?"

The name catches me off guard again, like it has every time she's used it. It makes my heart do a weird little trippy thing. I shake off that feeling and focus on Abi in my lap.

"Take it off."

She scrambles to obey, reaching behind herself and a moment later the bra has joined the dress somewhere on the other side of the room.

"You like it when I tell you what to do?"

She nods, looking uncertain for a moment. "I like not having to think." She cups her bare breasts, thumbs brushing over erect nipples. "Plus, this confidence looks fucking hot on you." She pinches and lets out a moan.

The sound goes straight to my dick. I want her to make good on her offer from earlier, but I'm still nowhere near ready for this to be over and I know once she wraps her lips around my cock I won't be able to last. It's bad enough with her grinding on me.

I drag my hands up her thighs until I'm gripping her hips

and shift her backwards. Her eyes immediately drop to the hard bulge in my jeans, the zip still only halfway down. She reaches for it but I bat her hand away.

"I thought you were doing as you were told," I mutter against her ear. She lets out a needy whimper and I have to take a deep breath to keep my control in check. "Be a good girl and sit on the table."

I don't know where this is coming from, this confidence to be able to tell her what to do, to sound like I know what I'm doing when I really, really don't. I'm grateful for it though. Grateful that I'm able to set the pace, and fuck it turns me on when she's so keen to obey.

Abi slides off my lap and perches her ass on the corner of the coffee table in front of the couch. I hope it's a sturdy one. She watches me with hungry eyes as I release my zipper and shove my pants down to take the pressure off.

"I can't see you with your knees pressed together like that," I say, voice a low rasp.

Abi's eyes slam closed, but her legs open as she rests back on her hands. The scrap of fabric covering her pussy is drenched, her tits heaving as she pants.

I palm my cock through my boxers, pressing down to try and stave off the need that's throbbing through me. I have no idea what I'm doing with Abi spread out before me like this.

Her eyes meet mine again and her desperate need is plain as day. "What now?"

"You're going to stay just like that," I say, "Until I tell you otherwise."

35

———

ABI

FLYNN IS GOING to kill me. I'm going to die right here, spread out on my coffee table wearing only a pair of very wet lace panties and cowboy boots. Why didn't I take the fucking boots off?

But Flynn's gaze keeps catching on them in a way that makes me think he's very into the cowboy boots staying exactly where they are.

I didn't expect Flynn to embrace the control as much as he has. I was hoping he would, because if he's in charge, my brain doesn't have to think. And I know Flynn well enough to know he's going to take care of me, in more ways than one.

So I do exactly as he says, and stay perfectly still.

He sprawls back on the couch, his eyes tracing over my body as he lazily undoes the buttons of his shirt. It's nothing I haven't seen before; the long, lean planes of his chest, the taut abs, the way his jeans fit around his hips. But my current position and the way he's taking his god damned time undoing that shirt makes me lightheaded. It's a good thing I'm sitting down. Or sprawled. It's definitely more of a sprawl at this point.

Flynn finally reaches the last button and stands to strip the shirt off his body. I sit up, expecting him to finally embrace my offer from earlier, but he places a hand on my shoulder and pushes me back down until I'm propped up on my elbows with him standing over me, between my spread legs.

He shoves his jeans down to mid-thigh, then his tight black underwear. He fists his gorgeous thick cock and slowly drags his hand up and down the shaft.

"See what you're doing to me, Rosie?"

"I want to do more to you," I say between short puffs of breath. He's barely touched me and I'm panting and desperate. I'm almost scared for the moment he does put his hands on me. I might explode.

"Yeah? What do you want to do?"

"I want to suck your cock. I want to ride it. I want to have you fuck me with it."

Flynn groans, pausing his slow jerks. "Patience. If you're a good girl, you'll get to do all of those things ... eventually."

"Now," I say, trying to sit up again, but Flynn leans down and presses his mouth to mine, keeping me in place.

"No," he says between firm, chaste kisses. No tongue, no teeth. "First, I want to taste you."

He drops to his knees, his hands ghosting up my thighs and sending goosebumps across my sensitive skin. He glances up at me, the confidence and control from a moment ago wavering and I can see his nerves rising to the surface.

"Fuck yes, sweetheart," I murmur. "Please." It comes out as

a low whine, my desperation clear and it seems to steady some-thing in Flynn.

He tugs my underwear down and I lift my hips to help him, pulling my legs up and together to let him remove them. He tosses the fabric on the floor and trails kisses up my leg, soft brushes of his lips. I relax into the gentle touch. Then he sinks his teeth into the soft flesh of my thigh and I hiss, but his tongue is there, soothing away the pain as I groan. He drags his nose along the crease between leg and body, then trails kisses back down my thigh. I don't know if he's teasing me, or if he's trying to find the confidence to put his mouth on me.

I reach down and thread my fingers through his hair. He glances up at me again and without breaking eye contact, drags his tongue across my pussy.

I jerk in surprise as electric shocks of pleasure and desire shoot through me. My fingers tighten involuntarily and Flynn takes that as encouragement, taking another slow taste of me.

He swirls his tongue, alternating with licks and flicks, the sensation sending me boneless. My hand slips from his hair and I collapse back onto the coffee table, staring at the ceiling.

His tongue stops moving and he nips at my thigh. "No. Watch. I want to see your face. I want your hand in my hair. I like that." He gives me a shy smile as I prop myself back on my elbows and caress his cheek for a moment before sliding my hand back into his hair, wrapping my fingers tight and giving a tug. He hums against my pussy and I feel the vibrations. "Just like that," he murmurs before resuming his taunting and teasing.

He works me over with his mouth, pressure building in my pelvis as he does. My eyes keep trying to close, but each time they do, Flynn pauses until I make eye contact again. I'm squirming on the edge of the table, so close to the peak of my pleasure, but unable to quite make it there.

Then Flynn slides a finger into me and after a moment, adds another. Using his mouth and hand in tandem, he has me crying out. I'm so close, but I still can't get there. The pressure is mounting, both the physical as he draws me higher and higher, but also the mental. That cloying fear that I can't actually let go.

I whine and writhe against him, desperation climbing.

"Come for me, Rosie. Then you can have my cock. It's desperate for your pretty lips."

His words do it. They send me over the edge and I cry out as my body is wracked by my intense orgasm. Thankfully Flynn doesn't pull away too soon. He holds just the right amount of pressure until the shudders subside, then he slowly withdraws his fingers, leaving me empty and whimpering. He presses a soft kiss against my thigh, then against my belly as he lifts himself up.

"Can I kiss you?" he whispers, leaning over me. I can feel his hard cock against my hip.

"You better fucking kiss me," I mumble and he chuckles softly.

"You look absolutely wrecked," he says.

"Mmhmm," I hum as he presses a soft kiss against my mouth. Words are too hard right now.

"It's the single hottest thing I've ever seen, and I've seen on you my motorbike in a fucking tight skirt and heels."

I laugh. He smooths my hair, running his fingers through it. It's all too soft, this moment. I'm supposed to have his dick in my mouth by this point, but instead he's draped over me—holding his full weight up on his elbow though so he doesn't crush me—caressing my hair.

"Give me like, another thirty seconds," I say. "Then I'm repaying the favour."

"Only if you want to," he says and presses a kiss against my temple.

Ugh, this man. He's too hot and sweet for his own damn good. I can't believe no one has locked him down yet. A tiny pang of disappointment shoots through me as I remember that whatever happening between us is a short-term thing. It's a physical thing. It's not a relationship. It's not dates and romance and falling in love. I don't have the capacity for that, and Flynn deserves it all.

I push against his shoulder and he shifts back, helping me sit up. "I started this by offering. I wouldn't have done that if I didn't want to do it."

Flynn resumes his place on the couch, his jeans still halfway down his thighs, cock still hard and standing proud.

I lick my lips. God, I want to taste him.

"I guess you better get on your knees then," he says and my gaze darts from his cock to his eyes. The sweet uncertainty is gone. I know he's faking the confidence, but it doesn't stop it being the hottest thing I've ever experienced. He reaches out and grabs my ass, squeezing tight. "Now," he says and without hesitation, I obey.

I kneel between his thighs and take his dick in my hand, wrapping my palm around it.

"Fuck," he grunts.

I hold eye contact as I lean forward and flick my tongue over the tip, tasting him.

"This is not going to last long. I'm sorry," he says.

"I'll take it as a compliment." I flick my tongue over his head again, then suck it into my mouth.

He grunts again, his hips twitching forward, pushing himself deeper into my mouth. "Sorry."

I shake my head as much as I can without releasing him, letting the heavy weight of his shaft slide over my tongue. I don't go too hard, not wanting to overwhelm him too soon. There's plenty of time for that. So I alternate long, languid licks with sliding my lips over his dick, enjoying the pleasant stretch.

"Fuck, Rosie," he grunts as I take him deep and his hips thrust up again.

This time I do release him. "You don't need to hold back," I say, then take his length in my mouth again.

This time when his hips push forward, he doesn't stop himself and the moan he lets out is worth it. He thrusts again, and again, never going too far, like I knew he wouldn't. Because he's Flynn.

"I'm going to ..." he trails off and the hand that's buried in my hair tugs, trying to pull me off him. I don't let him and a moment later his body tenses as warmth fills my mouth. He shudders as I draw him through his orgasm and when he's done, I slowly release his dick.

I climb into his lap, pressing our bare skin together and wrapping my arms around him. His hands rest against my back, large, warm and solid.

"Who looks wrecked now?" I whisper as I drop a line of kisses along his jaw.

"Both of us," he mumbles, still a little dazed and I laugh. "I'm ruined," he adds.

"Need some sleep?"

He nuzzles against my neck. "Mmm. You mentioned a bed earlier?"

"Yeah, I have multiple."

"It's okay. We only need one."

36

———

FLYNN

I STRETCH AND ROLL OVER, snuggling into the warmth at my side.

"Morning," Abi whispers into my shoulder, brushing a kiss against my skin.

"Morning," I mumble in reply. "Did you sleep well?"

"Sure did. You?" She curls into my side, tucking her head under my chin and tangling our legs together.

Fuck, I could get used to this. It's probably the wrong thing to think the morning after hooking up with your friend-slash-colleague.

But right now, I don't care, because I'm still riding the high from last night. I thought quick and dirty hand jobs against a wall was hot but last night ... that was something else. The images of Abi laid out for me, of her kneeling in front of me taking me in her mouth, they're never fading. They're going to be burned into my brain forever.

After the incredible sex and we returned to our senses, I

noticed the goosebumps covering Abi's bare skin and made her take me to bed.

Unlike the last time we shared a bed, this time there was touching. Nothing sexual, just some cuddling. It feels like her body was made for me to hold like this.

But I still don't know what any of this means. Surely friends with benefits don't snuggle?

"Flynn?"

"Yeah?"

"You okay?" Abi props herself up on an elbow so she can study my face.

"Yeah, of course. Obviously. Why wouldn't I be? Everything's great."

"Because you didn't answer when I asked how you slept and now you're rambling."

I groan and she grins.

"Remember what I said last night?"

"You're good with instructions?"

She blushes but rolls her eyes. "Not that part."

I think, but nothing else comes to mind. She called me sweetheart a few times, which did things to me I'd rather not acknowledge, but I'm not sure that's what she's getting at.

She scoffs and flops back onto her pillow. "Being honest with each other, Flynn. That's the most important part of this. Fucking typical man." She's trying to sound annoyed, but I can hear the laughter in her voice. "Now, are you okay?"

"I am," I say. "I'm just ... confused about where this leaves us now. Maybe we should have had this conversation before we took your clothes off."

She makes the same scoffing noise again. "Like you'd have taken anything in with your dick that hard."

It's the last thing I'm expecting her to say and a laugh bursts out of me. "You're not who I was expecting you to be," I say.

"Yeah, well, same goes for you. I'm desperate to know what you were expecting ... but I think we need to backtrack a little bit."

"Lay it on me," I say, rolling up onto my elbow so I can look down at her, spread across the pillows, still a little soft with sleep.

"What are you confused about?"

I rub the back of my neck, then trail my fingers through Abi's hair. "What happens next, I guess."

"What about it?"

"Do we really have to talk about it?" I pull a face and she giggles.

"Yeah, we do, sweetheart," she cups my face, brushing a thumb over my cheekbone. "Especially if we don't want to ruin our friendship, which I don't know about you, but I really, really don't want that."

"Definitely don't want that."

"Then we just need to set some expectations."

Okay, expectations. I can understand that. Hopefully it'll let me know when I'm allowed to touch her because 'all the time' doesn't sound like it's appropriate for our situation, even though it's exactly what I want.

Abi continues. "At work and in public we keep it quiet. When we're alone we take it as it comes? We can still hang out as friends, sometimes we can add sex. Staying over isn't going to be as easy as this again, not without raising questions."

It's a shame really, because waking up with Abi is incredible. But if I started staying in town at night there would be questions. If she stayed on the farm, there'd be questions. Too many damn questions.

It's probably for the best though. Hopefully distance will help me keep some perspective.

I take a deep breath and ask, even though I'm sure I sound like some naive little kid. "When am I allowed to touch you?"

"Whenever you want," she says, a soft smile curving her delicious mouth. "Obviously when other people are around we keep it friendly though."

"But when we're alone?"

"Touch me all you want." She rolls over, pushing me down and laying her naked body over my mine. "Just remember to keep talking to me, okay?"

"Okay, I can do that."

Then, because she told me I can touch her all I want, I reach up and capture her mouth with mine, dragging my hands over her bare skin.

I completely ignore the little thought at the back of my mind that tells me I'll never actually be able to touch her all I want, because I never, ever want to stop.

I HAD TO STOP. Eventually. And I haven't had the chance to touch Abi again in days.

Between our jobs and Abi spending time with Sadie, we've had no chance to spend time alone, which means the few times we have crossed paths I've had to keep any touches super casual.

I've decided it might just be easier not to touch her at all because as soon as my hand comes in contact with her, I'm overwhelmed with need, with desire, with this strange burning something in my chest.

I take the steps to Abi's office two at a time, pausing in the door to drink in the sight of her. She's sitting at her desk in a silky green shirt that matches her eyes and her hair pulled into a ponytail high on her head.

The professional business woman look is not something I thought I'd be into, but it works on Abi, especially when I know she can rock a pair of jeans and climb on a dirt bike.

And the cowboy boots.

We've actually made plans to spend time together this afternoon and as much fun as I'm going to have hanging out with her and maybe taking her and my bike back to the beach for another lesson if she wants, I'm hoping we'll end up naked by the end of the night.

Abi glances up as I lean against the doorframe. "Oh, hey," she says, sounding distracted.

"Hey, Rosie." I step across the room, taking in the sheets of paper spread across the desk. They're covered in lists and numbers. A quick glance at her computer screen shows the same. "This looks ... awful."

Abi groans. "It is. Budgets." She pulls a face.

"Ew." I mirror her expression. "Do you need to finish it now? Or are you nearly ready to head off?"

"Sorry. I didn't realise the time. I'll just finish up."

"No worries, Rosie. Take your time. What do you want to do?"

Abi pauses gathering up the sheets of paper. She's shoving them into a rough stack like she really hates them, but she drops the stack onto the desk. Her head falls back, hitting the headrest on her chair.

"No more decisions," she grumbles. "I'm all out of decisions. Between these budgets and trying to fill the bar staff roster with people who actually want to turn up to work and dealing with a particularly frustrating couple ... just no more decisions."

"Rough day, huh?" I stride around her desk, hands coming to rest on her shoulders. She lets out a pleasant little hum at the touch.

The sound goes straight to my dick, and it twitches. Now really isn't the time.

"Yeah," she sighs. "I just want to get out of my head for a bit."

She's said those words to me before and I take a moment to place the context. She said that to me about the day we made out on the beach. I don't know if her repeating them now is a hint, but I'm not going to let this opportunity pass me by.

I drag my thumb up the side of her neck and she lets out a breathy sigh. I trail my fingers along her collarbone, slipping them inside the edge of her shirt. Another little hum from Abi. My other hand strokes down her hair and when she relaxes into the touch I wrap her ponytail around my fist.

"I have an idea that could help you get out of your head," I whisper.

"Yeah?" Her voice is already wrecked and broken and I've barely touched her.

"Yeah. If you're up for it." I use my grip on her hair to tilt her head back so she's looking up at me. Her wide-eyed gaze locks with mine and she gives the tiniest nod, all she can with me holding her in place.

I drop her ponytail and remove my hand from where my fingers have been dancing across her chest.

"Finish tidying up your desk. I don't want to ruin anything important."

I swear Abi lets out a whimper as I cross the room to carefully shut the door and ensure the lock is in place. By the time I've turned around, Abi's desk is cleared and she's sitting primly in her desk chair, hands in her lap, legs pressed together.

"Do you want to do any thinking here?" I ask, standing across the desk from her. My cock is so hard and by the way Abi's eyes keep dropping to my crotch she knows all about it.

She bites her lip. "No. I want to do exactly what you tell me to."

I groan and give in, reaching down to rub my hand across my dick. It's aching for more.

I don't know if she's giving me control purely because she doesn't want to think, or if she realises what it does to me, having the control to pace things as I need to.

"You'd better stand up then. That chair is mine."

She leaps up so fast the chair shoots backwards. Her cheeks turn pink as she watches me.

Oh, holy shit. She's in one of those hot as fuck skirts; black, tight and clinging to the full roundness of her ass. As I step around the desk my gaze trails down. Sky high heels.

How I don't just come in my pants every time I'm around her I have no idea.

I pull my t-shirt off and drop it on the floor beside the desk. Abi doesn't move as I step behind her and slide a hand across her ass.

"Undo my jeans, Rosie," I whisper in her ear. My voice is already a low, lusty rasp.

She spins around, hands finding my waistband in an instant. She pops the button, lowers the zipper and pushes the fabric away from my aching dick.

"Don't touch it," I say, stopping her hand as it reaches for my cock. Once it's in her hand this will be over way too fast. I need to build some anticipation first. Then get her off.

I fall into the chair and pat my thigh. "Sit that gorgeous ass right here."

Abi steps closer and right before she lands in my lap I realise my mistake.

"Wait. Stand up again," I say.

"Everything okay?" she whispers, voice thick. Her blush is creeping down her neck and the desire filling her expression is so fucking alluring.

"Sure is. Just need to make an adjustment." I take hold of her skirt, one hand on each side and yank upwards, tugging the hem from just above her knees to barely below her ass. I grasp her hips and tug her down.

"That was a good adjustment," she breathes, leaning back into me.

"I thought so," I murmur, dragging my lips up her neck. My hands and mouth roam over her body as she sprawls across my lap. She's soft and pliable as I skim my palms down her chest, pausing to gently cup her tits, before continuing down her belly, across her hips and over her thighs. I hook one leg up and over the armrest of the chair, spreading her wide.

Thank fuck this office has a lockable door because holy shit I wouldn't want anyone to walk in right now. I should still be conscious of the time though. There's still plenty of people who could drop in unexpectedly.

Abi is squirming in my arms, panting lightly as she tries to angle her body so my wandering hands will stroke her where she wants it most.

"As much as I'm loving driving you crazy like this," I whisper. "I think it's time we move things along." I press my palm over her clit and she cries out, turning her face into my neck to muffle the sound. "Up."

A low keening sound comes from Abi, but she doesn't move.

"I said up." I catch her earlobe between my teeth. "Now."

She climbs to her feet and takes a single step away. She's a little wobbly. "I'm up," she says, sounding dazed.

"Elbows on the desk."

She does as I say while I roll the chair forward. I hook my hands under the hem of her skirt and slide it higher, exposing the black lace underwear hugging her ass.

"Now that's a pretty sight." I lean back in the chair, my eyes right in line with her pussy. "God, I want to fuck you so bad. But I'm not prepared for that, so you'll have to wait for my cock." I might have to start carrying condoms on me at all times.

Another long low moan from Abi has me smiling.

"Lost your words, Rosie?"

She nods and lets out a whimper. I chuckle.

I tease her for a moment longer, trailing my fingers down the backs of her thighs, tracing the edge of the lace.

"Need you," she whines. So apparently she hasn't lost all ability to form words. "Please, sweetheart. Touch me. Please."

"Because you asked so nicely," I say as I slide my fingers across the centre of her underwear. I hook it to the side and hold it in place with one hand while I use the other to tease her clit. She writhes against my hand but when I slip my finger inside her she goes a relaxed, boneless kind of still for a moment before slowly pushing her hips back.

"That good, huh?"

A guttural "yes" falls from her lips as I slide another finger in. She pushes back further, rocking herself on my hand. She moves faster, harder, until her thrusts start to lose rhythm.

I stand, giving myself better control. I take hold of the back of her skirt, pushing it around her waist and holding her in place as I work my fingers in and out of her tight, wet heat.

Abi trembles and finally lets go, crying out as her orgasm wracks her body. As she rides out the wave, she collapses onto her desk, holding up a shaky hand.

"I'll be right back with you. Just going to need a moment after that," she mumbles against the wood.

"Stay just like that," I say. "Don't move."

I slide her underwear back into place, then fit my hips against her ass, dragging my cock along her pussy, revelling in the feeling, despite both our underwear being between us. Abi shudders.

I finally fish my cock out and wrap my palm around it. The head brushes against her ass cheek and Abi turns her head to look back at me over her shoulder.

"How do you want me take care of that for you?"

"By staying exactly where you are." The words are interspersed with grunts as I thrust my hips forward, fucking into my fist.

Abi's eyes go wide with realisation and she pushes back up onto her elbows, trying to see more. I can't decide if I want to stare at her face as she watches me jerk off over her ass, or if I want to watch my cock as it slides through my hand, skimming her ass with each pass.

"That's the hottest fucking thing I've ever seen," Abi mutters and her words send me over the edge.

I come with a groan and manage to catch myself before I collapse on top of Abi. I fall into the chair instead, Abi's exposed ass right back in my line of sight.

I don't know what I've ever done to deserve this, but fuck, I'm grateful for it, whatever it was.

37

———

ABI

AFTER FLYNN MAKES me come on my desk, then comes all over my ass, we clean up and I get changed into what I'm now affectionately calling my farm clothes; a pair of jeans, a t-shirt and hoodie, all old and worn, but perfect for hanging out with Flynn, or Sadie, after work.

"Want to go riding at the beach again?" Flynn asks as I lock up the function barn.

"Riding? Or riding? I don't know if I have that in me again."

"Motorbike," he says, his grin wicked. "It's time you had some more practise. Because I definitely don't have that in me again. Not for a little while at least."

I laugh. "Sounds good, though I feel like I've completely forgotten how to drive that thing."

Shrugging, he points to his ute and I climb into the passenger side. "You'll pick it up again. I have faith."

I roll my eyes but don't reply as Flynn drives us around to the main farm entrance.

"Do I look like we've just been doing filthy things on my desk?" I ask as he pulls into the driveway. Slowing to a stop, he turns to study me.

"No, I don't think so. A little pink in the cheeks, but that's not unusual." His mouth lifts into a smirk.

I narrow my eyes at him. "Are you mocking me?" I fold my arms and stare him down, willing myself to hold it together and not laugh.

"Not at all." His sincerity, his openness, is one of my favourite things about him. He reacts out a thumb and brushes it over my cheek. "I love your blush, *Rosie*."

Oh.

That's where Rosie comes from? I just assumed it was a dumb nickname spurned from the flower debacle. Not an *endearment*.

Words freeze in my throat, but Flynn doesn't seem to notice. He just turns his attention back to driving.

We bypass the main house, though my gaze is searching, looking for Sadie. I don't spot her and as we descend the slight hill down to the barn I realise why. She's with Katie, putting Scout and Aurora back in their paddock. They must have been riding after school.

"Flynn," Sadie shouts as soon as he opens his door.

"Heya, sprout," he replies cheerfully, stretching his arms out to catch her as she leaps at him. "Look who I brought with me." He lowers her back to the ground and Sadie spins towards me.

She hesitates for barely a second before throwing herself at me too. "Hey, mama," she says.

My arms tighten around her as my heart freezes, then

swells. "Hey, sweet girl," I murmur against her hair, tears burning at my eyes. She's never called me anything close to mum before. So far she's pretty much avoided calling me anything, though I'm not sure anyone else, including Sadie, is aware of that.

"Hey, Abi, Flynn," Katie says, slinging the horses lead ropes over her shoulder and approaching us after she's finished latching the gate. "Hey, Sadie, I have to go check something, do you want to stay with your mum and Flynn while I do, or come with me?"

I had my reservations about Katie when I first arrived. Not about how she is with Sadie, but how she'd be with me and whether her relationship with Dallas is too new to handle my sudden appearance, but she's taken it all in stride. And I love how she gives Sadie choices, like this one.

Sadie peers up at me. "Can I stay with you?"

My breath catches in my throat again. I clear my throat and force words out. "Sure thing."

"I should only be about fifteen minutes," Katie says.

I nod, my heart still in my throat. As much as I've wanted more with Sadie, I haven't yet looked after her alone.

Before, this was the moment when everything would fall apart.

This is the time I'd have a panic attack and Dallas would realise he couldn't leave me alone with my own daughter.

I could once upon a time, but after Sadie and I had that horse riding accident ... I just couldn't anymore.

I tried, but every time Dallas went to walk out the door, my throat would close up, my vision would go dark and I'd lose it.

As if the stress of Sadie's injuries wasn't enough to deal with, then he had to deal with my complete breakdown as well.

That's why I left them, so Dallas had one less thing to worry about. Sure leaving him a single parent probably wasn't great, but at least he wasn't responsible for all of Sadie's care as well as me.

I've spent the intervening years in therapy and fine-tuning anxiety medication until I had my life back under control and now here I am, on the verge of losing my shit all over again, despite all that work I've put in.

I'm not even truly alone, because Flynn is here, wheeling his motorbike towards the ute.

Katie's still talking and I force myself to breathe and listen to what she's saying. "If you need something to occupy her, she needs to clean Scout's bit."

"Yeah, of course," I say, voice thick.

Katie studies me for a moment, her expression resolute. "You're fine, Abi. You've got this. Fifteen minutes."

I swallow and nod. She knows, and she has faith in me anyway. She climbs into the side-by-side, gives Sadie and Flynn a wave and heads down the farm.

"Hey, Sadie," I call out and she turns towards me. "Do you need to do something with Scout's tack?"

After a moment, her face lights up. "I need to clean it!" She skips towards me.

"Sorry," I say to Flynn, shoving my hands in my pockets to hide the fact they're quivering. I take a deep breath, exhaling the tremor of anxiety I'm feeling. "We can still go when Katie's back?"

"Of course," he says, leaning against his ute with his arms folded casually across his chest. "Never apologise for Sadie, okay? Never."

"Okay." I shoot him a smile and my heart gives a little flutter as he returns it. Then Sadie slips her hand into mine and I shove thoughts of Flynn out of my mind.

Focus on Sadie.

It's not hard to do when she chatters the entire time she's cleaning the bit in Scout's bridle. Once she's done with that, she cleans Aurora's for Katie, then asks me if I know how to clean the straps and when I say I do, from my childhood as a pony club kid, she asks if I'll help her, to surprise Katie.

It's impossible to say no to her, so we carry the saddles and bridles out into the sunshine to wipe them down and rub saddle soap into the leather.

"This looks productive." Katie's voice cuts into my contented thoughts.

Apparently fifteen minutes has passed and my anxiety hasn't spiralled since she left. Sitting out here in the sun, the smell of leather tack and saddle soap surrounding us, listening to Sadie ramble about her day, it'd be pretty hard to be stressed out.

"Surprise," Sadie says, jumping up to wrap her arms around Katie's waist.

"Thank you," she replies, bending down to drop a kiss on the top of Sadie's head. "And thank you." Katie turns to me. "All okay?"

"Yeah, great, and no worries about the saddle. It's been a while since I've cleaned one but Sadie showed me what to do."

"You guys hanging out?" Katie asks, tilting her head towards Flynn, who's loaded his bike onto his ute in the time I've been with Sadie.

"Yeah. He seems to think I should learn to ride that thing."

Katie's eyes widen and I recall Flynn saying something about his friends thinking he was crazy for letting anyone ride it. She doesn't say anything about it though, just nods once. "How do you feel about picking Sadie up from school tomorrow?"

The usual hit of panic shoots through me, but I push it down. It's collecting her from school and driving her home. That's it. I can do that.

I take a deep breath. "Yes, I'd love to." She grins. "Does Dallas know about this?"

Katie shrugs. "Look, I love the man, he's the best person I've ever met, but he's ... overprotective. I understand why he is the way he is, but that doesn't mean things should always stay that way. He needs a little nudge now and then, and it turns out I can get away with that."

"As long as it's not putting you two in an awkward position. I don't want to mess with what you've got going."

She smiles, and it's softer than I'm used to seeing from her. She's always so confident and self-assured and is clearly comfortable pushing Dallas's boundaries, which I admit is probably good for him.

"I know," she says. "I love Dallas, and I love Sadie too, which means we've got to make this work. He's anxious about pushing you too hard, too fast. But Sadie deserves her mum in her life, and you deserve it too," she adds and I feel heat prickling at my eyes.

Oh, god. Am I going to cry right now?

"Thanks," I whisper, just managing to hold the tears in.

"If the school pick up doesn't work, for whatever reason, let me know."

I nod and she calls out to Sadie, who's been carrying the bridles back inside, asking her if she's ready to go. Sadie waves goodbye to Flynn, then wraps her arms around my waist. The familiarity of the gesture makes me want to fall to my knees and cry in appreciation for everything that's brought me back to this point.

"Bye, Mama," she says.

"I'll see you tomorrow," I say, voice thick as I let the word Mama wash over me.

"You good, Rosie?" Flynn says, voice low behind me.

"I'm absolutely perfect," I say, turning to him with a grin.

"That you are."

38

FLYNN

MY RELATIONSHIP—FOR lack of a better word—with Abi settles into a sort-of rhythm quickly.

We work, we hang out like we always have, and occasionally, when time and circumstances permit, we get each other off.

Unfortunately even when circumstances allow it, the timing isn't usually great, so our orgasms have been quick handies and blowjobs and I haven't had the chance to curl around her and sleep next to her again.

Or have actual sex, even though I really, really want to.

Mind you, I'm not complaining about any time I get with her either.

Even if we aren't getting time to get naked with each other, Abi is a heap of fun to hang out with. Now that she's settling in and realising the people here are on her side, not against her, she's proving to be a lot of fun.

Especially when she nags me to take her riding. We've spent several evenings down at the beach, Abi in control of the bike, or perched on behind me, an arm stretched out to embrace the wind while she whoops and hollers in my ear.

Watching her let go in those moments is my favourite thing to do.

Abi's relationship with Sadie has evolved in leaps and bounds too, from Katie leaving Sadie with her that day, to Abi collecting Sadie from school the next afternoon.

I'm not sure how keen Dallas was with Katie's meddling in the situation, but those two seem as rock solid as ever, so he can't have been too put out by it. Or if he was, she managed to bring him around. I don't want to know how she did it.

There are some things I don't need to know about my best friend.

Since that day, Abi has spent more and more time with Sadie, including having her at her house for a couple of hours. When Sadie came home she was fizzing with excitement about the afternoon they spent together and while Abi watched on I could swear I saw tears in her eyes.

I'm so glad I was around when she dropped Sadie back out to the farm.

Abi's anxiety around being with Sadie is lessening as Sadie's level of excitement of having her mum back in her life grows.

I slow my bike to a stop and kick down the stand, already looking forward to the afternoon Abi and I have planned. First port of call is a quick dinner at Violet's, then I'm finally giving her a decent tour of the farm from the back of my bike. I know it's likely that at least one of the others will want to join us, and despite me constantly wanting time alone with Abi, I don't mind if our friends want to hang out with us either.

I stride into the function centre and stop dead. It's like déjà vu of the day of the roses.

Flowers everywhere and in the middle of it all, Abi, looking like she's going to burst into tears.

"I'm so sorry," she says the moment she sees me. Her voice wobbles and she clamps her teeth down on her lower lip. "I obviously can't go anywhere tonight."

"Hey." I stride across the room towards her. As soon as I'm within reach I stroke my thumb across her mouth, gently tugging her lip free of her teeth. "Take a breath, Rosie. What happened?"

"Same florist, didn't follow the order again. Now I have all these flowers to arrange. I'm going to be here for hours."

"What else do you need to do tonight?"

"Nothing, thankfully. Pretty much everything else is taken care of."

"Okay." I slide my phone out of my pocket and check the time. "First things first, dinner."

She opens her mouth to argue but I grasp her chin gently.

"You've got to eat, Rosie. Then we'll deal with the rest."

She exhales a heavy breath and I feel it wash over my skin. "Okay," she whispers and the next argument I had on my lips dies. I wasn't expecting her to give in that easily.

She follows me outside and climbs onto the bike, automatically sliding her body close to mine and wrapping her arms around my waist.

Her lack of hesitation hits me right in the chest as I release the clutch and twist the throttle, heading for the main house.

It's already loud and chaotic when we step inside, forever the last to arrive.

Dallas, Katie, Sadie, Olivia and Violet all greet us in various ways from simple greetings to a running hug from Sadie, as per usual.

Violet serves us massive plates of sweet and sour meatballs, rice and vegetables and we all dig in, conversation sliding into its usual easy banter.

"You two off somewhere after this?" Olivia asks Abi and I pause shovelling food into my mouth to see how she's going to respond.

"Ah, I have a little more I have to do before we're ready for this wedding tomorrow," Abi says, eyes not leaving her plate.

"I thought it was all sorted?" Olivia asks, her eyes narrowing. "What happened since lunchtime when I was down there?"

"Um, well, the flowers arrived and the florist got it wrong again."

"Wrong how?" Olivia asks, voice steely and Abi's cheeks turn pink. "And what do you mean again?"

Abi opens her mouth, but no words come out. She lifts her chin, her gaze crashing into mine across the table.

"Hey," I say to Olivia. "It was the florist's fuck up, not Abi's. They sent the flowers, but they aren't arranged. And she means again because this isn't the first time it's happened."

Olivia instantly turns sheepish. "Sorry, Abi," she says. "I wasn't meaning to sound pissed at you. You're right about it not being the first time either. I think we need to find a new one." She pauses, moving her food around her plate with her fork. "Why didn't you tell me about the first time?"

"Ah, I didn't want to let you down," Abi mutters, her cheeks turning even redder as she realises everyone in the room is paying attention to her.

"Well, we're all here to help you," Katie says. "I'm not sure flower arranging is really in my skillset but I can give it a go. You can find a new florist next week."

Abi glances at Katie, shooting her a small smile, then looks back to Olivia.

"What she said," Olivia agrees, gesturing to Katie. "Sorry about your evening though."

"It's fine." Abi shrugs. "Was only going to be hanging out with Flynn anyway." She shoots me a smirk.

"Rude," I exclaim. "I'm excellent company."

Katie pats my arm. "Sure thing, sweetheart. We all know Livvie and I are better."

Sweetheart.

The name registers in my brain, but coming from Katie it doesn't mean a damn thing, except that she's an annoying little shit.

When Abi calls me that though ... then it means everything.

I scoff, then glance back across the table at Abi. Her mouth curls into a smile and she quickly glances around the table before sending an air kiss in my direction.

Conversation resumes around me, with Abi explaining how the flowers need to be arranged and as soon as the meal is done, everyone, including Violet, Dallas and Sadie, pile into vehicles to head back to the function centre. I expect Abi to get in one of the utes, but she follows me straight to my bike and slides on behind me.

As we pull in the driveway, a little red hatchback is coming along the road from the opposite direction. It rolls to a stop and I smile as the driver's window lowers to reveal Tilly Sheridan.

"Everything okay?" Tilly asks.

"Hey, Tilly," Abi says, surprising me. They must know each other from Sugar, because I can't think where else they would have crossed paths. "Just a mishap with the flowers for a wedding tomorrow. It's apparently all hands on deck to get it sorted."

Tilly lifts both her hands from the steering wheel of her car. "Want another set?"

"Oh, no. It's okay. You must already have plans."

"Nope. Nothing important. Was just going to see the family. But it's fine. I can see them anytime."

"Well, we'd appreciate the help," I say, then head up the driveway, with Tilly following close behind. As we pull to a stop and I wait while Abi climbs off the bike I ask her how she knows Tilly.

"She makes those amazing cupcakes at Sugar." Abi smooths her hair down. "I thought about asking her if she wants to do cakes for some of the weddings here, but ..."

"But?" I prompt.

"She's a Sheridan isn't she? Aren't I supposed to stay away from them?"

"No. Max is the only one who isn't welcome around here. Tilly and her parents are fine."

"I appreciate that," Tilly says from behind us. She turns to Abi. "Please don't lump me in with my idiot brother. I've been meaning to ask actually if you need more bar staff?"

Abi's smile grows. "Yes. Always. Please. Can you start tomorrow?"

Tilly laughs. "Sure can, but you said something about flowers?"

Abi leads us inside, where the rest of the team are already waiting.

"Woah," Tilly breathes, then turns to everyone else in the room to say a quick hello.

"What do you need us to do?" Olivia asks Abi and after the tiniest hesitation, Abi takes a deep breath and explains what needs doing. Everyone picks up a task and before I know it, the flower arrangements are coming together, surrounded by chatter and laughter.

I pause as I pass Abi carrying a finished arrangement to a table across the room.

"You don't need to say I told you so," she mutters and I let out a low laugh.

"I would never, Rosie. I just wanted to say how proud I am of you. Look at you, complete and total boss babe, emphasis on the babe."

Her cheeks flush. "Shut up, Flynn," she mutters, but as I move away her fingertips on my wrist make me pause. "But thank you, for everything."

It's my turn to fire an air kiss in her direction. "Any time, Rosie. Whatever you need."

39
———
ABI

"MAMA," Sadie cries out as she sees me at the door and automatically flings her body into my arms.

"Heya, Sadie," I murmur into her hair, squeezing my eyes shut against the burn of tears.

You'd think by now I'd be over crying every time my little girl refers to me as her mother, but I'm not and I don't think I ever will be.

I've even spent time alone with her, with me the only adult around, without panic attacks. In fact, where Sadie's concerned, there doesn't seem to be anxiety anymore. It makes me wonder why I spent so much time away.

I squash those thoughts and remind myself what my therapist told me last week when I'd mentioned it to her on one of our virtual sessions. I took the time away because I needed to, so I could be the mum Sadie has now.

I squeeze her tight, then set Sadie's feet back on the ground and step into the kitchen, expecting to see the table laid out ready for the usual chaotic dinner, but while there's some serving dishes of food lined up down the centre of the table, there's nothing else.

"Everyone's in here," Sadie says, taking my hand and leading me through into the dining room. I've never actually stepped foot in this room, just had glimpses of it through the door. It's never been used for any of the meals I've joined the family for.

But we're clearly using it tonight.

When Violet asked me to come tonight—it was more of her strongly suggesting I be here, rather than an invitation—she had mentioned it was a bit of a special occasion, but she didn't say why, and I didn't even think to ask someone about it. I should have asked Flynn.

I glance around the room, looking for him, but I already know he's not here. He would have greeted me already. I try not to feel the disappointment. He'll be here soon. He's as much a part of the Austin family as Olivia herself, he's not going to miss this special occasion dinner.

Instead of seeing Flynn and receiving one of his beaming smiles, I acknowledge who is here; Dallas is setting cutlery out on the huge wooden table, Olivia is opening a bottle of wine and Katie is lining up glasses along the sideboard.

They each say hello and we settle into our usual conversations, with Olivia asking how things are going down at the function centre and me reassuring her it's all fine.

The second flower fiasco was handled much quicker than the first, with so many hands on deck, and the wedding itself went off without an issue, especially with the new addition of

Tilly to the bar staff. She seems to have a natural instinct for customer service and managing the moods of the staff. I'm already considering urging her to get her manager's license so she can run the entire bar for me. She's sure easier to work with than the grouchy woman I currently use, but I'll wait to see how Tilly goes for a few more events first.

Violet dips in and out of the conversation as she flits between the kitchen and dining room and when I hear heavy footsteps in the hallway I turn expectantly for the door.

But it's not Flynn who steps through.

The guy is tall and solidly built. He's wearing tidy, dark wash jeans and a charcoal grey button up shirt, the sleeves rolled to the elbows. His hair is dark blond and short. He probably shaves it himself over his bathroom sink.

Clear hazel eyes scan the room, assessing each of us.

"He's not here, is he?" the guy asks, his tone gruff.

Violet releases a soft sigh. "Not yet," she says, voice gentle.

"Hunt's here!" Katie—who I hadn't even noticed wasn't in the dining room when this guy arrived—yelps as she steps back into the room. She grins at him, but he simply glares back at her.

"Don't call me that."

"Okay, apologies." She doesn't sound the slightest bit apologetic and the smirk on her face confirms it. "Hunter," she says, dragging out his name with plenty of emphasis on the 'r'. "This is Abi. Abi, this is Hunter." Hunter, as in Flynn's brother? "Flynn's grumpy-as-shit big brother."

"Hi," I say, suddenly nervous. This is Flynn's only family and he seems less than impressed as his gaze skims over me. He jerks his chin in greeting, then turns to Violet.

"I knew he wouldn't go for it."

She looks a little defeated. "I know, but I was hoping."

Katie sidles up beside me and mutters under her breath. "Don't be put off by my buddy Hunt. He doesn't like anyone. Grumpy fucking bastard."

That tugs a tentative smile from my lips. "Are they talking about Flynn?" I ask, indicating Hunter and Violet with a tilt of my head.

Katie sighs, the shit-eating grin slipping from her face. "Yeah. Do you know what today is?"

I rack my brain, but nothing comes to mind. I shake my head.

"It's the anniversary of the day their parents died. It happened ten years ago today."

My breath catches in my throat and my heart aches for Flynn. "And he's not here?"

"No." Katie's usually wearing a grin, she's usually joking and teasing, but her face right now is unnaturally serious.

"Mum thought he wanted to be with us to acknowledge it this year," Olivia says, slipping into the conversation. "When she asked him about it, he seemed fine with the idea. But he's just text me to say the planting is taking longer than he thought and he'll let me know when he's done."

"He's not coming then," Katie says, resigned. "He can make tractor work last all night if he wants to."

Olivia agrees, then goes to speak to Violet and Hunter. Violet looks sad, but accepting, Hunter looks ... well, he looks pissed. He runs a hand roughly over his hair and turns towards the door, but

Violet stops him with a hand on his arm. He spins on her and my heart leaps into my throat as he towers over her. I'm wondering how this is all going to play out when he suddenly deflates.

"Just leave him be," Violet says, voice soft.

"I'm sorry, Vi," he mutters.

"No one needs to be sorry. Now if you don't mind, I've spent half my afternoon making your mother's apple pie and I'd really like to be eating it and we have to get through actual dinner first."

"Do we really need to do dinner first though, Vi?" Katie asks, pushing through to find her humour again. "We could just eat the pie."

"I do like the way you think," Violet points at Katie. "What do you think, Sadie?"

Sadie glances at Dallas, then at me, before looking at Katie and back to Violet. "Pie!"

"That settles it," Violet says. "Dessert for dinner it is."

Hunter rolls his eyes but follows Violet into the kitchen, returning a moment later with a stack of bowls. Olivia grabs a tub of ice cream and Violet serves up her apple pie, leaving a piece in the pie dish.

Eating dessert first feels wrong on all kinds of levels, but everyone else digs in and I lift a spoonful to my mouth.

"Oh my god," I murmur. I want to moan but manage to suppress it when I catch sight of Hunter across the table, studying me closely. "This is amazing," I say, turning to Violet and ignoring Hunter's gaze.

Violet grins and holds up her own spoonful. "Isla Woods

was truly the queen of the kitchen." Her smile softens with nostalgia.

"Do you remember that peanut butter slice she made?" Olivia asks and Violet blinks away the moisture in her eyes.

"Yes," she groans. "That was the best."

Olivia and Violet chatter about Isla, and as the conversation progresses, their stories spread from Isla and her incredible baking, to Flynn's dad, Trent, as well, then the memories the two families shared. Katie, Dallas and Sadie ask questions and laugh along with the two Austin women, but Hunter sits silently, barely contributing unless he's asked a direct question. And even then, if the question comes from Katie he scowls and ignores her. In his defence, she does seem to be trying to piss him off on purpose. I have to admire her gall to do that. He seems scary enough not pissed off.

Once the pie is demolished, except for that single slice, Violet serves us dinner, though none of us are particularly hungry after the dessert.

During the clean up, I find myself in the kitchen with Katie and Olivia, who's piling food onto a plate and wrapping it in clingfilm.

"Flynn's almost done," Olivia says. "Do you think he'll come down here tonight?"

Katie shakes her head. "We won't see him tonight. Should we take it up to him?"

"Yeah," Olivia says.

"Do you want to take it?" Katie asks. "Or should we both go?"

I want to offer. I want to open my mouth and say I'll do it.

But no words come out, and I know this isn't my place. I'm Flynn's friend with benefits. His *secret* friends with benefits. I'm not his best friend like these two are. I'm not his family. In the whole scheme of things, I'm the least important person here.

The plate I'm loading into the dishwasher slips and crashes into another, thankfully not breaking either plate.

"You all good?" Olivia asks.

"Yep." I nod. Then, to hell with it. I open my mouth again. "I can take the food to Flynn. You two stay here with your family." My bravado slips away from me. "I mean, if you want, but I'm heading out anyway and …" I trail off and I feel the heat crawling across my cheeks. Fabulous. I turn back to the dishwasher.

"That's a really good idea," Olivia says. "I think he'd like that."

"Rude," Katie says. "Are you saying he wouldn't like to see this beautiful face?" She indicates her own.

"Not at all. But you need to get Sadie home to bed anyway and Abi is on her way out." Olivia holds the plate in one hand, then wraps her free arm around me, surprising me by pulling me in for a quick hug. She surprises me more when she whispers in my ear, so quietly I know the words are only for me. "Make sure he's okay?"

I squeeze her back. "Of course."

40

FLYNN

I TURN OFF THE TRACTOR, then swing open the door and climb down, jumping the last few feet.

My boots hit the dirt with a satisfying thud and the tractor door slams with another satisfying sound.

I feel like slamming my head in it to get it to shut up.

I shouldn't be out here. I should be down at the main house with my damn family who went to a whole lot of effort to make today nice for me, and I blew them all off.

Violet asked me last week if I was happy for her to have a family dinner to acknowledge the anniversary of my parents' passing and I said it sounded like a good idea.

I meant it at the time.

But today, when my usual knock-off time rolled around and I thought about going down to the house to talk about my parents and the family I used to have, I couldn't go through with it.

So I chickened out and told Olivia I needed to finish the

planting. Which was a shit excuse because she's the boss and she wouldn't have made me work until this late to get it done.

I stomp up the hill towards my flat, my head down and filled with storm clouds.

Movement in the dark startles me and my heart leaps into my throat as a figure stands from the shadow of the front step.

My mind immediately goes to Abi, then I scoff at myself. It's probably Hunter here to yell at me for being a shithead. There's no way Abi would be sitting on my front step waiting for me. There's just no way.

Except as I get closer I can make out the dark spill of her hair and the full curves of her body.

She's here.

I want to reach out and pull her to me and never let her go. I want to wrap my arms around her and slide my hands into her hair. I want to have her do the same to me.

"I brought you some dinner," she says.

"Thanks," I mutter, shoving open my front door. Abi follows me inside and slides a plate and a bowl onto the counter. There's apple pie in the bowl and the sight of the cinnamon sugar-crusted top makes tears threaten to spill over.

Abi trails her fingers down my arm.

"I can't tonight," I burst out. "I just can't. Not tonight." My voice cracks and threatens to break.

Abi pulls her hand back, but steps closer, right into my space. "What do you mean?"

"Sex, hooking up, whatever. I can't be what you need tonight."

Her soft hands cup my cheeks, lifting my chin so my gaze

meets hers. "I'm not here for that, sweetheart. I'm here to make sure you're okay." She brushes her thumbs across my cheeks and I'm horrified when a tear spills down my face. She swipes it away without comment. "I can go if you want me to, or I can stay and look after you for once."

I should ask her to leave. I'm in no state for being around people tonight. It's why I spent all day in a tractor out the back of the farm planting the summer feed crops. I can't make my voice work though, and when Abi drops a hand from my face and wraps her arm around my waist, tugging me to her, I don't pull away.

I fall into the embrace, clinging to her as the endless ocean of emotions swirls around me.

"Do you want to eat or shower first?" she asks against the base of my throat. Her warm breath sends shivers over my body.

"I just want to sleep," I mumble.

"Soon," she soothes, sliding a hand into my hair.

"Shower," I mutter. "I'm filthy."

"Yeah, you kind of are." Abi pulls back and wrinkles her nose as she takes in my dusty state.

"I can't believe you hugged me when I'm like this." I try for a joke but I don't know if my execution lands it.

Her hands are back on my face in an instant, connecting my gaze to hers. "I will always hug you when you need it, okay?"

I nod and when she slips her hand into mine and leads me to the bathroom, I follow.

She turns on the hot water then returns her focus to me. "Do you want help?"

I shake my head, then nod, then shrug hopelessly because all I want is for it to be ten years and one day ago.

"Come on, sweetheart." Abi steps in close and slides her hands under the hem of my shirt, lifting it off over my head.

Her hand glides back down my chest, but the movement isn't teasing, it isn't meant to turn me on. It's comforting, it's reassuring. She pauses when her hands reach my fly, her eyes searching mine for consent.

I nod, then drop my forehead down to her shoulder. I can do this myself. I should be doing this myself. But right now, I just can't. Being taken care of feels too good.

Abi pushes my jeans from my hips, down over my ass, taking my underwear with them. She pushes them down my legs and holds my arm as I step out of them.

"You don't have to do this," I mutter as she leads me to the shower, heat on my cheeks. This is mortifying, but I'm all out of emotions that make me want to give a shit.

"I want to be here for you," she says. "I'm going to let you shower."

"No." I reach out for her. "Stay. Shower with me?" My voice is pathetic and pleading and Abi hesitates.

She takes a step backwards and my already aching heart feels like it's just been driven over by a tractor.

Then she strips off her clothes and steps into the shower.

Water spills down her perfect body and I trace the drops as they skim over her shoulders, down her chest, across her belly to the sexy as fuck silvery marks she got from carrying Sadie, one of my favourite humans.

"I'm going to need you to stop that," Abi says through a gasp as my fingertip traces the outline of her hip. "I'm trying to look after you, and if you keep touching me like that I'm going to be begging you to fuck me against this wall, which isn't what you need."

Maybe not, but it does sound pretty fucking incredible.

It's a shame I'm so completely exhausted from the emotional turmoil that I can't truly appreciate that Abi is here with me.

I groan. "I want to, so bad," I whisper against her wet skin.

"Maybe one day, but not right now."

"Tease," I mutter and she huffs out a little laugh.

"You're the one that made me get in here."

"I hardly held you at gunpoint," I say and for the first time today I feel a smile tugging at my mouth.

Abi just shrugs and takes my soap from its little shelf, lathers her hands with it, then glides them over my body, washing the dust and grime from my arms and shoulders. I take over as she strays lower, because her washing my dick is where I draw the line, at least if it's not in a sexy way. Maybe we could revisit this showering thing another time.

As I rinse the soap off, Abi grabs my shampoo, squeezing a dollop into her hand before gesturing for me to turn around.

When her hands settle on my scalp I can't even be embarrassed by this whole situation anymore, because it feels like magic. She massages the shampoo into my scalp. It makes me want to melt.

The hazy fog of grief that's clung to me today clears ever so slightly as she cares for me.

I know how lucky I am with the family I've ended up with, despite losing my parents.

I know how lucky I am to have Hunter, who put his entire life on hold for me, and Violet who stepped up to mother me when I needed it, while never overstepping.

I know how lucky I am to have best friends like Katie and Olivia, and Dallas and Sadie.

I know how lucky I am to have Abi here with me right now.

And I know, despite me letting them all down by not showing up for dinner tonight, they're all still going to love me tomorrow.

Well, except maybe Abi.

Because I'm pretty sure friends who are just hooking up aren't supposed to love each other the way I'm in love with Abigail Fletcher.

AFTER WE SHOWER, I force feed Flynn, making sure he eats something.

He perches on a stool at his kitchen bench, wearing only a pair of dark boxer briefs and I do everything in my power not to stare at the long lines of his body. I fail repeatedly as my gaze lingers over the smooth muscle. I want to draw constellations with the freckles scattered across his shoulders.

Instead, I tell him about us eating the apple pie first and a soft smile plays at his lips.

"Mum would have loved that," he murmurs, reaching for the bowl.

Once he's fed, I lead him to the bedroom, pulling back his blankets for him as he climbs in. I tug the duvet up around his shoulders as he settles in, then take a step back.

"Do you need anything else before I go?"

"For you not to go," Flynn says, voice already sleepy. "Please, stay."

"People will think that's strange."

He lets out a frustrated little noise and it's kind of adorable. "We'll just tell them we were hanging out to make me feel better and you fell asleep here. It's the truth."

I sigh as Flynn peels open his eyes and stares up at me. It's become really, really hard to say no to that face. "Fine."

"T-shirts are in the second drawer if you want one to sleep in," Flynn says, voice slightly muffled by the pillow he's burrowing into. "Or I wouldn't complain if you didn't wear anything at all."

"Go to sleep, sweetheart," I say. I grab a t-shirt from the drawer, tug the dress I put back on after our shower over my head and slip into the shirt. It's incredibly soft and smells deliciously like Flynn.

Crossing the room, I slide into Flynn's bed behind him, wrapping my arm around his waist and tugging him back into me.

He snuggles in and within minutes is asleep, his breath soft and even.

I try not to be jealous as I lie in the dark holding him. Sleep eludes me and if I was alone, I'd be tossing and turning constantly. But here, I lie still and hold Flynn to me, his warm body an anchor.

Eventually I give up and slip from the bed, padding silently to the kitchen for a drink before sneaking back into bed.

"Where'd you go?" Flynn murmurs. "I woke up and you were gone."

"Just to get a drink. I'm not going anywhere. Go back to sleep."

He relaxes back into the mattress, but as I settle beside him, his arms snake out and wrap around me, tugging me into him.

I go willingly.

"You smell like my soap," he whispers against my hair.

"That's because I used it."

He snorts a tiny laugh. "Obviously." He pauses, then draws a long breath. "I didn't mean to force you to stay. You can go if you'd rather not be here."

"Hey." I roll towards Flynn, cupping his cheeks with my hands. "There's nowhere else I want to be." I stroke my thumb along his cheekbone. "I mean, I wouldn't mind getting some actual sleep, but I'm not sure that's happening tonight."

"You can't sleep?"

"Nope. But it's okay. Lying here with you is still better than being at home alone."

"I might be able to help with the sleeping. Or at least relaxing ... maybe." Flynn's hand skates down my spine and tingles shoot through me.

"You're supposed to be sleeping," I murmur against his lips, only now realising how close we're getting.

"I can't sleep while you're not."

"The last couple of hours beg to differ."

"Hush, Rosie," Flynn says against my mouth, before pressing a soft, slow kiss to my lips.

His hand lands on my hip, rubbing a smooth circle before sliding under the hem of the t-shirt to trace the outline of my spine.

"I'm supposed to be looking after you tonight," I whisper.

"You are. Mutually beneficial arrangement, remember? It'll

help you sleep, and you can still take care of me." He pauses and pulls back. It's just light enough in the room that I can make out the gleam of his eyes and the furrow in his brow. "If you want to. I don't think I can do all *that* tonight, as hot as it is."

By that, I assume he means leading our hook ups, the control I hand over to him to help me get out of my head. But tonight, I don't need that.

Tonight, I just need to care for this incredible man. It's all I want.

"Of course I want, but are you sure? You're not exactly in a great place today."

He snorts. "Rosie, I'm sad and miss the family I lost ten years ago, but that's never going to stop me from wanting you." He snags the waistband of my underwear with his thumbs and tugs them down.

I kick them off my legs, then roll towards him, pushing him onto his back as I land on top of him. "I can work with that." I thread my fingers into his hair and am rewarded when he lets out a soft moan. "Can I turn on a light? I want to see you."

Flynn reaches out, his arm flailing in mid-air for a moment before connecting with the bedside lamp and a moment later soft light surrounds us.

I blink a few times, waiting for my eyes to adjust, then wriggle further onto Flynn's body until my knees land on the mattress on either side of him. I sit up, straddling his waist, and gaze down at him.

His eyes are soft on me as he trails his gaze down my body, his hair mussed against the pillow.

"Fuck, you look good in my clothes." His hands close around my bare thighs, teasing the hem of the shirt.

"I look better without them though," I say, and tug the shirt over my head.

Flynn lets out a low groan. "Agreed." His hands skim over my hips, lifting to cup my breasts. His thumbs brush over my nipples and a breathy, needy moan leaves me.

His simple, soft touches have me desperate for him, heat already pooling in my belly, the ache between my legs building.

I slide my hips back so I can get at his thick, hard cock. I shove his underwear down his thighs, freeing him. I wrap my hand around his shaft, giving a few slow pumps while Flynn drops his head back and lets out a gravelly low groan.

"Do you want to fuck me?" I ask, wanting to make sure we're on the same page with this. We haven't had sex yet, just used hands and mouths and I don't want to push him too far if he's not there yet. He'll be losing his virginity. I don't want him to regret it because it happened on an emotional night when he wasn't feeling himself.

"Does it count as me fucking you when you're up there?" Flynn's voice is breathy and broken with need.

"Sure, we can go with that," I say, leaning forward to suck his tip into my mouth. He lets out another guttural noise, his hands finding their way to my hair and tugging me off. I pout.

"I won't last, and I'm not blowing now if you're offering to ride me," he says through gritted teeth.

"That's fair," I say. "Do you have condoms?" I ask as I lean down and capture his mouth for a long, wandering kiss.

His arm flails about again until he hits his hand against his bedside table and breaks the kiss to curse. "Fuck that hurt," he mutters, then turns his attention to the drawer, indicating the box inside.

I fish out a foil packet, rip it open and roll the condom onto him.

"Do you need anything?" he asks, pushing up onto his elbows. "A warmup round?"

I grin at him. One of the best parts of being with Flynn is how fun it is, even when we're in the middle of a super hot hookup, it's still fun. He's constantly making me crack up laughing, even on the brink of orgasm.

"See for yourself," I say, rising up onto my knees.

Flynn drags his hands across my body again, sending shivers and goosebumps spreading from every place he touches. He cups my pussy and slides a finger inside me.

"So wet," he says, voice filled with bliss. "I assume this means you're good?"

I grind down on his palm and he groans.

"Very, very, very good. Now, let me at your dick."

He chuckles, the sound warm and soft and landing right in the middle of my chest.

I move up his body again, then ever so slowly sink down onto him.

"Oh holy Jesus fucking Christ on a cracker. Oh, god."

"Nope, no god here. Just me," I say. My voice is barely audible, just a breathy whisper of lust and desire as I feel myself stretch around him.

His jaw clenches and eyelids flutter, but he never closes his eyes, never takes his gaze from me.

When my ass presses against his thighs he lets out a sexy as hell grunt.

"*Fuck*, Abi. Fuck, you feel amazing."

I lean down and kiss him, sliding my tongue into his mouth and exploring, losing myself in him while he's inside me.

His hands grasp my hips, holding me in place and I'm not sure if it's because he's worried I'm going to run away, or if he's trying to stop himself giving into the need to take more.

I tangle my hand in his hair and drag the fingers on the other hand down his throat. I push off his chest so I'm sitting upright again.

"You haven't felt anything yet," I say, in a ridiculous husky voice.

Then, I begin to move.

___

42

FLYNN

I MIGHT DIE.

Right here, with Abi straddling me, riding my cock.

She moves her hips in the slowest, most sensual movements I've ever seen in my life as my hands bracket her waist, skin soft under my palms.

This is different to our other hook ups. Those have been hot and heavy, usually hurried and desperate.

But this ... this is less about getting off and more about sharing this experience.

And Abi is sharing it with me.

Fuuuck. We're having sex. Like actual sex, not just ultra-horny versions of foreplay that end in my coming way too fast. She feels amazing. Hot and tight and so incredible I have to fight to keep focussed and not simply lose myself in her.

She trails her fingertips across my face, along my jaw, down my throat, like she's tracing me and committing me to memory.

I tell my poor deluded heart to shut up because I know what

this is for Abi, and it's not love. It's not forever. It's friends helping each other out.

Except I've ruined it all by falling in love with her.

Abi leans down, pressing her lips to mine and I push all the thinking from my brain, focussing on this moment as she lifts her hips and lowers down on my cock, over and over.

The sounds Abi is making are desperate and needy as she rides me, alternating between bouncing and grinding.

Tingles are shooting down my spine, the world spinning as all of my focus comes down to Abi and the feel of her surrounding me.

Her hair falls in a curtain around my head. She keeps her lips on me as she moves her hips and I'm so close. So, so close.

I need to come, but I need her to as well.

"Are you going to come for me, Rosie?" I whisper against her mouth.

She whimpers, then lets out a frustrated noise. Sitting up she increases her pace, but her rhythm falters. She lets out a hiss, then another desperate whimper.

"Come for me, Rosie," I say, tone firmer this time, knowing how much she likes me in control.

She lets out a choked sob, collapsing on top of me, her body going still. "I can't," she mumbles. "Not like that. I'm sorry."

Shit. Panic seizes me. She's not enjoying this. My arms immediately wrap around her body, my hand smoothing her hair.

"Rosie, I'm so sorry."

She pushes up onto her elbow to look down at me. Her

expression is wrecked. "It's not your fault. I just sometimes can't get there when I'm on top."

"What do you need?" I ask, cupping her cheek and bringing her face to mine for a soft kiss.

She slides off me and I want to pull her back, but I refrain. "Come here," she says, lying back and reaching for me.

I roll towards her, settling between her legs. She wraps them around my waist, tugging me closer. I let out a low hum when my cock slides against her wet pussy.

"I want you to fuck me like this," she murmurs. "I want to feel all of you."

I blanket her body with mine and push into her. Her face is pressed against my neck and I feel her exhale ghost over my skin as I enter her.

I tuck my arms around her and hold her close.

Abi riding me was incredibly sexy. Everything about her is.

But this moment right here, this intimacy, this is what I really needed tonight.

I thrust my hips and Abi moans, pressing a kiss against my throat.

She drops her head back to the pillows and stares up at me. Our gazes lock and with long, deliciously slow thrusts, I build her up, dragging her closer and closer to the edge.

"You're so fucking gorgeous," I murmur. "Incredible. Beautiful. Determined. Brave."

Each word causes her to tremble a little more until the last one, which sends a full body shudder through her.

Her palms press against my face and while instinct wants

me to throw my head back and fuck her harder, her hands keep me grounded, intent on her.

I lose myself in her. I'm not just Flynn anymore. She's a part of me, I don't know who I'll be without her.

When I can't hold back anymore and my orgasm hits, I tumble over the edge, Abi following me right over, her finger-nails digging into my shoulders, legs locked tight around my waist, eyes still on mine.

"Fuck me," I gasp, ragged pants making me shudder over her.

"I just did," Abi replies, a soft smirk on her lips and I laugh as I let my head fall to her shoulder, then collapse on top of her.

She drags her hand up and down my spine, the caress almost too much for my heart.

"Go clean up, then go to sleep, sweetheart," she murmurs against my hair.

"Only if you stay right here with me." It's a stupid thing to say. I shouldn't want her to stay. I should be creating some distance between us, before I blow this entire thing up in our faces with my feelings.

I'm going to have to end it before I get myself in any deeper, if that's even possible at this point.

Our reality is that we aren't supposed to be together. There are too many things to consider. Sadie for one and how she might feel about this. Abi was supposed to be here for Sadie and only Sadie. Yet here I am, diverting all the attention.

Plus, there's our jobs to think about. Not that Olivia seems to have an issue with employee fraternisation. No, it's not her I'm worried about.

It's Katie and Dallas.

Katie and I drifted apart while she wasn't living in Kauri Creek and now she's back, do I want to jeopardise one of the best friendships I've ever had by admitting to this thing with Abi?

It's all too much, too complicated. And I don't do complicated. I tell myself it's why I've avoided any relationships until now, because I can't deal with complexities and emotions and the hard stuff. The fact I've never found someone to have a relationship with is irrelevant. I'm the good time guy. I'm definitely not the guy Abi should be relying on while getting her life back on track. She's so close to everything she ever wanted.

I head to the bathroom to deal with the condom, then slide into bed beside Abi again.

She curls into me, expanses of her warm, bare skin against mine.

"Sweet dreams, Flynn," she whispers to my shoulder, then presses the softest kiss there.

My arm reflexively tightens around her. "Goodnight, Abi."

Then we sleep, both of us, so tangled up in the other I can barely tell where one of us begins and the other ends.

And I'm not just talking about our bodies.

THERE'S a banging coming from somewhere, but I'm too busy nestling into the delicious warmth of my bed.

"What the fuck is that noise?" Abi mutters and I let out a soft chuckle.

"Flynn! I'm coming in so you'd better make sure you've got clothes on." The voice shouts from the front door.

"Okay, so that's my brother."

"Oh, shit." Abi throws back the duvet, then hunts for her clothes. She pulls on her underwear, then the t-shirt of mine she'd worn last night. "I had the pleasure of meeting him last night."

I roll out of bed and narrow my eyes at her. "Was he a dick?"

"No. Just … he's not like you is he?"

I let out a laugh, but it's not particularly amused. "An irresponsible idiot? Nah, not really. Hunter very much has his shit together."

"I meant fun and happy."

I toss her a pair of sweatpants. I'm not particularly concerned about Hunter catching an eyeful of me, but I'd rather he didn't make Abi feel uncomfortable. She's just tugging them into place when Hunter hollers through the door again.

"Time's up. Hope you're not naked."

At least he's prevented me from having to reply to Abi's comment, because I have no idea what I'm supposed to say to that. She didn't acknowledge me saying Hunter has his shit together and implying I don't, so does that mean she also doesn't think I have my shit together? I mean, I know I said it, but it still kind of stings. I'm too wrung out from emotions and the most incredible sex to ever happen to deal with all this today.

The door creaks as it swings open and Hunter steps inside. I've managed to get my own underwear on, and a pair of jeans halfway up my thighs when his gaze lands on me.

"Didn't I give you enough time?" he asks, tone as grouchy as ever.

"I was asleep," I mutter.

Hunter scans the room, eyes landing on Abi. "Asleep. Sure. Late night, huh?"

"Uh, I'll leave you to it," Abi says, folding her dress over her arm and holding it against her body like a shield. "I'll see you later. Hunter." She gives him a nod as she passes my brother and steps outside before I have the chance to reply.

"Why are you here so early?" I mutter once the door is closed.

"I stayed at Violet's. You'd know that if you bothered to turn up to dinner."

"I was working."

"Like Vi gives a fuck about the crop. Family is what matters to her. You know that better than anyone."

"Did you just come here to be an asshole, or did you have an actual purpose in mind?"

He sighs and runs a hand over his face, rubbing at the stubble on his jaw. "I came to check on my little brother. I didn't realise I would be interrupting."

"You weren't interrupting anything. Abi's my friend. She brought me some dinner." And then fucked my brains out. Probably shouldn't tell my brother that part though, even if I kind of do want to shout it from the rooftops because holy shit, it was the best moment of my life.

"I'm aware." He talks to me like he's talking to a child. "You think that's really a good idea? To have her spending the night?"

"Fucking hell, I'm not a kid," I snap.

"No." Hunter runs his hand down his face again, a sure sign he's exasperated. "What you do with her is your own business, just be careful. She's got a lot of baggage, and you, little brother, do not. Don't let it weigh you down."

"Nothing is weighing me down. We're friends. That's it. There's nothing else there."

"Fine, if you say so." He glances around the room, taking in the small space, his gaze lingering on Mum's flowers painted on the ceiling. "You should get the dog."

"What?"

"You were talking about a puppy when I saw you last. I think you should. You were supposed to get one, that Christmas. Mum and I were going to go and choose it for you ..." His voice drops. "The day after the accident. Obviously we never made it."

"Okay." I lower myself onto one of the kitchen stools, a little dumbstruck over his revelation. Hunter doesn't talk about our parents, not to me anyway. We don't talk about much. He became my guardian and worked his ass off to keep our heads above water, but emotionally he cut me off, not that we were ever particularly close. "I'll keep that in mind."

"You've wanted one since you were six. You went on and on about every dog you ever met. Never shut up about them. Plus, it makes sense for you to have some company out here."

"Some without all that baggage, you mean?"

Hunter sighs. "Just trying to look out for you. Make sure you're nice to Vi today."

"I'm always nice to Vi," I mutter. Always. I love that woman. Without her who knows where I would have ended up, because she provided me the emotional support I needed when Hunter couldn't.

"I know you are. I need to go, but are you alright?"

"Yes, Hunter. I'm fine. Sometimes I'm just allowed to be sad and not want to hang out with everyone, okay?"

"I know." He gives me a look. One that says he gets it, but still wishes neither of us had to understand this feeling. "I'll see you later."

And after that wonderfully uplifting conversation, my big brother disappears back out my front door, leaving me alone with my feelings, and the horrifying realisation that I've fallen in love with Abi.

Somehow I need to get through this, ideally with our friendship, and my heart, still intact.

One thing is for certain though, I'm in over my head and I need to get out before I drown. This thing with Abi, it needs to end. It was always going to, but if I do it now at least it's on my terms.

I just hope our friendship survives, because I don't think I can handle losing her completely.

43

—

ABI

I BURY myself in work the week following my night with Flynn.

Well, I try to anyway. It's not easy when my mind keeps straying to thoughts of him.

Of his body wrapped around mine.

Of his hair tangled in my fingers.

Of his hands caressing my skin.

Of his face as he fucked me, gaze never straying from mine.

Except that wasn't exactly fucking. It was more than that. I know it was, I just really, really don't want to admit it.

I keep waiting for him to turn up at the function centre. Every time a vehicle arrives I catch my breath, my heart doing a little skipping thing in my chest.

But he never shows.

I shouldn't be surprised.

Not after what he said to his brother.

I shouldn't have lingered, but once I was out on the porch,

the door closed behind me I worried that I'd left Flynn too soon. Maybe I should have stayed with him for the conversation with his brother.

But then it quickly turned to me. His voice echoes through my head as I recount the wine glasses we have on hand for the third time. I can't concentrate enough to get it right.

"Nothing is weighing me down. We're friends. That's it. There's nothing else there."

His words shouldn't have hit me as hard as they did. Because it's the truth, but my heart still gives sad little pangs every time I remember.

Then there's the radio silence this week.

I've text him twice, asking first if he was free Sunday afternoon to hang out and he'd replied with a very brief, vague excuse about being too busy.

I messaged him again later, asking him to let me know when he would be free.

He didn't reply to that one.

I refocus on my counting. I need to determine how many glasses were broken at the event over the weekend so I can charge the client for the loss and I've let it drag on far too long already.

The sound of a motorbike approaches, the crunch of gravel, then the sound of the engine cuts off.

I curse, because I've lost count again, but then I turn my attention to the doorway, my heart in my throat.

Dallas steps inside.

I deflate, but try not to let my disappointment show.

"Hey," he says, smile wide and relaxed.

"Hey," I reply, and drop my clipboard on the table beside me.

"You have a minute?"

"Yeah, sure. Want to go sit outside?"

Dallas nods and we head around the side of the old barn, towards the gazebo. It's a gorgeous day, with endless blue skies meeting the Wildflower Ridge hills, all lit by stunning early summer sunshine.

We sit side by side in the gazebo, looking out over the pond.

"How are things?" Dallas asks.

"Yeah, they're really good." I smile. Things really are good. Great even. Except where Flynn is concerned, but I can't think about him now.

"You're happy with how things are going with Sadie?"

"Things with Sadie are amazing. Thank you for everything you've done."

He loops an arm around my shoulders and pulls me against him in a side hug. I love that even after everything we went through, we can still be friends.

"How do you feel about having her this weekend?"

"Yeah, sure. Saturday or Sunday? I have no events on."

"Saturday and Sunday."

"Overnight?" My breath stutters and Dallas must feel my body go stiff.

"Only if you want to. Katie and I are going away for the weekend and we thought you might like to spend the time with Sadie. But Violet can have her if it's too much."

"No," I say, but my voice is a rough croak. "No." I try again. "I'll have her. I'd love to. Of course."

"Well, she'll love it too, she hasn't shut up about your spa day."

I take a breath, then another, making the exhales long and slow. The spa day was a lot of fun. I painted Sadie's nails, did a conditioning treatment in her hair and gave her a mini-facial, then while our face masks were on we lay on my couch and watched silly animal videos. Afterwards we went out for lunch where Tilly complimented Sadie endlessly on her glowing skin and pretty nails. That girl is a customer service dream.

I spent the whole day with Sadie that day. I can do that again and include an overnight in there. Dinner, bath, bedtime. A long expanse of time when Sadie will be asleep, safe in her bed.

Absolutely no reason for anxiety. No reason for panic attacks.

I can do this. I've spent years working towards being able to do this again, and the baby steps Dallas and I have used to reintegrate me into Sadie's life have been the perfect stepping stones. I haven't had a panic attack since the very beginning and this is the next step in being Sadie's mum again. It's one I'm sure I can manage.

"I can't wait," I say to Dallas.

He studies my face, turning on the seat to get a good look at me. "Are you absolutely sure about this?"

"Yes. Violet will be here if I need anything, but I won't."

"Katie and I aren't going far anyway, we'll only be about forty minutes away."

"That's barely going away, Dal." I pat his shoulder with a laugh.

"I know. But I haven't spent a lot of time without Sadie being more than a paddock away. It's going to take some adjusting for all of us."

"For what it's worth, and I'm sure you already know this, but you're an amazing dad. The best. I knew I could focus on myself and not have to worry about Sadie, because she had you." I pause and drop my eyes, taking a deep breath before making eye contact again. "But I am sorry, for all the things I put you through."

Dallas uses the arm still around my shoulders to tug me to him, his other arm wrapping around me. "You didn't put me through it, Abs. That was all that anxiety. It's not you."

He releases me and I sit back. "It's still a part of me."

"Yeah, and it's made you who you are today, which is an amazing, strong woman. A mum. Plus, it brought us to this place." He gestures around, at the function centre, the sprawling hills, the vast open skies.

"It's a pretty great place," I say, leaning against him as he turns back to face the pond.

"And we're pretty great parents. *Both* of us."

With his words, something settles in me.

We may have had an unconventional route, but this place, this family, it really does feel like home now, for all of us, and I can't wait to watch my daughter grow up here.

44

FLYNN

I'M BEING SUCH a little baby over my life right now, but I can't snap myself out of it.

It's been days since Abi was at my place, curled around me as I slept, protecting me from my loneliness.

I haven't been to see her and I ignored the last text she sent me.

Well, I didn't exactly ignore it. I don't think it's classed as ignoring it when I've reread it a million times and thought of all the ways I'd like to reply.

But I can't.

It's why I can't go and see her either, because I don't trust myself not to blurt out that I'm head over fucking heels in love with her.

And I really don't want to do that. She made it clear what this was. A mutually beneficial arrangement between friends. I just hope that these feelings fade soon and we can get back to the being friends part.

The mutually beneficial arrangement, well I'm going to have to leave that in the past.

Friends only from this point forward.

If only I could figure out how to tell Abi, because while I'm hiding from her, I'm aware I'm being a shitty friend.

As well as avoiding Abi, I've also been avoiding everyone else. I went to see Violet after Hunter left to apologise for missing dinner. She reminded me I don't need to apologise to her, like she has every time I've tried to be sorry for the times I've screwed up. Then she asked if I was okay and wrapped me in a long, tight hug, even though I told her I was fine.

I've been hiding from Olivia and Katie too. My best friends. Because I can't bear to tell them what happened between me and Abi, but it feels weird to lie to them about it.

So, I've tied myself in such a huge knot I can't unravel it.

And hiding from everyone in my life just means I'm even more lonely.

I sigh and tug on the wrench I'm using to tighten the hydraulic hose I've just replaced on the tractor. The wrench slips off the coupling and rebounds off my hand.

"Mother fucker!" I drop the wrench, barely missing my foot, but at least I have steel cap boots on so that wouldn't have hurt as much as hitting my hand with it does.

"Flynn?" Fuck. Olivia. Come on, Universe. That was shitty timing. I can't exactly hide from her now.

"Yeah," I croak through the pain and she rounds the corner of the implement shed, face filled with concern.

"Are you okay?"

I nod. "Wrench slipped. Hit my hand." I've been pressing my other hand over the site of the injury, thinking applying pressure would help a bruise. I have no idea if that's true, but it's helping steady me.

"Need some ice?" She steps closer, takes my arm and pries my uninjured hand away. She inspects the red mark on my skin. It's already looking a bit purple. "Yes. Ice. Come on."

She doesn't release my arm and leads me gently to the side-by-side. I climb in beside her, knowing arguing is worthless. When Olivia's set her mind on something there isn't much point trying to change it.

Maybe I'll get a muffin out of it or something. Some real food at the bare minimum. I'm not exactly enjoying living off a loaf of bread and jar of peanut butter. But to get the good meals I have to be around all the people I'm trying to avoid.

Olivia zooms down the driveway to the main house and I follow her inside. She goes straight to the freezer and grabs an icepack, wrapping it in a tea towel, then pressing it against my hand.

I hiss and try to take the icepack from her. "I can do it."

"I know but let me."

Weird, but okay, I'll indulge her. We sit at the kitchen table, my hand on the table with Olivia holding the icepack over it.

"What's up, Flynny?" she whispers after a long, awkward silence.

"Nothing," I sigh, running my free hand through my hair.

"Oh, yeah, sure. That's so convincing. Obviously you're fantastic." She spins her legs around so she's facing me. I keep my eyes firmly on the tabletop. "Something's up. You're avoiding everyone. You haven't even come down for food."

I keep trying to cut her off, to argue, but she steamrolls over me every single time.

"I'm your best friend. You're bound by law to tell me what's going on."

"By law?" I shoot her a sceptical look, then refocus on the table. The wood grain here is super interesting.

"Yes. The official law of my life." She grins and I roll my eyes.

"It's nothing, Liv."

She lets out a heavy breath. "Fine. But you know I'm always here for you if you need to talk about shit. Always, Flynn."

The words leave my mouth before I have a chance to catch them, or even filter them. "I slept with Abi."

My cheeks flame hot and I know how aggressive my blush will be right now. Oh my god. I can't believe I just threw that out there. I wasn't supposed to tell anyone, let along the person who holds both our jobs in her hands. What if, despite all outward signs of peace, things aren't actually good between Abi, Dallas and Katie? Have I just fucked us both over?

"Okay," Olivia says, her expression barely flickering at my confession.

"Okay? That's it? Why aren't you freaking out?"

"I'm trying to work out why *you're* freaking out. Was it really bad?"

"What? No. The opposite."

"Are you worried she thinks you were bad?"

Oh god. Does Abi think it was bad?

No. I'm fairly certain she was fully in the moment, or moments as the case may be, and she had a good time. A really good time.

"Ew. Stop thinking about it while I'm sitting right here."

"Ew? What's ew about it?" I'm mortified. Horrified. Was it ew?

"You're like my brother. I don't need to know details about your sex life."

Oh, thank fuck it's only that.

"It wasn't bad, Liv. It was definitely as far away from bad as you can get."

"I still don't understand why you're freaking out."

"Because ... it was supposed to be one thing, and I've turned it into something else. Something it was never supposed to be."

Her eyes widen. "Shit. This got involved didn't it?" She pokes me hard in the chest, right above my heart. I give her a look, but don't need to say anything else. "I'm not surprised."

"You're not?" I thought this would be a shock to her. But she's taking it way too calmly.

Fuck. Maybe she has cameras in the office at the event centre. That would be very, very bad. So bad. I'm going to have to ask her and hope she doesn't have too many questions.

Before I have a chance to fully panic about that, Olivia continues.

"You have so much love to give, it doesn't surprise me that you fell for her. She's pretty cool, a strong, badass woman and obviously gorgeous, so it all makes sense."

"Nothing about this makes sense, least of all you being so calm about it. Does nothing faze you?"

She snorts. "Plenty of things faze me, but my friends being happy doesn't. Am I supposed to be pissy that you two hooked up? If it doesn't affect your jobs then I don't care." She points across the paddock to Dallas's cottage. "Exhibit A."

I lean towards her and rest my head on her shoulder, the contact familiar and so, so comforting.

"I want to get a dog," I say. I really have zero tact or conversational skills today. "One of those puppies you showed us the other week."

"Sounds good. I considered it, but I don't think I'm ready."

"That's it?" I ask, lifting my head to look at her. "No jokes about my lack of responsibility?"

Olivia looks puzzled for a moment, then her expression clears, before quickly turning apologetic. "I'm sorry. We were just joking, but we should never have said what we did."

I sigh and drop my head again, leaning into my best friend. "You were right though."

"No, we weren't. You have lots of responsibility. If you want more, just let me know. You can have some of mine."

I snort. "You'd trust me with it?"

Olivia shifts away and I'm forced to sit up again, then she places a hand on my leg and drags it towards her, forcing me to twist in my seat so I'm facing her, our knees touching. She places her hands on my shoulders and leans in close.

"I trust you with everything, Flynn. I trust you with a puppy. I trust you with your job. I trust you with this whole fucking place. One of the reasons I can get through each day is I know that you're here to back me up, always. I know you'll look after this place, and my family, like it's your own, because by this point, it is yours. This is your home, Flynn, it always will be. If you want more from it, you say the word."

"A puppy seems like a good place to start," I say, trying not to let the wobble in my voice show.

"You don't have to ask my permission," she says. "You know that right? About the dog, or about Abi."

"The thing with Abi is over," I mutter, turning back to the table because while I could look my best friend in the eyes while she told me I'm a part of this place, I can't do it while I talk about falling in love with a woman I can't have. "I need to make some space."

"Is that what Abi wants?"

"Abi wanted casual. She has her own priorities and I don't make the list. That's okay, I just need some time to deal with my feelings over it all."

"Makes sense. Just maybe check—" Olivia's phone rings and she groans as she pulls it from her jeans pocket. "Fucking thing never stops."

She answers the call and talks for a few minutes before jabbing violently at the screen to end the call.

"You need to go?" I say.

"Yep. I'm sorry to cut this short."

"I'm not," I say, a small laugh slipping out of me.

Olivia laughs as she stands. "I mean hanging out with my bestie," she says. "Making you squirm was just a bonus. But don't shut me out when things get hard, okay? I need you."

"I promise." I reach up and wrap my arms around Olivia's waist before she has a chance to step away. I squeeze her tight and she hugs me back, then pats me on the head and as much as I scowl and swat her hand away, I love the attention.

As Olivia leaves the kitchen, still muttering about whatever it is she has to go and deal with, I pick up my phone and navigate to the puppy listing. I'm going to choose one this weekend. At least with a puppy to keep me busy I won't have time to wallow in my stupid feelings.

45

———

ABI

I'M WAITING outside Sadie's school, still marvelling that this is my life now.

I'm a fully present part of my daughter's life and this weekend she'll be staying with me overnight.

I never thought I'd get back to this place, not after Sadie's accident, when suddenly I couldn't cope with being left alone with her for five minutes for Dallas to have a break.

Our snails-pace reintroduction to each other has been exactly what I've needed to manage my anxiety around having Sadie solely in my care. I appreciate it more than Dallas could ever know.

The bell rings and hordes of children spill from the classrooms. Laughter and chatter echoing around the school.

"Mama!" Sadie shrieks and throws herself into my arms.

I laugh and scoop her up, squeezing her tight before setting her feet back on the ground. She immediately slips her hand into mine.

I want to burst into tears right here in the middle of the sea of children and students.

"Hi," another mother says to me, a little girl Sadie's age beside her. "Are you Sadie's mum?"

"Yeah." I grin. "Abi."

"I'm Quinn. This is Ruby. Her and Sadie are good friends."

"So nice to meet you," I say, meaning every word.

"Mama, can we play?" Sadie asks, tugging on my hand.

I glance at Quinn and she nods. "Just for a few minutes, Lady Sadie." She drops my hand and grabs Ruby's, then they skip off towards the playground together.

"Chances of getting them back anytime soon are slim to none," Quinn laughs. "Let me give you my number and maybe we can set up a playdate for the girls sometime, and while they're playing we can have coffee, if you want."

My heart swells. "That would be amazing." I pull out my phone and tap the digits in as Quinn recites them to me, then I send her a text so she has my number too.

"This might be too forward, and sorry if it is. I'm just exceptionally nosy, but I don't always see you here picking her up? And not until recently?"

My cheeks heat. But it's reality and I shouldn't be ashamed of it. I was strong enough to come back, and that's what matters.

"Yeah. She's usually with her dad and if he's not picking her up it could be his girlfriend, or one of the people we work with."

"We? You work with your ex?" The look on her face is pure horror.

I laugh. "Sort of. We don't really have much to do with each other at work. The whole thing sounds more complicated than it is, but everything between us is extremely amicable. Dallas is a great dad, Katie is fantastic with Sadie and the people we both happen to work for are incredible. We're all like this big, weird family. I kind of love it."

"That sounds amazing. I'm going to need the full breakdown and probably a diagram or two when we catch up." She grins and I send one right back to her.

"I'm sure that can be arranged."

Quinn glances at her phone and sighs. "I need to get going." She pulls a face, then calls out to Ruby who comes trudging back, Sadie at her side. "Lovely to meet you," she says, giving me a warm smile before turning to the girls and farewelling Sadie, before leading Ruby away.

"Ready to go, Sadie?" I ask and she nods.

"Do I get to have a play with Ruby?" she asks, eyes bright with excitement.

"If you'd like to. I'm sure we can arrange something."

She squeals and bounces up and down. "Yes, yes, yes, yes," she chants.

"I can see you're thinking about it."

Sadie giggles and climbs into her car seat without argument.

The whole drive back to Wildflower Ridge she's chatting about Ruby and her other friends and all the fun things they could do together.

I pull in the driveway, heading straight to the main house. I've got a venue viewing this evening, so I need to drop Sadie off with Violet before heading back down to the function centre to show a potential couple around.

I park beside Violet's car and help Sadie out of her seat. She grabs her bag and races up the porch steps, calling out a goodbye as she goes.

I watch her go, leaning against the bonnet of my car. As she reaches the door she lets out a yelp and I immediately go on alert, then relax as Flynn steps through.

"Where's the fire, sprout?" he asks her.

She folds her arms across her chest and stares up at him, eyes narrowed suspiciously. "Did you eat all the cookies?"

Flynn glances at the fistful of cookies he's holding before sliding the hand behind his back. "Absolutely not," he says, mock offended. "I would never."

"Yes, you would." She spins away and heads into the house. "You better have left me some," she calls back, the words echoing down the hallway.

I let out a laugh and Flynn glances up at the sound, registering me for the first time.

"Oh, hey," he says, strolling down the steps and coming to a stop just a little bit too far away from me for my liking. "Cookie?" He holds one out to me, but I shake my head.

"No, thanks. I've got to get down to the venue, but I'm having Sadie this weekend. My first time overnight." I grin and Flynn sends one back to me. I try to convince myself it's my imagination that makes it feel half-hearted.

"That's great," he says, taking a huge bite of cookie.

"Do you want to come and hang out with us for a bit? Maybe watch a movie or something?"

I've missed him something terrible this week, even though I've been trying to lose myself in work and Sadie. It hasn't worked and at the back of my mind there's been this longing ache that I know can only be filled by one thing: more time with Flynn.

Not just the physical part of our relationship, but just him in general. His humour and bad jokes, his sense of fun and adventure, the way he looks after me but never hesitates to push me outside of my comfort zone.

I miss all of that. I miss him, and while that should be sounding alarm bells, because this is how friends with benefits arrangements always go bad, I ignore them.

Flynn chews slowly and eventually swallows. "I don't think that's a good idea, Abi."

Not Rosie. Abi. At least it wasn't Abigail, I suppose.

I open my mouth to ask why, but he answers before I even have to ask.

"We're fuck buddies. Friends who hook up. I'm not the guy you bring around when you're with your daughter." He sounds so bitter, not like the Flynn I've come to know and lo—oh shit. Love.

I might be ignoring the alarm bells, but can I ignore I've fallen in love with him? Right as he's apparently decided to not just push me away, but shove me.

"I think this mutually beneficial arrangement should probably end now," he says, gesturing between us. "I've got to get back to work, but I'm really happy things worked out for you and Sadie. You deserve it."

He spins on his heel and strides away. A moment later I hear his motorbike engine kick to life and he tears off down the farm, driving way, way faster than normal.

I'm left standing in the driveway, right in front of the main house, my heart feeling like it's been trampled, and tears threatening to spill down my cheeks.

I climb back into my car and head around to the function venue. As I pass under the Wildflower Ridge sign on the main gate, the tears spill over, my control on them finally slipping.

I let myself cry until I turn into the road that leads up to the function centre, then I take several deep breaths and push aside all those emotions.

I'm strong enough to get through this. I've made it through everything else life has thrown at me.

I'll give Flynn some space, then hopefully we can rebuild our friendship.

And these feelings I have will fade over time.

They have to.

46

ABI

SADIE and I are having the best day.

I picked her up from Dallas's first thing this morning so he and Katie could make the most of their weekend.

Sadie and I headed to Sugar where Tilly treated Sadie to a free cupcake and I grabbed coffees for myself and Quinn.

We met at the school so the girls could play on the playground, while Quinn and I sat in the sun and I gave her the full rundown on the situation at Wildflower Ridge. I told her all about how I co-parent with Dallas, Katie, Violet and Olivia. I briefly mention Flynn, but when my heart pangs I quickly move onto the next topic, pushing thoughts of him to the back of my mind, like I have been every time he crosses my thoughts since he told me he wants to end our arrangement. I need to focus on Sadie, like I should have been this whole time.

When Quinn needs to go to pick up her son from his football game, Sadie and I head home, ready for an afternoon of girly pampering and treats, before snuggling together to watch a movie.

It's going to be perfect. Everything about it.

Until I ask Sadie what she wants for lunch.

"Nothing," she mumbles from her position sprawled across my couch.

"Aren't you hungry?" I ask, sitting down beside her, instantly worried I've filled her up on junk food and treats instead of proper food.

"Sore tummy," she says with a little moan.

I study what I can see of her face. The rest is smooshed into one of the cushions that live on my couch. She looks a little pale and maybe a little flushed at the same time.

Is that a thing that can happen?

She groans, louder this time and rolls over, curling into a ball. "Hurts," she whimpers.

I stand, scooping her up into my arms and cradling her against me as I scurry down the hall towards the bathroom.

Her forehead falls against my neck and I pause. She feels hot.

When I reach the bathroom I place her on the edge of the bath, making sure she can hold herself up before pulling a small towel out of the cupboard and wetting it with cold water. I press it to her face and she winces.

Is that normal? Or is that bad?

"It's bright in here," she mumbles, closing her eyes.

She sways, whimpers again, then lets out a low moan that tears at my heart.

That's when the vomiting begins.

SADIE IS sick over and over, until there's nothing left to bring up, but that doesn't stop her tiny body trying.

She cries, and moans, then falls asleep between bouts of dry retching.

She's hot to the touch, but I don't own a thermometer so I can't take her temperature. I've been frantically searching the internet for what to do, and what's normal when a child is sick.

Could it be that she just ate too much junk food and her body is rebelling? But when I think back over what she ate today, it doesn't feel like it was that bad.

Is she sick? She must be sick. But is it something that will pass on its own? Or does she need medical care?

Sadie lets out another cry from where I have her laid out on my bed, surrounded by towels to try and protect the bedding. I clamber off the floor where I've been resting with my back up against the side of the bed while she's been resting somewhat peacefully.

I gather Sadie to me as she thrashes. I smooth her hair back and hold her while violent heaves rock her body.

After what feels like an eternity, she goes limp in my arms and I lay her carefully back down.

I slide off the bed and head into the bathroom to wash my hands. I've been doing it every time I touch Sadie, because the last thing I need is for me to get sick too, especially before Dallas gets home.

The cool water trickles over my hands as I stare at myself in the mirror.

Dark hair, tired green eyes, pale skin.

My image fuzzes in and out.

I can do this, I remind myself. I'm her mother and I can do this.

Except I can't, because I have no idea what I'm doing. I don't know if keeping her here is the right idea.

I could be doing it all wrong.

I must be, because she's getting worse.

She's limp now, barely with the energy to lift her head. She's barely reaching consciousness when the bouts of dry retching hit.

Oh, god. I'm making it all worse.

My breathing stutters. I can't be trusted with her. I can't make the right decisions.

I can't even figure out what went wrong with Flynn. I shouldn't be trusted with a child.

I can't draw breath. There's a weight crushing my chest and it's stopping me breathing. My vision goes dark around the edges.

Panic attack, I think somewhere in the depths of my fog-affected brain.

I slam my hand on the tap to shut off the water and scramble for my phone.

My fingers are too wet to work the screen and I swipe my hands across my clothes, willing them to dry faster.

I slide to the floor, breath coming in short, pained gasps.

I hit at my phone screen again and I pull up the first name I can think of.

The call connects.

"Help," I gasp. "I need help."

47

———

FLYNN

I'M SITTING in my ute hating myself just a little bit.

I've been to see the puppies and chose the one I want to bring home with me in a few weeks when they're ready to leave their mother.

The fact that I chose the one Abi thought was the cutest when we first looked at the listing is completely irrelevant.

He chose me more than I chose him.

The puppies were roaming in a large pen and when I stepped in and sat on the grass, he raced over to me and immediately climbed into my lap. The other puppies all came for a look and played with me, but none of them had the devotion of the one with the half pink nose. He didn't leave my side the entire time I was there, alternating playing with me and napping while sprawled across my thighs.

But the whole time, I kept thinking I should have taken Abi and Sadie with me.

Sadie would have loved meeting all the puppies and I would have loved watching Abi coo and gush over them too.

I've been working long hours all week, though I'm trying to hide less from my friends and family. I've been to dinner a couple of times since my talk with Olivia and I've tried not to isolate myself.

But that's how I ran into Abi that day she was dropping Sadie off after school.

And seeing her again felt like my heart was being ripped out.

All I wanted to do was take her in my arms and love her.

But instead of doing that, I turned bitter and grouchy.

What is *wrong* with me?

It's easier this way. That's what I keep telling myself anyway. Space. That's what I need, and my behaviour that day ensures I'm going to get it.

It's just really fucking unfortunate that what I need is in direct opposition to what I want.

I start the ute. I've been tempted to swing past Abi's on my way home to tell her and Sadie about the puppy.

But that's overstepping, so I head straight out of town, bypassing the road to Abi's house and head for Wildflower Ridge.

My phone blares through the ute's Bluetooth and I hit answer before I see the name flash up. It'll be Olivia. Because she is the only one who ever calls me.

"Hello," I say.

"Help. I need help."

The voice is raspy and barely audible, but somehow I recognise it instantly.

Abi.

"Abi," I say, pulling over to the shoulder of the road and when the car behind me has passed, I do a U-turn.

"I know you don't want to hear from me," she says, panic threaded through her voice. "I don't know what to do." Her voice cracks over her words and she lets out a huge, heaving sob.

"What's wrong?"

"Sadie's sick. I don't know what I'm doing. I can't do this."

"Yes, you can. You can do this, Abigail. You're her mum. You're already doing it."

She doesn't speak, just lets out a few more sobs. She's trying hard to control them, but her control is slipping with each one.

"Where are you?" I ask.

"Bathroom. On the floor."

"Where is Sadie?"

"On my bed."

Okay, just across the hall. She's still nearby. I let out a breath and calm myself. There's no use in me arriving panicked.

"Sadie's sick," Abi whimpers. "She won't stop throwing up."

I pull into her driveway, parking beside her car and disconnect my phone from the Bluetooth before turning off the engine.

I stride up the driveway and take the three porch steps in one. I push open the door, lifting it just right to stop it from sticking.

I race down the hallway and peek into Abi's room. Sadie is curled into a tiny ball on a layer of towels, a bucket sitting on the floor beside the bed. She's resting peacefully so I spin around and step into the bathroom.

Abi's on the floor, curled into a position much like her daughter's, tears running down her face and her phone clasped to her ear.

I end the call between us and Abi pulls her phone away from her ear, staring at the screen.

"Flynn?" she whispers, voice completely broken. She drops the phone to the floor and lets out a sob that wracks her entire body.

"I'm here, Rosie. I'm here."

I fall to my knees beside her and pull her to me, wrapping my arms tight around her. She buries her face against my neck, her fingers twisting in the front of my shirt.

"I've got you. Take a breath for me, Rosie," I say, dragging my hand down her spine in long, soothing strokes. She sucks down a lungful of air. "Another one, then tell me what you can hear."

I'd usually start with what she can see, but right now it's only my shirt, so we'll start with hearing. I just need her to focus on right now, in this moment, and not the chaos happening inside her head.

"Your voice," Abi says with a soft sigh. "I can hear your voice."

"Atta girl. Can you hear anything else?"

She pauses for a moment, drawing in another breath, this one easier than the last. "Your heart," she murmurs. "Thub-thump. Thub-thump. Thub-thump. I can smell you too. You smell so good," she mumbles.

I smooth the hair back from her face and she lifts her head. I use my thumbs to wipe the tears from her cheeks.

"You're here," she says.

"I'm here," I agree. "You called."

"I'm sorry," she mumbles, pushing herself off my lap. She inhales and it shakes. "I know you don't want to see me, but I didn't know what to do. Sadie ..."

She shoots to her feet and races out of the room, straight across the hall to her room. When she sees Sadie still asleep in the centre of her bed, Abi releases a sigh, her whole body slumping.

"What's wrong with her?" I ask, stepping up beside Abi. I want to wrap my arm around her and pull her to me again. "You said something about her throwing up?"

"Yeah, for hours. So, so much. She's hot and all limp. She hasn't woken up for ages, even when she's throwing up, she's not really waking up anymore." She turns to me with wide, watery eyes. "I don't know what to do."

I'm so out of my depth here. I know nothing about kids and tummy bugs, or things worse than tummy bugs. But I take a deep breath and make my suggestion. "Why don't we take her into the hospital to get checked out? The worst that can happen is they'll say it needs to pass on its own, but if there's something more serious going on then they can deal with it."

Abi wrings her hands in front of her, but nods.

"You get what you need, I'll bring Sadie out to your car and get her buckled in."

She nods again, then picks up her phone and a bag and starts tossing things in. A phone charger, her wallet, a spare towel, a bottle of water and a protein bar. I'm a little dumbstruck at her quick efficiency as she slips in and out of Sadie's room, a change of clothes for her going into the bag.

I shake my head, a tiny smile touching my lips. She's got this way more under control than she gives herself credit for.

I lift Sadie off the bed and Abi grabs a couple of the towels that we tuck around her once we have her buckled into the seat.

I take the keys from Abi's hand as she heads for the driver's side and though she looks like she's going to argue, she doesn't.

She slips into the passenger seat and flips down the visor, opening the flap to check herself in the mirror. She swipes at the mascara under her eyes and smooths her hair, then lets out a disgruntled noise and flips it closed again.

I want to tell her she's as beautiful as ever, but now isn't the time. I don't know if I'll ever have the privilege of saying those kinds of things to her again.

But before I can worry about anything between me and Abi, I have my favourite little person to worry about, so I shove my relationship woes out of my head and get Sadie to the hospital.

48

——

ABI

SADIE IS GOING to be fine. She's mostly fine now, but the doctor wanted to keep her nearby for observation since she was getting too close to dehydration for comfort.

Her nausea and bouts of vomiting have subsided since we made it to the hospital and her rest is actually peaceful now.

We have to wake her regularly to make her drink an awful electrolyte drink and while she grumbles about it each time, she's also gaining more strength from it.

I'm lying beside her on the hospital bed, with Flynn sitting in a chair across the bed from me, holding onto Sadie's hand.

I thought he'd drop us off and leave us to it, but he hasn't. He's barely left the room.

I still can't believe I called him in the middle of my panic attack. I was supposed to call Violet if I needed help. She was who I planned to call when I picked up my phone, and I didn't realise I hadn't until I heard Flynn's voice through my speaker.

I still don't know how he was there as fast as he was, unless my attack lasted longer than I realised, though the timing of that doesn't stack up.

I stare down at the bed, where Sadie's hand rests in Flynn's. He leans forward and rests his cheek on the bed beside their hands, his gaze flicking to mine for a moment before he looks away again and the longing that shoots through me would take me to my knees if I weren't already lying down.

I want to reach out and stroke my hand through his hair, tangling my fingers in those dark red curls. But I hold back.

"Flynn." A voice comes from the door and I glance up to see a nurse standing there, a soft smile on her lips.

Flynn slowly raises his head, blinking a few times before focussing on the woman. "Clarissa," he croaks and I wonder if he fell asleep for a moment there.

The woman—Clarissa—steps closer, picking up Sadie's chart from the end of the bed, then rests a hand on Flynn's shoulder as she reads it over.

"How's miss Sadie doing?" she asks me.

"Good, I think. She drank some of the electrolytes. She seems to wake up a little more each time."

Clarissa smiles. "That's excellent." She makes a note on the chart, replaces it on the end of the bed, then returns her hand to Flynn's shoulder. He leans into the touch. "And how are you two doing?"

"We're good, Riss," Flynn says, glancing at me. "This is Abi, Sadie's mum. Abi, this is Clarissa Sheridan. Her and her husband own Constellation Station."

"Tilly's mum?" I ask, the pieces of the puzzle slotting

together. I decide against mentioning Max Sheridan, who I assume is Clarissa's son.

"That would be me," Clarissa says with a smile. "She told me about her new job at the function centre. She's very excited about it."

"I am too. She's a natural when it comes to customer service."

"She's a good kid. Spends lots of time with me, unlike some others I know." Clarissa ruffles Flynn's hair.

He groans. "I know, I know. I'm sorry. I'll visit more. Do you give Hunter shit about it?"

"You bet I do." She turns her focus to me. "I'm going to get the doctor to come and see you again. I think miss Sadie might be ready to go home."

I thank Clarissa and she heads out of the room.

"She seems nice," I say to Flynn, who's already lowered his head back to the mattress.

"She is," he says, voice muffled. "Violet and Clarissa were my mum's best friends."

This time I let myself reach out and brush my hand over his hair. He startles at the touch, then stays tense. "Every time I learn something about your mum, I think how she must have been the coolest person ever." I withdraw my hand, placing it carefully along my thigh and pressing down into the muscle to fight the urge to continue touching him.

"She really, really was."

We lapse into silence, the usual hospital noises the only thing between us. My phone vibrates in my back pocket and I shuffle until I can get it free.

A text from Dallas. I should have messaged him hours ago, when Sadie first got sick, but I didn't want to ruin his weekend. He so rarely gets to spend time with just him and Katie.

I slide off the bed as I read the message.

DALLAS:

Just checking in to see how your day was.
Give Sadie a kiss goodnight for me.

"I need to call Dallas," I say quietly and Flynn raises his head, nodding. "Are you okay to stay with Sadie?"

"Of course," he says, voice soft. "I'm not going anywhere."

"Thank you," I whisper, then head down the hall, looking for a quiet spot where I can call Dallas and confess.

Confess that I couldn't look after Sadie without help.

Confess that his faith in me was misplaced.

I hit call on his name before I can chicken out.

"Abi?" he says after only one ring. "Is everything okay?"

"Yes," I say. "Mostly. It is now."

"What's wrong?"

"Sadie's sick," I say, forcing my voice to remain steady, or at least not crack and break. I take a deep breath.

"Do I need to come home? Or have you got it handled?"

"No," I say. "I mean. No, you don't need to come home. But I wanted to let you know what happened. She was throwing up all afternoon. Flynn brought us to the hospital and she's doing heaps better now. The nurse thinks we'll be able to go home soon but she's just checking with the doctor. She just needs to rest and rehydrate."

"Okay, thank you for calling," Dallas says, his voice calm

through I can detect a tiny thread of worry in there. "We'll come home first thing in the morning, but let me know if you need me there sooner."

"It's alright, I think we're okay now," I say, the control I have on my voice beginning to crumble.

"You did the right thing, Abi," Dallas says. He pauses. "Are you okay?"

I take a breath "I had a panic attack," I whisper. "I needed Flynn to snap me out of it. I'm so sorry." I fight the emotion welling in my chest.

"You're okay, Abi. You're okay and Sadie is okay. Is Flynn still with you?"

"Yes," I choke out.

"Okay, good. He'll take care of you. Let him help you, okay?" His voice is so calm, so soothing. He doesn't sound ruffled by my breakdown at all.

"Yep, I will. Thank you, Dallas."

"We'll see you tomorrow." He ends the call without waiting for my response, which is probably for the best, because if I had to form any more words all that would have come out was sobbing.

He handled it so well, just took it in his stride, like he always does.

Though maybe things will be different tomorrow when he gets home. Maybe it just needs a little time to sink in that I'm still not a competent caregiver for a child.

I sigh, then retrace my steps to the room Sadie's in.

My breath catches in my throat at the sight. Flynn has climbed onto the bed in my absence and Sadie is curled into him, her tiny fist clutching his t-shirt, his lips resting against hair, like he was giving her a kiss goodnight but fell asleep in the process.

"He's a good one, that one," Clarissa says beside me and I startle. "Sorry love, didn't mean to scare you." She gazes fondly at Flynn. "But yeah, he's got a heart of gold."

"I know. He's the best person I've ever known."

She squeezes my arm. "Sadie's all good to go. Here's the paperwork." She hands me a bundle of paper and points out where I need to sign. "Look after your little girl," she says, handing me my copy of the discharge papers. "And that boy for me, okay?"

"I will," I say, hoping I have the chance to do just that.

Hoping he gives me that chance.

49

FLYNN

ABI WAKES me from where I'm curled on the hospital bed beside Sadie, telling me it's time to go.

It's getting late now and I don't know how Abi is so awake, especially considering how exhausting a panic attack must be.

I carry Sadie to the car and Abi insists on driving us home, where I carry Sadie inside and tuck her into Abi's bed.

Abi watches me and follows me to the kitchen once I'm done.

I turn to her. "You okay here?"

"Yeah, but you can't drive now, Flynn."

I glance around the room, looking anywhere but at her. I could handle being around her when Sadie was the focus, when the worry about her was overwhelming anything else.

But now that I know Sadie is going to be fine and just needs some sleep, I can't handle being around Abi anymore.

"Stay, Flynn. You've been falling asleep half the night. You wouldn't let me drive when I was less tired than you are right now."

I sigh. "Fine. Sadie's room? Or the couch?"

"Sadie's room is fine." Abi's face drops as some kind of realisation hits. "You're going to sleep in there before she is."

Oof. Sadie was supposed to be in there tonight, in the room Abi has carefully been putting together since she moved here. What a milestone.

And instead she spent half the night at the hospital and I'll be sleeping in there the rest of the night.

"I don't have to sleep in there," I say. "The couch is fine."

She gives me a look. "Like you'll fit on that couch." She glances at it, her gaze lingering and her cheeks turning pink. I refuse to think about what I know is currently on her mind. The night I spread her out on that coffee table. The night she knelt before me and rocked my world as I sat on the couch in question.

Yeah, so I'll be sleeping in Sadie's room.

"You want to know something?" I say as I step past her. "It was my room first anyway."

Abi's eyes light up. "Please tell Sadie that tomorrow. She'll love it."

"Alright."

Then I head to bed, alone, and thank fuck I'm as exhausted as I am from all the late hours I've done this week, because I fall asleep after only a small amount of angsting over Abi and how much I miss feeling her skin under my hands.

More than that just missing her body, I miss her, in general.

All of her. I'm in way too deep and I don't know what to do except let myself drown.

CAR DOORS SLAMMING wakes me from a restless sleep. I crack my eyes open at horse posters plastered over the walls and when I roll over I almost fall off the side of the single bed.

Sadie's bed.

Ah, that's right. I guess my plan to wake up early and slip out isn't going to work anymore.

I can hear Abi's voice filtering down the hallway, then Dallas's.

Fuck, is this going to be weird? At least I'm not in Abi's bed this time.

I push myself up and find the jeans and t-shirt I dumped on the floor last night, pulling them on before heading down the hall, following the sound of voices.

Abi, Dallas and Katie meet me in the middle of the hall, on their way to Abi's room.

"Hey," I say, acknowledging Dallas and Katie. "How's Sadie?" I ask Abi.

"She's good," she answers. "A bit tired, but feeling heaps better. Come see for yourself." She gives me a soft, grateful smile that's lined with a touch of anxiety as I turn and lead them into Abi's room.

Sadie's curled on her side on the bed, her eyes fluttering open as we walk into the room. I lean against the wall, posture relaxed, which is a far cry from Abi's as she stands beside me. It takes every tiny piece of self-control I have not to reach out for her, to soothe her stress with my hands.

"Daddy," Sadie whispers.

"Hey, Sadie girl," Dallas says, perching on the edge of the bed. "How are you doing? Your mum said you weren't feeling well."

Sadie curls into his side, shaking her head. "I wasn't. Such a sore tummy. I had to go see the doctor."

"Are you feeling better now?" he asks and Sadie nods.

"Little bit," she whispers before snuggling into him more.

Katie sits on the bed on the other side of Sadie and murmurs soft words to the little girl, trailing her fingers through her hair.

I watch the three of them, feeling a little bit like a creeper, and insanely jealous. That's what I want. Somehow. A family of my own. The Austin's are incredible and somewhere deep down I know my brother loves me. I know I have a family, but it's not that same as having your person.

I just had to go find, then fall in love with, a person who's unavailable for more than anything casual. I know I could have handled the whole situation better. I know I shut her out as soon as the realisation I'm in love with her sunk in. Maybe I should have talked to her about it, like she was so adamant we needed to do.

But the fear of her saying she doesn't want me ... it's easier to just end it. Then I can still pretend she at least likes me as a friend.

I've always been a dramatic motherfucker.

Dallas glances up, mouth open ready to speak, then his expression shifts, confusion crossing his face. "Where'd Abi go?"

I glance beside me, startled to realise she's slipped out of the room without me even noticing. Apparently I was too caught up in my feels over being all alone to notice her leaving the room.

Dallas moves to stand but I hold up a hand.

"I'll go find her," I say. I don't know what possesses me because it's the exact opposite of giving her space. I just know if she's anxious right now, Dallas might not be the person to go after her.

I head down the hallway into the kitchen. She's not there. I scan the open-plan area, taking in the couch, the dining table, the empty back deck.

Maybe she just went to the bathroom. I honestly can't remember if the door was open or closed as I came down the hall.

Then a flash of movement, in the room right at the end of the house catches my eye.

Sadie's room. The one I just came out of.

When I step inside, Abi is sitting on the far corner of Sadie's bed, leaning against the wall, clutching the pillow to her chest.

She startles when she sees me, then relaxes again, turning her face into the pillow.

"Hey," I say.

"Hey," she replies, the word muffled by the pillow.

"Can I?" I gesture to the bed beside her and she peers at me over the top of the pillow before giving a short nod.

I slide onto the bed next to her, my back against the wall and legs stretched out in front of me.

"Are you okay?" I whisper.

She leans into me, but doesn't answer. I wrap an arm around

her pulling her closer, inhaling her delicate scent. It makes my heart twinge. This is a special form of torture.

A moment later, Abi's body shudders and sobs burst from her. She presses her face into the pillow and I know if I were to pull it away, it would be soaked with her tears.

"Rosie, hey, no." I pull her closer, scooping her up and depositing her on my lap, wrapping both arms tight around her shaking body.

She shoves the pillow away and instead presses her face—wet with tears as I expected—into my shirt. Her fingers latch onto my shoulder, anchoring her and I revel in the feeling of being able to be this person for her.

I hold her close, knowing it's likely the last time I'll ever have the chance. After this, I have to let her go.

Properly.

For good.

Long moments pass as Abi cries into my shirt and I whisper reassurances to her. As her sobs fade I slip my hand under her chin, lifting her gaze to meet mine.

"Talk to me, Rosie," I whisper.

She shakes her head and tries to slip out of my grasp.

"Please. I need to know how I can help."

"You can't," she says, voice thick with tears. "I can't do this. I don't know why I thought I could. I'm not supposed to be Sadie's mum. She doesn't need me. She has her family now." She waves towards the wall with Dallas, Katie and Sadie on the other side.

"She does need you, and you are her mum."

"No, I'm not. I brought her into the world sure, but I haven't been there for her. I haven't raised her. I tried and the first chance I get, I fail." She lets out a heavy breath. "I'm going to leave them to it and stop trying to force something that's not meant to be." Her voice breaks again and more sobs tear free. She tries to shove off my lap, but I hold her tight, trying to process everything she's saying.

"You're going to leave town?" I ask, dumbstruck. She can't leave. She just can't. She belongs here now.

"There's nothing for me here." This time when she pushes away from me I don't have the strength to hold her in place. She curls back into the corner, pulling the pillow between us like a shield. "You made it pretty clear where you stand the other day, and I'm sorry I dragged you into this mess."

"Where I stand?" I echo, still trying to process that she wants to *leave*.

"That you don't want anything to do with me anymore. I'm sorry I pushed you too hard that night. I should have left you alone, like you wanted."

"I've never wanted you to leave me alone," I blurt out. "The opposite. I want you too much." She blinks at me and I barely register what I've said because I'm still stuck on her wanting to leave ... not me, but *Sadie*. "You can't leave Sadie. There's so much for you here. This place is your home."

"Sadie has everything she ever needed with her dad."

"She still needs her mum. Trust me. She needs her mum. And yeah, she has Katie, but why limit her? Why can't that little girl have all the love in the world? She fucking deserves it, and so do you." I reach out and swipe my thumb along a stray tear that trickles down her cheek. I hesitate, then play the guilt trip.

"Take it from someone who misses his mum every single day, Sadie needs you."

Abi narrows her eyes at me, the corner of her mouth tugging up. "You really went there?"

I shrug. "If that's what it takes, then yeah."

"But, I couldn't even look after her." Her voice is a broken whisper.

"Yeah, you could. You did everything right. Ask Dallas. He'll agree with me. Sure, you had an attack, but you called me. You asked for help when you needed it. It's okay to have help. This family sticks together, and now you're a part of it. Being Sadie's mum gives you automatic entry."

I watch as Abi slowly lowers her defences, her posture relaxing, the pillow shield drooping, the tension in her expression softening.

"Please, don't go," I whisper. "For Sadie's sake."

For mine too, I want to add.

But I don't, because after today, I'm letting go of everything I feel for her.

Or at least I'm going to shove it right to the back of my mind and bury it so it never sees the light of day again.

50

—

ABI

FLYNN'S STARING AT ME, pleading eyes fixed on mine.

"Okay," I breathe and his expression immediately melts into relief. "I'll at least talk to Dallas and see what he wants to do. He needs to know about the panic attack."

I can't actually remember if I told him that last night when I called him.

The whole night is a blur. The entirety of yesterday is a blur. It feels like it happened years ago, not just twenty-four hours.

"If he's going to be a dick about it, he's not the man I thought he was," Flynn mutters and I can't help the smile that tugs at my mouth at his protectiveness.

I sigh, because what Flynn said right then lets me know exactly how Dallas is going to react. With concern for me, then he'll do everything in his power to work through it so I can stay a part of Sadie's life. Because that's the kind of man he is.

So, my declaration that I needed to leave might have been premature and a little dramatic.

Stupid, fucking anxiety brain. I should stop listening to it and start listening to Flynn, because he always steers me right. He balances me, taking away the anxiety, bringing me fun and a soothing sense of calm whenever we're touching.

I toss the pillow aside. I was hugging it because it's supposed to be Sadie's, but I'd forgotten Flynn spent the night resting his head on it, so all I could smell was him. Why smell a pillow when the real thing is right here beside me?

I wriggle closer, sliding my legs back over his and leaning into his shoulder. I'm not in his lap like I was earlier when I cried all over him, but I'm almost there.

"You want me too much?" I whisper, terrified of where this might be going, but chasing it anyway.

I'm feeling reckless and too emotionally drained to care.

Flynn groans and tips his head back so it thunks against the wall. "Hush."

"You think I'm going to let that go?" I ask. I snuggle closer and his arms come around me, pulling me up into his lap so I can bury my face in his neck.

"I wish you would," he mutters against my hair, then presses a kiss to my forehead.

My eyes flutter closed and I lean into the sensation of being wrapped up by him. "Is there something else for me here, aside from Sadie?" I whisper, holding my breath after the words spill out.

"If you want there to be," he whispers, voice barely audible, but I feel the words brush over my skin, caressing my hair as he presses another kiss to my forehead and tightens his grip on me.

I don't know how to answer him. I need to sort things with Sadie out first. I need to be clear where I stand with Dallas, whether or not he still wants me around.

His head jerks up and his body goes stiff before I have the chance to formulate my reply and I glance up at him.

He's staring at the door, mouth ajar, like he's trying to come up with words himself. I glance towards the hallway and it all makes sense.

Katie is standing in the doorway to Sadie's room, eyes wide in shock. "I'm so sorry. I didn't mean to interrupt," she babbles. "I'll come back. I just wanted to check that Abi was okay. I'm sorry. I'll go now."

"Katie Kat," Flynn says. "Wait."

She stops where she's already turned back down the hall and glances back at us over her shoulder.

I slide off Flynn's lap and he scooches forward until he can stand, then crosses the room to her. He places his hands on her shoulders and they murmur a few words before she leans in to hug him quickly. Disentangling himself from her embrace, he shoots me a soft smile, promising to finish our conversation later, then heads down the hall, back to my room and Sadie.

Katie steps into the room, looking the most awkward I've ever seen her. She bites her lip. "I'm really sorry about interrupting ... whatever that was." She waves a hand, encompassing where I'm sitting in the rumpled bed.

"It's fine," I say, trying to smile. "Sadie okay?"

"Sadie's great. Just a little tired you know? But how are you? Last night sounds like it was a lot."

"It was." I fiddle with the blankets, then reach for the pillow, hugging it to my body. "I assume you know why I left in the first place? The anxiety and panic attacks?" Katie nods. "It happened again last night."

"Are you okay?" Katie asks, reaching out to slip her hand into mine and squeezing tight. "It must have been scary."

"It was. It always is. That's when I rang Flynn. I barely remember doing it. Then he was here, making everything better ... but ..." I take a deep breath. "I couldn't look after Sadie, not on my own."

Katie's grip on my hand tightens. "You know you don't have to be on your own, right? It sounds a bit cheesy, but Wildflower Ridge is like a big, mostly happy family. You're part of that now. Everyone at that place has your back."

I blink, tears blurring my eyes. "That's pretty much exactly what Flynn said."

Katie laughs and I can't help smiling along with her. I'm not quite ready for laughing though.

"I'm not sure I can do it, that's if you and Dallas want me around still."

Katie stares at me, expression more shocked than earlier when she first walked into the room, which I didn't think was possible. "In what world would we not want you around? Aside from the fact that you're Sadie's mum, you're doing a great job with Olivia's dream business and I get the feeling you're making my other best friend really fucking happy. Of course we want you here."

"Even if I can't look after Sadie like I should be able to?"

She shrugs. "We'll work on it. I tell you what, she had a bug a couple of months back—nowhere near this bad—and Dallas nearly lost his shit. Your anxiety is understandable, and we'll work with it." She squeezes my hand again. "Sorry, but you're stuck with us now."

A sob catches in my throat, then bursts free and I fling myself at Katie. She catches me and wraps her arms around me. She lets out a soft laugh and holds me until I pull back and swipe under my eyes.

I cough, clear my throat and give her a sheepish look. "Sorry about that. But thank you. I can't tell you how much that means to me."

"There's just one condition," she says, lifting an eyebrow at me. "You look after our boy's heart. It's solid gold and he deserves nothing but the best. Can you give that to him?"

I take a fortifying breath and look her dead in the eye. "I'm going to damn well try," I say and she nods.

"Good."

51

———

FLYNN

I SENT Abi a final smile where she was sitting on the bed, looking way too vulnerable for my liking, but I knew Katie would be gentle with her.

I made sure of it before I stepped out of the room.

"I didn't realise I'd be walking into something," Katie whispered when I slid off the bed, leaving Abi behind.

"It's fine, but be kind, okay? She's been through it over the last twenty-four hours."

"I know she has, and of course I will be," she said, then gave me a sly smirk. "Protective looks good on you, Flynny."

I told her to shut up, rolled my eyes and left her to it. I can only hope she's doing as she promised and looking after Abi, who's so emotionally wrung out I'm not sure she knows which way is up.

I peek into Abi's room where Dallas is stretched out on her bed, Sadie tucked into his side fast asleep. I'm about to carry on down the hall when Dallas waves me in, patting the other side of the bed.

I hesitate. He wants me to lie down beside him and Sadie?

"Come on, Flynn. It's not like you aren't family."

I shrug and crawl onto the bed, slipping my hand into Sadie's, even though she isn't aware of it. It soothes me though.

"So when does she get to start calling you her stepdad?" Dallas asks and I choke on my breath.

"What?" I croak.

"You're not going to tell me there's nothing going on between you and Abi are you?"

I glance over at him, terror in my veins, but he's smirking back at me. "What?" I repeat. "How?"

"She called you in the middle of a panic attack?" he asks, and I give a tiny nod. I stare at him, unable to form words as a smug smile tilts his lips and he continues. "Abi doesn't let just anyone in like that. You obviously mean something to her."

I take a breath, then turn my head to meet Dallas's eyes straight on. "I hope so."

He smiles, nods and turns his gaze to the ceiling. "Katie and I will get out of your hair soon so you can figure it out for sure."

"You're not pissed off?"

He glances back at me. "No. I want Abi to be happy. Same goes for you, obviously. I know you two are friends, but if there's something more there, then I'm always going to support that, just like you did for me and Katie."

"Is it weird though? It's weird right?"

Dallas laughs. "Little bit."

"Abi's worried you won't want her around Sadie since she's still having panic attacks."

Dallas's laughter dies as I blurt out the words. "You know that's not the case right?"

"Yeah, that's what I told her. I assume Katie's telling her the same thing now."

"Yep, and I'll tell her as many times as I have to, until she believes it. She's Sadie's mum and they both deserve that relationship."

I exhale, tension I wasn't even aware of melting away.

"You and Abi also deserve your relationship, whatever that looks like."

"Thanks, man."

"Of course, Flynn." He laughs quietly to himself. "We really are all family around here, huh?"

"Sure fucking looks that way."

DALLAS, Katie and Sadie leave when Sadie next wakes up.

Dallas has a quiet word with Abi before they go, reassuring her that he has no issues with her being around Sadie. We watch from the front porch as Dallas backs out of the driveway, Sadie giving us a tired wave as they drive away.

Abi turns to me as they turn at the end of the street and disappear. "Apparently we have things to discuss. That's what Dallas said as his reason to take Sadie home anyway."

"He's right, and it's probably better we do it without her around."

Abi nods, then plays with the end of her ponytail. She looks exhausted, completely and utterly wrung out. I want to take her inside and look after her, like she did for me on the anniversary of my parent's accident.

But we have to clear up whatever is going on between us first. Katie and Dallas both seem to think we're together. It's time to find out for sure.

"Why did you want to end it?" she asks.

I sigh and lean against the porch railing. "Because I freaked out and then I broke your single rule. I should have talked to you about it, but I was in too deep. I was scared I'd lose you completely and I figured if you were going to leave me anyway, that I'd get in first and we could just go back to being friends."

"It didn't work out, huh?" Abi asks, a tiny smile playing at her lips.

"Nope," I say. "I'm in love with you." The words tumble out of my mouth. Wow. Smooth. I wanted to word it right, to ease into the declaration, to explain all the reasons why, and the second she's standing in front of me I throw that at her. We haven't even got off the front porch.

Abi blinks, mouth falling open into a soft 'o'.

"Fuck," I mutter and run a hand through my hair. "Well, that just came out."

Abi giggles. "Yeah?"

"Yeah. I think you're fucking incredible. You're generous and loyal, loving, gorgeous and so, so strong. I want to be with you all the time. Like I actually can't stop wanting to be around you all the damn time. It's a miracle I've actually got any work done since you moved here." I take a deep breath and step towards her, lifting her hands in mine. "I'm in love with you."

Abi twists her hands and for a second I think she's going to pull away, but before my heart can shatter at my feet, she links her fingers through mine.

"Good. Because I love you, too. You're my perfect balance. You can handle my anxiety without making it feel like a burden and you always make me laugh, no matter what we're doing. Being with you steadies me in a way I can barely explain, but all I know is I want to be with you all the time too."

I'm speechless, because while I was optimistic about Abi wanting to build some kind of relationship with me, after both Dallas and Katie's comments, I wasn't expecting her to love me back. That's taken me by surprise.

I drop her hands and eliminate the space between us, wrapping my arms around her waist and hoisting her up so I can rest her ass against the porch railing. Abi lets out a tiny yelp as I lift her, but settles against me. She tucks her ankles behind me and tugs me closer with her heels, then slips her fingers into my hair, dragging my lips towards hers.

She touches our mouths together, once, twice, three times and just as I'm about to fully lose myself in her a catcall comes from the street.

We glance up to see Dallas driving slowly by, a shit eating grin on his face as Katie screeches out her window at us.

She lets out a wild wolf-whistle and blows us a kiss while Sadie grins and waves out the back window.

Abi bursts out laughing, burying her face in my shoulder

while I hold her in place on the railing, my arms tight around her waist.

"How about we relocate this?" I whisper.

"Sounds great to me. Does the coffee table work?" She pushes me back with a hand on my chest and I groan as memories of the last time we used the coffee table flash through my mind. It's a really fucking excellent thing Sadie isn't here right now. I'm going to thank her dad later.

I take Abi's hand and lead her inside, making sure I lock the door behind me, because as much as I love Katie, I don't trust her right now and I do not want this interrupted.

She follows me down the hall without question and when she tries to turn into her bedroom, I tug her in the opposite direction, into the bathroom.

I reach into the shower and turn the water on before turning back to Abi and taking in the loose t-shirt and sinfully tight leggings she's wearing.

"Off with these I think," I murmur, tugging the hem of the t-shirt up over her head. She raises her arms and lets the garment fall to the floor.

"This isn't what I was expecting," she says, hooking her thumbs into the waistband of her leggings, then pausing.

I nod and she slowly works them down until she's standing in front of me in only a soft bra and panties.

I want to throw all my plans out the window and devour her right now. But she needs something else first and I have a favour to return.

"There's plenty of time for all that, Rosie," I say with a smirk. "Got to look after my girl first."

I grip the band of the bra when I realise it doesn't have hooks and pull it over her head, watching her tits fall free from its hold. Leaning in, I kiss the top of one swell, then the other.

My self-control is crumbling so I nudge her towards the shower. "Hop in. I'll be right back."

She pouts over her shoulder as she shimmies her ass at me, sliding her underwear down her legs. "You're not coming in?"

I step up behind her and wrap my arms around her, cupping her breasts and marvelling at the soft skin and gentle weight of them. I drag my lips down her neck, leaving a trail of goose-bumps in my wake.

"Soon, Rosie. I promise. Be a good girl and get in the shower for me."

She moans, a soft, breathless sound, but does as she's told, stepping out of my embrace and into the shower.

"Good girl. I'll be right back, then I'll take care of you."

"You better fucking take care of me," she groans. "I need you to fuck me so bad."

"Patience. Do as you're told, then maybe I will."

I shoot her a wink, then turn and walk out of the room, pulling the door closed behind me as her moan echoes around the bathroom.

"Oh, and Rosie?" I say, poking my head back in. "Don't you touch that pussy. It's all mine."

52

ABI

I STAND and wait in the shower, practically vibrating with need.

In truth, a shower is an excellent idea because I probably smell like hospital and vomit.

But I need Flynn, desperately.

I want to touch myself, but he told me not to and even though he'd never know, I want to please him. Instead I stand under the water, letting it spill over my head, soaking my hair.

Flynn returns a few minutes later, promptly strips off his clothes and steps into the shower with me.

The water is near scalding, making the small space deliciously steamy. Flynn hisses as the water hits his skin, but when he wraps his arms around me again he seems to forget about the temperature of the water.

"Did you behave?" he asks, nipping at my skin with his teeth, then soothing with his tongue.

"Yes," I gasp, arching back into his touch.

"That's my girl."

I reach around, my hand searching for his cock that's already hard and pressing up against my ass. He swats my hand away.

"Patience, Rosie," he says, then steps back.

I moan at the loss of contact. He's got me so needy and desperate I can't think straight and when a bottle clicks open I barely register. Not until his hands slide through my hair and he begins to massage shampoo into my scalp.

For the next long stretch of time—it feels like eternity, but realistically is probably ten minutes max—Flynn washes my hair, then soaps up my loofah and gently scrubs me from head to toe. His touch skims over all the most important parts; my nipples, my pussy, and barely caresses my ass before moving onto washing the next part of me.

By the time he shuts off the water I'm panting. I thought I was desperate before, but this is next level.

Flynn wraps me in a towel and gently dries off my skin, before doing the same to himself.

"Come on," he says when he's finally satisfied. "Let's get you to bed."

"Why does that sound like you're putting me down for a nap?" I ask, voice laced with suspicion.

He shrugs and when we step into my room I realise where he disappeared to earlier. In the corner of the room is a pile of soiled bedding and towels. He stripped the sheets off my bed and remade it with clean ones.

If I didn't already love him, that tiny act of kindness might have pushed me over the edge. I don't remember the last time someone made a bed for me.

Flynn leads me to the bed, then tugs free the towel wrapped around me and lets it drop to the floor while he pulls back the blankets and urges me in.

"You too," I say, terrified he's going to leave me here alone, to sleep.

"Absolutely," he says with a smirk. He drops his towel and slides in beside me, resting his back against the headboard.

I curl in beside him, my gaze lingering on the outline of his hard cock through my sheets. God, I want it so badly.

Flynn's fingers play with my still damp hair. "What do you want, Rosie? A nap? Or ..."

"Or. Definitely or." I push myself up from my prone position and slide into his lap, my pussy brushing against his cock as I shift into position.

Flynn stutters out a groan, his eyes slamming closed as he grits his teeth. "You're already so wet for me."

"That's what happens when you tease me and don't let me touch myself."

"I can't wait to be inside you again," he whispers, breathless.

"In the drawer." I indicate with a tilt of my head and he immediately reaches out, pulling free a condom.

I lift my ass up to give him room to roll it down his length and as soon as it's in place, I knock his hand out of the way and position his cock.

Flynn lets out a grunt as I lower myself down on his length, his hands gripping my hips so tightly I'll likely have bruises tomorrow. When I bottom out, my ass flush with his thighs, I lean in and capture my mouth with his.

"I love you, sweetheart," I say against his mouth.

His eyes flash open, gaze colliding with mine. "I love you, too, Abigail," he breathes. "So fucking much." He glances down at where or bodies meet. "You want to do it like this?"

I nod, lifting my hips and dropping down again, watching his expression shift and change as I ride him slowly, then increasing my pace. "For now. But soon I'm going to want you to bend me over and fuck me until I can't see straight."

"Fuck. Like that day I had you in your office? You want to be all spread out for me?"

"Just like that," I say. I lean in and bite down on his neck. "But this time your cock's going to be inside me."

"Get up, Rosie," he growls, almost lifting me off his lap in one swift movement. His dick slips out of me and I moan at the emptiness. "Up," he says again. "The faster you move, the faster I can be inside you again."

I scramble off the bed, almost tumbling to the floor in my haste, but Flynn catches me, gently guiding me into place beside my bed, my feet on the floor, my hands pressed into the mattress.

He presses between my shoulder blades and I drop my torso lower, resting on my elbows. Flynn's hand drags across my left ass cheek, then my right. He drags his fingers down my pussy, pumping two inside me once before pulling back.

I whimper, pushing my ass towards him.

"Stay still," he says, voice taking on that husky rasp that makes me want to swoon.

I freeze, expecting he'll place his hands on me again, but he doesn't. The only reason I know he's still behind me is I can hear the harsh inhale and exhale of his breath.

"Fucking gorgeous, Rosie," he mumbles and I chance a peek over my shoulder.

He's standing half a metre back, hand gripping his shaft but not moving as he gazes at me. His eyes flick up to meet mine as he steps forward, dragging his cock over my wet pussy before thrusting home.

Our moans are simultaneous and guttural, but after another thrust he stops.

"Not like this," he says, pulling out. "I want to see you. I'll fuck you like this some other time."

I immediately roll over, wrapping my legs around his hips and pulling him closer. He slides into me, then blankets my body with his.

"Better?" I whisper, dragging my tongue down his throat.

"Yes," he gasps. "I can't believe this is my life. I can't believe I'm yours."

"And I'm all yours, sweetheart. All of me. My body, but most especially my heart."

Flynn groans at my words, then slams into me, thrusting over and over, lifting me higher with each one, until the world shatters around me and I tumble over the edge, my body and my heart protected and safe in Flynn's solid embrace.

EPILOGUE
FLYNN

I STRETCH out on the lawn behind the main house at Wildflower Ridge and enjoy the last of the summer sun warming my skin.

New Zealand Easter is excellent. It's the last chance to soak up all the best bits of summer: sunshine, barbecues, long hot days, beach trips and Abigail Fletcher in frilly sundresses that show off more cleavage and leg than my poor dick knows what to do with.

I close my eyes, listening to the sound of Abi, Olivia and Katie chatting from the picnic table.

This truly couldn't get better.

I could melt into this grass right now, I'm so utterly relaxed. Mostly because Abi woke me up with her mouth so I'm still rocking a post orgasm glow.

"Oof," I moan as a small fluffy bundle lands on me. Not so

relaxed now. I pry open my eyes, right as my puppy, Jett, drags his tongue across my face. "Ew, gross," I grumble, pushing him away.

Sadie's giggles are the only warning I get before she lands on me too.

I push myself to sitting and grab her before she has a chance to wriggle away from me. Jett bounces around us, his tiny, playful barks utterly adorable.

"I've got you now, sprout," I say, skittering my fingers across her stomach. She shrieks and giggles harder. I'm not sure if she's actually ticklish or just pretends to be, but either way, this is one of our favourite games.

After a few minutes of us struggling back and forth, both trying to out-tickle the other, Sadie cries out stop and I immediately settle my hands on her back, tugging her in for a quick hug where I drop a kiss to her blonde curls before releasing her.

She leans into me, staying put even when I drop my arms back to prop myself up on my elbows. Jett scrambles onto us, draping himself over Sadie's lap and she pats him with gentle hands.

"Is it time for egg hunting yet?" Sadie asks.

"Pretty soon, poppet. We're just waiting for Uncle Hunter," Abi says, lowering herself to sit beside us. I lift my chin and she immediately leans in and presses a kiss to my mouth.

We've only been together a short time, barely a few months, but I know: this is never going to get old.

Abi grounds me in a way I didn't know I needed, giving me the security I've always craved and dissolving the aching loneliness I've felt for so many years.

Her anxiety is more stable now, though she still has bouts where she spirals about things, but I've learned how to allow space for her fears, and gently guide her back to herself.

She hasn't had a panic attack since Sadie got sick, even though she's had Sadie in her care more times than I can count, and while sometimes I'm with them, other times I leave my girls to bond. They're still building their relationship and that's still Abi's number one priority, but I think she's got it pretty well in hand by now.

Tyres crunch on gravel, a car door slams and a moment later, Hunter appears around the side of the house.

"Uncle Hunter!" Sadie cries and leaps off my lap, poor Jett ejected from his cozy spot. It takes him barely a second to recover before they both race towards Hunter.

Sadie grabs his hand, tugging fiercely. "You're here! We can start hunting now!"

Hunter stares down at her, his face as impassive as ever.

Sadie doesn't seem to notice his lack of enthusiasm before she drops his hand and races to Katie and Olivia, trying to usher them inside to get the first clue for her Easter egg hunt.

Jett races along behind her, his stubby puppy legs stumbling and tripping.

"Oh, come on, Hunt," a voice says from the porch. Olivia's older sister Willow leans against the railing, a mug of coffee in her hand and a smirk on her lips. "It's the world's cutest kid and a puppy. A teensy tiny smile won't break your face."

I flick my gaze towards my brother, just long enough to see him scowl at Willow, but as she turns and follows everyone else inside, Abi gasps, her fingers digging into my forearm.

"Holy shit," she whispers, staring at my brother. "He does smile."

I glance up and watch Hunter's face soften, his mouth curving up as he watches Willow disappear into the house.

"Only for Willow," I say, leaning in to brush a kiss along Abi's temple.

She hums, sliding her arm around my waist and leaning into my touch. I grasp her chin and tilt her mouth up, tracing her lips with the tip of my tongue.

"Muuuum," Sadie calls from the porch. "Stop kissing Flynn and come get your clues!" She heads back inside, but not before I catch her muttering, "Why's everyone always *kissing* around here?"

"You've been told," I murmur, pressing a final kiss to Abi's lips before standing. I hold out my hands and she lets me pull her to her feet.

"So I have. Good thing I'm good at doing what I'm told," she says, shooting me a smirk over her shoulder as she hurries up the porch steps.

And now I'm spending Easter morning hunting for eggs with my family sporting a boner.

Fucking awesome.

I could do without the hard dick right now, but as far as everything else goes, my life couldn't be any more perfect. It's all coming up roses.

ALSO FROM ELLE ASHWELL

Want to read more about the Wildflower Ridge family?

Katie and Dallas's story - In Full Bloom - is available now.

Flynn's darling big brother Hunter gets his second chance with Willow next! You can preorder Forget Me Not now.

If you haven't read Violet and Henry's story, you can read No Shrinking Violet for FREE by signing up to my email newsletter here:

One of the best ways to support your favourite indie authors is to leave a review. I'd truly appreciate if you could leave one for Coming Up Roses on your preferred platform.

Don't forget to follow me on social media to keep up to date with my work: @elle.ashwell.author

See you soon at Wildflower Ridge

ACKNOWLEDGMENTS

The last year has been a crazy ride, from starting drafting In Full Bloom to now releasing Coming Up Roses.

I wouldn't be here without so many people, but there are a few I have to mention specifically.

Ashleigh Van Arkkels from AVA Book Editing, who takes my final manuscript and polishes it to a shine. Thank you!

Jenn Rackham - cover designer extraordinaire. These covers are never not going to amaze me. I can't wait to see what you come up with next.

Kelsey, Natalie and Mon get to read the first version of each book (the lucky things get to see the absolute hot mess it starts as). Your thoughtful words and sweet praise both made this story so much better and kept me on track. Thank you for being my on-call cheer squad.

Ana - for her epic proofreading skills, spotting all those ninja typos! Thank you so much for using your keen eye to give these books their final polish.

For my readers and the other authors who have read In Full Bloom and/or supported me through the crazy, amazing release of my adult debut, I couldn't have done it without you and I'm forever grateful.

Finally (but definitely not least), to my husband and daughters, thank you as always for your support of my author career. I couldn't do it without you.

ABOUT THE AUTHOR

Elle Ashwell has always been a hopeless romantic.

Dedicated to the swoon and happily ever afters, it makes perfect sense to combine her love of all things romance with the charm of small town life in New Zealand.

Her romances are sweet and a little spicy, with green flag guys and ride-or-die friendships.

When not lost in fictional small towns, Elle works in administration, is a farmer's wife and mum of three girls in rural New Zealand.

www.ingramcontent.com/pod-product-compliance
Lightning Source LLC
Chambersburg PA
CBHW030929120726
47906CB00002B/555